"The sun isn't setting there. I'd s
to do without your aid, but bl(
gets, and you are particularly resist(
people to protect you."

"But—"

"In the meantime, order the usual shipments for the next month. Have your second-in-command coordinate emergency blood drives with the Red Cross. Start at our own open offices, in fact. And put your staff on daylight hours, same as the other businesses."

"How in hell am I going to rationalize that?"

"Convincingly," Hesha frowned, "if you want to save their lives. Should the enemy take the clinic while the staff are still there, our people will be massacred. Understood?"

There was a pause. "Yes, sir."

"And all of you: Cut communications between branches of the organization to a minimum. Close what channels you can. I want our holdings concealed from onlookers as much as possible. I want the four of you speaking to each other as little as possible. Thompson has briefed you all on the emergency procedures; start using them.

"Any questions?" Silence fell. "Further business?

"Yes, sir." Thompson darted up the stairs and back again, holding several plastic-wrapped bundles on a tray. He wore gloves to handle them. "Family letters for you, and a few others that Mrs. Lindbergh had a feeling about."

"There are messages waiting on your private line, as well," said Janet. "And I show a call from Miss Dimitros's number."

The Asp snickered.

Copyright © 1999 by White Wolf Publishing
ISBN 978-1-950565-98-6
All rights reserved. No part of this book may be used or reproduced in any manner
whatsoever without written permission except in the case of
brief quotations embodied in critical articles and reviews
For information address Crossroad Press at 141 Brayden Dr., Hertford, NC 27944
A Mystique Press Production - Mystique Press is an imprint of Crossroad Press.
www.crossroadpress.com

Crossroad Press Trade Edition

VAMPIRE

THE MASQUERADE

CLAN NOVEL
SETITE

BY KATHLEEN RYAN

WHITE WOLF

To my Mom, for her birthday

part one

new york

Saturday, 31 July 1999, 12:33 AM
A studio apartment in Red Hook, Brooklyn
New York City, New York

She sat in the exact center of her own apartment and waited.
The collar of her crisp, white cotton shirt lay open, just as he had left it. The blood on her neck had dried, and the tender skin there itched under the sticky crust. The handcuffs, finally, lay still. Tested, the chains and shackles had held, and she was weary of fighting them.

With the irons, *he* had bound her to and through an old, heavy office chair—solid walnut, too sturdy for her to destroy, even if she wanted to. And, she thought, *he* would have known that she wouldn't. Though the ruddy scratches on her wrists pained her, the knowledge that her struggles had scraped the foul and dirt-encrusted bonds over the polished antique— uselessly, by God—hurt almost as badly. Wrist to wood to steel to wood to wrist, the hated things left broad, brick-red stains on her skin, on the shining walnut, and on the center pillar of her home, and there was nothing she could do now but watch, and wait, and remember.

He hadn't left a light burning in the apartment, but through the windows—the enormous, beautiful, north-facing, morning windows she'd rented the loft to have—the city gave her enough light to see by.

The neon, the cars, the street signs silhouetted the studio, her workshop, and gave the apartment its own skyline. There, the easel and its half-cleaned painting, standing tall above the borough. Beside it, a modem skyscraper, all angles and difficult curves: her quilt stand, stretched with a cavalry flag and draped in mending linens. The workbench, a little apart from the better neighborhood, was a warehouse and factory, the roof busy with neat rows of bottles, cleansers, jars, brushes, boxes of gloves and cotton swabs. The desk, large, straight-lined, imposing, was the—

The desk, dull and dark by streetlight, was real, true cherry. It would glow like copper when the real, true light struck it— when the sun rose, and shone like a god through the beautiful, huge, north windows—

That was the desk, she thought, and remembered.

Monday, 21 June 1999, 11:46 PM
Rutherford House, Upper East Side, Manhattan
New York City, New York

The desk was a wreck. Dusty, dirty, scarred, paint-smeared, neglected, its dovetails were falling to pieces, and the patent mechanisms that had made it "state of the art" before the term was invented had been broken for years. The center lock had, at some long-forgotten date, been sawn through and removed completely. The three side drawers had their locks, but so filthy were the mechanisms that even their right keys could never shut them again. Not that she had the right keys; she wasn't sure, in fact, that the wood around the locks would have survived the experiment. The cabinet side squeaked and rasped when opened, and the swinging table inside sang like a dying elephant if she dared make it emerge.

She wrung a cut-up cotton T-shirt nearly dry of the warm water and wood soap, and began to lift the grime from the desktop. There was too much grit on the surface to risk wiping the rag across it, even along the grain, so she pressed the wet rag flat, and picked the dust up through sheer water tension and the knit of the cloth.

With infinite care, she removed the drawers. The center drawer and one of the side three shimmied in her hands; they would have to be trued-up and pinned solid again. The one cut for storing stationery had been repaired before, horrendously. She shook her head at the huge blobs of wood glue that lined the joints. The fourth drawer, unexpectedly, was sturdy, and all the slats and dividers missing from the others were sliding around

inside it. Three were original to the desk, and she smiled over
the thin sheets of wood like a child over a Cracker Jack prize.

She opened the cabinet side, pulled the table up and out—
with a noise, this time, less like an elephant and more like a
broken merry-go-round—and crawled half beneath it. She put
the bucket and duster aside for the moment, and dug in her hip
pocket for a flashlight.

A voice erupted gently behind her, clearing its throat. "Is
this," said the voice, "for sale here?"

Startled, the woman dropped the flashlight to the dusty
boards. She pulled her head and shoulders out of the cabinet's
maw, and looked up with dark-amber eyes. The store was dark,
the workroom lamps were facing the wrong way, and the man
was standing still further shadowed, in the calm, low light of
the stairway leading to the owners' offices.

"No." She slid the grimy bandanna from her long, straight,
chestnut hair, embarrassed. "Maybe." With the cleaner side of
the kerchief, she wiped the dust from her face and squinted into
the landing. "It could be, I guess," she went on, leaning against
the comforting bulk of the thing. "It's mine. I'm afraid it's hardly
Rutherford House quality..."

"I'm not really looking to buy. I was just curious..." The
man's tone left the conversation open.

"I went to a sale with Amy Rutherford and saw it in the odd
lot. When she bargained for the pieces she wanted, we brought
it in as part of a package deal."

"Why?" And, somehow, the voice was genuinely interested,
and she found herself talking on.

"Urn...because it wasn't worth anything, really. Because we
were really interested in some early Marathi—sorry, some early
Indian brassworks. And of course, if the dealer knew that they
were what Amy was after, he might have double-checked his
appraisal. As it was, we paid a few dollars too many for the
desk, and picked up his 'souvenirs' for pennies. There's one in
the niche behind you," she said, gesturing to a display on his
right.

"But why all this?" One elegant hand pointed toward the
bucket, the cleaners, and the drop cloths.

She smiled, and gestured vaguely with the bandanna. "Because I like it."

The man walked out of the stairwell and into the workroom. He was tall and straight, wearing a charcoal-gray suit that could make a tuxedo look casual—or denim overdressed. He was bald or shaved, but the bones of his skull were beautifully shaped. He wasn't handsome; he didn't have to be; he was complete, and perfectly sculpted, and his dark skin gleamed like candlelit mahogany. He walked into the workroom with the polite diffidence of a guest, picked up the nearest of the glaring lamps, and turned it to shine on the old desk.

"It's good. It's not a bad piece. Why do you say it isn't worth anything?"

"The pull-out," she replied, tapping on the swinging table. "It's built to conveniently store and conceal your typewriter, circa 1920. Patent pending. The estate thought they might be able to sell it to an office-supply place. But hardly anyone wants desks without file drawers, and no one, but no one, uses manual typewriters anymore. Some fool would have taken out the poor creature's guts and drilled holes through him to convert him to the computer age." She stroked the beaded edge of the desktop, murmuring, "And I couldn't let that happen to him."

"To him?"

The woman half-blushed, and put on a more businesslike face. "Sorry. I'm just a little animist. Is there anything I can do for you?"

"You might give me the honor of an introduction."

"Oh." She wiped off her right hand, and gave it to him. Her grip was firm, warm, and confident; his was strong, cool, and dry. "Elizabeth Dimitros. I'm on staff here."

"I'm Hesha Ruhadze. It's a pleasure to meet you."

"The same." She paused, trying to place him. Late visitors weren't uncommon, but she'd never seen this customer before. "Were you here to see Amy?"

"Agnes," he said, naming the senior partner. "She was saving an alabaster figure for me."

"The Old Kingdom ushebti?"

"Yes. You saw it?"

Elizabeth nodded. "I helped authenticate it. It was the best piece the Rutherfords had, this side of the Atlantic." She looked at him, curiously. "Are you interested in Egyptian art?" She stepped out of her sneakers and left them on the drop cloth. With her stocking foot, she touched a power strip, and the blazing workroom lamps flickered out. With her clean hand, she turned up the dimmers that controlled the display system.

The main floor of Rutherford House glowed softly in the lights. The walls of the gallery were the color and texture of eggshell, curved and molded to provide shelves and niches for the treasures they held. The artifacts—few of them were young enough to be merely antique—were masterfully displayed. There was harmony, and tradition, and a feel for Anglican upper-class aesthetics. But there was also a contrast in the groupings that spoke of a more modern hand, one that understood the shock of Zen and the unmindfully disciplined dash of Chinese calligraphy. Ruhadze followed her across the thick, soft carpet to a shelf draped in velvet a shade darker than the walls. A slender collar of lapis and gold beads lay in the hollow.

"This is terribly common of course," she said, "compared to your latest acquisition, but the ibis inlaid in the clasp is the finest carving of the—"

Hesha swayed, suddenly disoriented. There was a bright flash inside his own eyes, and the echo of a waking mind, just beyond his own—with shock he thought he recognized the sensation. *The Eye? Active?* He strained to catch hold of the traces, throwing all his energy into the effort. His body, neglected, began to buckle.

"Sir? Sir!"

He found himself falling against the wall, and the woman sprang to keep his head from cracking open on the shelf. He ignored her completely, and concentrated on following the emanations.

"Are you all right?" Her arms wrestled with the weight of him. She braced her knee behind his back, and turned his unresisting body over. His eyes were closed. "Lie down." He felt her raise his legs and prop them up on something hard, and then a soft, yielding cushion was placed beneath his head.

Her hands fluttered at his cheeks and forehead, and he could feel her leave. He was glad; even the slightest distraction made focusing more difficult.

For an instant, the vague and slippery phenomenon held steady in his mental grasp: It was the Eye, he had no doubt now. Somewhere in the world it had been...freed. He had the statue with him in New York; that last-minute decision to bring it with him had been irrational, but thank Set for the omens that brought him to do so. He must go to it as quickly as possible.

A quilted blanket, smelling slightly of attics and moving vans, was spread across him, and his would-be nurse reached for his wrist to take a pulse.

Hesha motioned her away. "I'm all right." He sat up, accepting help he didn't need. Outwardly, he was grateful, and with half a thought spun an effortlessly plausible lie to explain his fall. His inner self was well-masked and racing with questions, analyzing the brief flash of clarity he'd achieved. Elizabeth kept a doubtful watch on him, but his steps were steady and his manner as polished as before the 'faint.' He drew his appreciation to a slow close and checked his watch.

"I really must be getting back to my hotel now," he said. "Thank you again, Mrs. Dimitros."

"Miss," she said, casually. "But call me Liz; everyone does."

He looked into her face thoughtfully. For a moment the mask was set aside and the problem of the Eye left alone. There was a question still unanswered here; the tiny puzzle charmed and tempted him.

"Would you mind," he began, "being Elizabeth to me? I'd hate to blend in with the common herd."

Elizabeth laughed, and her business face dropped away entirely. "Please."

"Would you mind," he asked, "putting that necklace aside for me to look at the next time I come?"

"Of course."

"And would you mind," he said again, "having dinner with me Thursday night?"

"I wouldn't mind at all," she said, laughing in surprise. And after he had gone, and the front door was locked behind him, it was some time before she remembered that the bucket, the rag, and the desk were still waiting.

A black sedan pulled up to Hesha at the curb. The rear right door opened for him automatically, and he slid into the sleek passenger compartment without hesitation.

The car was custom made for him. Its rear windows and the privacy panel were tinted; with the panel raised and the tint made black, the back seat was proof against the noonday sun. It held a laptop and a compact office; it had phone, fax, a modem, and scramblers for security of all kinds. It was bulletproof, by the driver's insistence—Hesha's own plans were laid to avoid firefights, rather than to protect against them, but he respected the fears of his retainer.

"To Greenwich, Thompson, as fast as you can."

Hesha picked up his phone and dialed the number of his ally, Vegel. The younger Setite was in the position of junior partner in Hesha's quest for the Eye. He would be eager to hear that the Eye was on the move, and as mystified as Hesha that someone else had gotten to the artifact before them...the phone rang for the sixth time, and Hesha began to worry...Vegel would be needed in Baltimore immediately. Hesha was glad he'd sent a full team to Atlanta for this Toreador lunacy; having a Cessna waiting would...the phone rang for the eight time...the ninth...

The phone company informed him that the cellular number he had reached was not responding; the subscriber might be away from his phone or outside the range of their calling area.

Hesha flicked open the laptop and brought up a list of numbers. He punched one into the phone.

Tuesday, 22 June 1999, 12:08 AM
Parking garage, the High Museum of Art
Atlanta, Georgia

"McDonough," said Hesha.

"Sir!" The faintest hint of awe undercut the sharp, professional manner. Vegel's driver had heard the chief's voice before, but not often.

"Vegel's number is down. Find him. Have him call me back."

McDonough sat for a moment, thinking. He tried Vegel's line himself, and when the saccharine voice of the telephone company started its speech, cut the connection and left the vehicle. He double-checked the car's alarms, and walked slowly through the underground garage to the elevator. The eyes of other men and women were locked on him the entire way: guards, drivers, enforcers, playthings, and monsters waiting for their masters to return from the party above. He gave the tight knot of smokers by the exit booths a wide berth and approached the elevator. The doors opened on a heavily built, unsympathetic-looking gentleman in a tuxedo. McDonough kept his hands in sight and steady. His voice was level. "Mr. Vegel has an important call. I need to communicate with him."

"Step in."

The two men rose to the basement level of the High Museum, and McDonough was received by a further eight guards, all in tuxedos. They reminded him of a matched set of knives; sleek, beautiful, deadly.

"Wait here," said the elevator man. Ten minutes later, he returned, holding the door open for a woman—a woman more beautiful and more deadly than any 'knife' in the room. Her dark curls floated around her head as she walked toward him; her plain white, sleeveless gown rippled and flared with each step. She smiled at him, and the rest of the room ceased to exist; she spoke, and he had trouble remembering his own name. "I'm sorry. Vegel seems to have left my party, Mr...."

"Mc...McDonough."

"You had a message for him?"

"Mr. Ruhadze called. Vegel's phone isn't working. I thought..."

"He isn't here. Let me take the call."

And McDonough pulled a phone from his pocket—too fascinated by the green eyes to notice the guards' hands automatically reaching into their jackets—and called the car in New York.

"Hello," she said, walking to a corner of the room. Her lackeys edged out of earshot.

"Who is this?" asked Hesha, evenly.

"This is Victoria. Victoria Ash."

"It's a pleasure to speak with you, Ms. Ash—"

"Victoria—"

"To what do I owe this unexpected delight?"

"I have your man here...a Mr. McDonough...who came running an errand for you. Of course, Mr. McDonough wasn't welcome above stairs...so as a courtesy to you, I looked for your errant friend myself."

"And?"

"No one's seen Vegel since midnight. A pity; he was a most enchanting conversationalist." She paused. "Is there anything else that I can do for you, Hesha?"

"No," he said, and there was as little emotion in that one flat syllable as there was enticement in hers. "Thank you for your efforts, Victoria. If Vegel should reappear..."

"I'll tell him to call you. He has the number?"

"A great many people seem to have this number. Good night, Victoria."

"Good night, Hesha."

Tuesday, 22 June 1999, 12:50 AM
Near Abingdon Square, Greenwich Village, Manhattan
New York City, New York

Hesha sat cross-legged, stripped of his coat and shirt, gazing intently into an eye of stone. In his hand he held the cord of a hollow bronze amulet. As the flashing, fickle energies twitched at his mind and his muscle, the swinging weight traced a pattern on the paper beneath it. A trickle of fine-ground, burnt powder fell from the pendulum's tip. At last, he broke away from the focus, and looked down at the record of his work.

Five lines radiated from the center. One thin, and terribly short...another locus in New York, perhaps. Another, a third of the way around the compass from the first, was almost as small in length, but the powder there was piled high into a ridge, so strongly and frequently had the string been pulled to that side. A line as thin as the first stretched far, far to the west. The longest, thickest line ran off the paper to the east...the carpet spoiled the tail of it, but it suggested Asia.

The last line, sharp and distinct, led southwest. He would measure the charcoal carefully, later, and find where the longest line ended, if he could—but he knew, with a certainty that drove his fine, elegant hands into fists, that the track south would be roughly a thousand miles long, and that the Eye of Hazimel was loose in Atlanta.

He called for Thompson. Speaking as calmly as could—there was no use putting ideas into the man's head before the facts were available—he commanded, "Thompson, get me a report from your team in Atlanta. I suspect...I want to know where Vegel is."

Tuesday, 22 June 1999, 12:53 AM
Parking garage, the High Museum of Art
Atlanta, Georgia

McDonough heard the shots before he saw anything. He started the engine.

A handful of guards—the smokers—flew from the exit to their cars, firing at an unseen menace, and they trailed dark ribbons of something behind them. The ones that looked back, or tripped, or had to look for their limousines were cut down first—not by guns, but by the ebon tendrils.

Car alarms went off in every direction. Ghouls stepped from their master's cars and drew weapons on the black mass that streamed unchecked down the ramp.

McDonough watched a gentleman in a pearl-gray suit turn and throw burning smoke into the darkness. The fire disappeared, and he lost sight of the grenadier. Other people—things—began to emerge from cover of the moving night. Vegel was gone...

The driver cursed, put the car in gear, and shot forward. He ran over a teenage girl whose arms were nothing but bone blades and sped through a firefight without giving either side a chance to blink. The exit was blocked, he knew—he pulled into the straight lane that led to the entrance—there were orange and white gates down, but by God, the limo could slam through them...and then McDonough saw a heavy trailer pull up to the curb, completely blocking the way out. It was hauling cement sewer-pipe rings and piles of iron rebar. Swarms of the enemy crawled out of the long gray cocoons. The streetlights behind it disappeared as shadow moved in...

McDonough drew his gun with one hand and reached for the phone with the other. The emergency code: A single button and the transmit command—but he was startled away, cringing as a monster—a boy, a skinny kid with filthy, flimsy clothes—leaped on the hood, firing over and over into the bulletproof glass. It splintered, and the red-fisted child laughed, threw the gun away, and punched a claw into the cracks.

The windshield tore apart, and the other taloned hand reached down.

McDonough was pulled from the car by his hair. The shatter-cubes of glass tore at his eyes and cheeks and hands. Half blind, he shot a full clip into the side of the beast who held him. The maddened vampire shook himself like a dog, and black blood spattered the concrete around them. Then he sank his fangs deep into the mortal neck, drained him dry, and howled.

Inside the remains of the car, the cell phone's faint blue light blinked over and over and over again: "SEND?"

Tuesday, 22 June 1999, 2:36 AM
Near Abingdon Square, Greenwich Village, Manhattan
New York City, New York

The Eye was closed again, and the traces were cut dead. As mystified as Hesha had been to know it open and in another's possession, he was twice as frustrated by the sudden silence. He rested his head on the high back of his chair and listened as Thompson called man after man. No driver—neither agent from the hotel—no pilots waiting at the plane. He called Fulton County police and reported the limousine stolen, and was told there were enough emergencies as it was—or wasn't he watching the news bulletins? Call back tomorrow.

Thompson put his phone down for the last time. "Nothing, sir. I think...I think they're dead." His voice cracked. Ronald Thompson had chosen the team that escorted Vegel to Atlanta. They were his own agents, and some were even friends.

"We won't jump to conclusions, Thompson. No one pushed their panic button?"

"No sir."

"We'll hope, then, that they've gone to ground somewhere." With a keystroke, he put the news page onto the dashboard screen. "Tomorrow they may have time to get word to us," he said. "They may even be on their way out already." Patiently, Hesha let Thompson stay in the room, giving the old cop time and...companionship.

The mortal would need a day or two to adjust to the deaths. In Hesha's own mind Vegel and his team were already six corpses—to be written off and replaced as soon as possible.

Wednesday, 23 June 1999, 2:24 AM
Near Abingdon Square, Greenwich Village, Manhattan
New York City, New York

Hesha turned on his laptop and called up a news site. Atlanta was having, apparently, a terrorist attack.

Historic Charleston lay in arsonous flames. Flare-ups in Savannah were being linked with a militia organization, denied by mayors and police departments, connected to the Atlanta incidents, isolated from the Atlanta incidents—it was a familiar pattern: the Masquerade. By tomorrow morning, the official reports would have settled into human history. He would have to find the truth (or what passed for it among the Cainites) along the grapevine or not at all.

"We're going out, Thompson. When you're ready."

"Baltimore, sir?" asked the driver, hopefully.

"Not yet." The Eye could be anywhere, now, and even the greater faculties available to Hesha in his own haven would be no help in finding it. There were, however, the two short traces close at hand. Somewhere in New York, there was a clue to Hazimel, and Hesha meant to find it. "I have questions for a few friends. Weapons and full jacket, Thompson, just in case. And call the Asp. There will almost certainly be beggars at our door; I want room found for them. Have him join us tomorrow."

Wednesday, 23 June 1999, 7:30 PM
Rutherford House, Upper East Side, Manhattan
New York City, New York

"Miss Dimitros?" the querulous voice of Agnes Rutherford called.

Elizabeth closed the crackling diary before her, stored it neatly in its case, and presented herself at the door of the bindery. "Yes, Miss Rutherford?"

"I am leaving now for London. Call the car around." Elizabeth obeyed, and looked up from the phone to see her employer still poised in the doorway.

"Mr. Ruhadze's secretary called and asked that you stay to show him the Thoth necklace." Elizabeth nodded her acquiescence, and Agnes went on. "I wouldn't ordinarily leave you alone to deal with one of our most valued clients, but he seems to be willing to settle for an associate on this occasion. Please remember our standards, Miss Dimitros. Your manners and deportment are not always what we could wish for in our staff," she said, looking the younger woman up and down like a statue of particularly dubious provenance, "although I will admit that you do better than most Americans I have employed in the past. And keep those clothes on, Miss Dimitros—"

Elizabeth blushed bright red, eyes wide in indignation.

"I looked over the security tapes from yesterday, and I advise you not to run around tonight in greasy T-shirt and torn dungarees. This is Rutherford House, *not* a jumble sale."

"Yes, ma'am." Liz straightened her shoulders beneath her navy silk dress, and tried to remember whether her plain leather pumps had been polished this week, or the week before. "I brought a smock to work in today, Miss Rutherford."

"Be sure you aren't wearing it when you answer the door, Miss Dimitros."

"Yes, ma'am." Elizabeth escorted her employer to the street door, bid the old lady a polite and properly subservient good night and safe flight, and set the alarm after her.

Delicately, wearing thin cotton gloves, she took the collar from its display and brought it to the viewing table. With care she draped and pinned it on a velvet model of a woman's neck and shoulders, and stepped back to see that the clasp fell correctly, into the hollow of the throat. From the files upstairs she brought the provenance papers—the photographs of the site at which the necklace had been found, copies of reports of its discovery, its sales, the bankruptcies and inheritances, the final auction that brought it to the Rutherfords—and set the House's signature, cream-parchment, gold-embossed folder on the table beside the treasure. At the customer's chair, she laid a jeweler's loupe, calipers, a fountain pen, and a pad of cream-and-gold stationery for notation. Prepared, she turned down the front lights and slipped back through to the workroom. She donned her smock, and set to work on her desk with a home-coming smile.

"Good evening, Mr. Ruhadze. Please, come in."

"Call me Hesha?"

"Whatever you like." Elizabeth reset the door, and turned to her customer. "Miss Agnes wanted me to tell you how sorry she was not to be able to attend to your needs herself." She paused. "If you'd follow me..."

An hour and a half later, Rutherford House's claims for the necklace had proved—so far as could be told by loupe, light, and letter—genuine. The sum agreed to was lower than the first mentioned by Elizabeth, higher than the first suggested by Hesha, and comfortably above the mark Miss Agnes would have been pleased by in person.

They'd passed into companionable conversation, finally. The mutual embarrassment of their last meeting was gone. The assurance was building that the night to come would be, at least, intellectually interesting, and they had discovered considerable tastes in common. "So, Elizabeth. How did you come to know all this?

"Oh. It started with a bachelor's degree in art history, which my father promised me would lead nowhere. After I graduated, it looked like he was right, so I hung the first diploma on the wall and went after another."

"Something practical this time?"

"It was supposed to be an M.B.A."

"But it wasn't?"

"My master's thesis was The Dissemination from Mesopotamia of Key Motifs in Neolithic Pottery.'" She grinned weakly. "Wall Street expressed no interest. My father had a fit." They watched each other across the table for a moment. "Would you like some coffee?" she asked.

"Never this late, thanks. It'd keep me awake all night. But don't let that stop you."

"In a while. I'll need it to drive home." She tilted her head and returned a cooling question: "How did *you* learn all this, Hesha?"

"I just grew up with it. My family had a rather…eclectic collection of North African household goods from the fifteenth century. Don't ask me how Grandfather came by it all." He thought for a moment. "How is your desk coming along?"

"Fine," she replied, mildly surprised. "Very well, actually. I was just putting it back together when you came."

"May I see?"

Elizabeth blinked, and smiled. "Sure."

The desk stood magnificently, whole once more and polished—where polish could help its scarred hide—to a high sheen. She took the last of her tools and buffers away with the smock, and watched her companion approach the edifice. Hesha Ruhadze slid three fingers across the right side panel. He kneeled to see light on the grain's edge. He rubbed one thumb over the curved saucer of a drawer-pull, and finally slid his dark hands flat across the smooth surface of the restored top.

Elizabeth realized, suddenly, that she was frowning; that

she didn't like the way his eyes roamed over the wood. Almost hostilely, she asked, "Why are you so interested in my desk?" It was the first time she'd used the word 'my' aloud for this possession; it was a defense, and she realized it once it was spoken.

"I'm not." He withdrew his touch. "I'm interested in why you care so much about it." Hesha leaned against the wall, and brought out a charming smile. "Why is the desk a he, and not a she, Elizabeth?"

She exhaled, less as a sigh than as an exasperation. Tension fled from her neck to her shoulders. Resignedly, she walked to the cabinet corner, and traced the grain of the old cherry with the index fingers of both hands. "Sleipnir, may I present to you Mr. Hesha Ruhadze. Hesha—Sleipnir." She performed the mock introductions, and paused.

"Sleipnir," said her listener, sardonically.

"This desk, Hesha, has eight legs. Look here—" she pointed to the feet, originally carved to resemble vases on pedestals, "—eight hooves, chipped by steel-wheeled chairs and cloven by his handlers. Someone cared for him properly, once. You can see the difference between the finish by the center drawer and the finish farther away—there was a blotter to protect his hide; you can still tell the dimensions of it by feeling for them.

"But there was a right-handed owner who was sloppy with his coffee. There was a typist who liked their machine facing the same way as the rest of the desk, and who didn't bother to repair the case of their typewriter. Hundreds of lines of ink were tattooed in by the carriage return. Here and here and here—" she struck with her knuckles at dark, ovoid burns on the varnish, "he has seen fire; there were cigarettes left carelessly to die in his company.

"Vandals have pierced him with arrows—God only knows why they wanted to fire nails and screws into the poor thing, but there are the holes to bear witness. There is red paint that spots him like blood, and there is white that flecks him like froth. He is missing parts of himself; his drawers have been jarred to the very bones and were ready to collapse within him. He has been cut and burned, but he perseveres. He has seen battles and carried the writer through; he has probably survived more enterprises than will survive him.

"He is a war-horse, eight-hooved. Sleipnir." She finished defiantly, standing between a worklight and the old desk. Her brown eyes flamed clear golden, and her profile was as sharp as the moon's.

Hesha Ruhadze stood watching her, and said nothing. The Eye was in his thoughts, and the death of Vegel and his retinue, and the memory of a daymare: Thoth with a woman by his side who was remembered, later, like the moon in Inundation. He waited, testing the moments before she spoke, or broke, or moved, but silence was no good weapon against her. "You picked up the art of a skald when you studied the Norsemen," he said.

Elizabeth searched his face. He seemed serious. "Thank you," she said, gravely.

"No," he began slowly, "thank you. And please pardon my intrusion into your privacy. I…felt a mystery here, and my particular passion is…detective work. Will you forgive me?"

She waved a vague hand. "For *my* being incredibly silly and melodramatic over a typewriter desk? Of course."

But he could see that it still bothered her, and he considered carefully what next to say to the mortal. If he let it go lightly, the resentment would take root, and a useful tool perhaps be lost. If he took the matter too seriously, she would suspect mockery again, and resent that as well. Hesha took three measured strides to close the gap between them, and looked into the brown eyes of the half-lit woman. "Still. It was an intrusion, and I'm sorry." He paused, as if contemplating the scornful lips tilted up towards his own. "Where will Sleipnir go from here, Elizabeth?" asked Hesha, looking away, returning to a business voice.

"My home."

"Good." He started toward the front of the shop, and held the door to the show floor open for her. "You said the other day that no one uses typewriters anymore. I have to confess that I still use an old one, every now and then. I've nearly worn down the question mark; I'll try," he said, facing her across the table that held the collar, "not to wear you out with questions tomorrow." His black eyes held concern in lightly wrinkled lids. "If you're still available?" She smiled faintly, and nodded. "Meet me at Charles's Fifth at seven?"

She smiled more broadly and replied, "I'll be there."

Hesha settled himself in the back seat of his car. He put the jewelry case and the folder that went with it into a hidden safebox. His driver waited in silence. "Thompson. I have further business in Queens." The black car ceased idling, sliding into traffic like a shark into a school of lesser fish, and began to trace a path south off of Manhattan. "You'll drop me off at a brownstone," and he gave the address. "Take the necklace to our own place here. Have Alex take the shipment down to Baltimore tonight."

"Yes, sir."

"Place a call to the agency. Use one of the corporate names; start a background check on an Elizabeth Dimitros, middle initial 'A,' residing in or around New York, currently employed by Rutherford House Antiques. I'll send a note to Janet later with some details I'd like looked into."

"Yes, sir."

"Be back at the brownstone by three o'clock. I don't expect that you will have to wait very long."

Thursday, 24 June 1999, 10:17 AM
Rutherford House, Upper East Side, Manhattan
New York City, New York

Amy Rutherford walked into the bindery holding a mug of coffee in one hand and the check for the Egyptian collar in the other. "Lizzie?!"

"Yes, Mrs. Rutherford?" asked Elizabeth, glancing up from her silk work on the diary.

Her boss flinched, nearly spilling her morning cup down her dress. "Aunt Agnes is an ocean away, and so is *she*. You call me by my mother-in-law's name again, and I'll have you tarred and feathered. Oh, Lord. You didn't hear that. Do you realize I live in fear of your finding a job somewhere the Rutherford family doesn't demand the royal treatment from their own damn staff? Where the hell was I? The check. The collar! Liz? Have you any idea what you've done?"

Elizabeth looked up in shock. "Wasn't the price high enough?"

"The price? Do you realize you brought it in a quarter percent higher than we've ever gotten out of Ruhadze?" She shook her head. "You're going to have to teach me your sales technique."

Elizabeth stared at the diary for a moment. "I played it by the book, Amy. I swear. I followed Miss Agnes's instructions to the letter."

"Then they worked better for you than they ever did for Aunt Agnes."

"I just…went over the provenance and talked about the workmanship."

"Did he quiz you?"

"Yes," she said, emphatically. "It wasn't an easy sale, Amy. I felt like I was defending my thesis before the board again." She leaned back in her chair. "And then we got to talking about my desk—"

"That reminds me, dear, Antonio and the boys are making a delivery in your neck of the woods today. Is it ready to go?"

"It's fine. Solid as a rock." Elizabeth made a note on the pad beside the bindery phone. "I'll call the super to let them in. They can pick up the paintings while they're there; the three by the door are cleaned and crated again.

"Wonderful. The desk. Ruhadze was interested in the desk?"

"Sort of." Elizabeth pressed her fingers to her temples. "Amy, what do you know about this guy?"

"Why?"

"I'm having dinner with him tonight."

Amy Rutherford stopped with her mug at her mouth. A lesser woman, a woman who did not have Rutherfords as in-laws, might have choked or spluttered. "You deliberately waited until I had hot coffee in my mouth." She tapped her well-manicured hands on the chair's arms. "Do you mean dinner as in a date?"

"I'm not sure. I think so."

"Oh, Lord. Do you realize—no, of course you don't. Look. We have five clients on our books for whom we will drop anything. Aunt Agnes and my sweet, sweet mother-in-law roll over and play dead for these people. One of them is royalty, three are corporations, and one is Hesha Ruhadze. He's insanely rich, incredibly well-connected, particularly for…well, I hate to sound prejudiced, but, for a black man…and knows more about real antiquities than…than Mother. I think he made his money in the business."

Elizabeth nodded. "But I want to find out about *him*, not his credit rating, Amy."

"He's supposed to be some kind of recluse. At least, he's not showy. There are so many 'celebrities' grabbing the headlines that even the Ford heirs can't make the news without a robbery." She threw her hands into the air. "He's polite. He's charming. I don't think he's married."

"That's always nice to know."

"Yes." Amy shook her head, looking at her employee. She'd always thought of Liz as a plain-Jane, compared to the kind of fashion product New York turned out by the thousands and called beautiful. Bookish and intelligent, a quick learner with a cool head—whether in spite of or due to that bizarre imagination of hers—but that sort of thing seldom led to dinner invitations from millionaires. "Tell me all about it, dear. Oh, Lord. What on earth are you going to wear?"

Thursday, 24 June 1999, 6:58 PM
Charles's Fifth Avenue, Upper East Side, Manhattan
New York City, New York

The taxi lurched to a stop at the awning of Charles's Fifth, and a doorman stepped smartly forward to attend the passenger. A young woman in a long, gunmetal-silver satin evening dress stepped delicately onto the pavement. She leaned into the window to pass a note to the driver. The sun, which was turning New York smog into something like ochre mist, brought out a few strands of copper in her hair, and turned her light tan deep umber. The cab pulled away.

As the glass doors were opened for her, Elizabeth took one last survey of herself. Amy had tried to drag her to some ridiculously couture boutique; Liz put her foot down at the idea of entering anything that couldn't call itself a store or shop and mean it. The gray gown would do, and although Amy had at last admitted it, she informed the younger woman that further dates with Ruhadze would mean that Liz would finally need more than one "real" dress.

Elizabeth entered the salon, and after a moment's doubt, approached the man at the podium at the end of the room. He snatched upon the hesitation, and began before her: "Miss Dimitros? Mr. Ruhadze's secretary called ahead; Mr. Ruhadze has been detained slightly. He asked me personally to see that you were comfortable." He led her through the crowded restaurant to an alcove with a small, linen-covered table and two luxuriously upholstered chairs. A waiter appeared at his side, holding a tray; the tray held a water glass and a small phone.

"Would you care for something to drink, Miss Dimitros?" asked the patriarchal maître d' as his minion set the water and the phone at her place. "Our wine list—"

"No, thank you. Water will be fine while I wait."

At 8:19 the phone rang, and Elizabeth watched it for a moment as though she had forgotten what phones were for. She swallowed the last of her soda and picked up the tiny handset. "Hello?" she asked the machine.

"Elizabeth? This is Hesha. I'm terribly sorry. I'm at a business meeting. My lawyers have just ordered in and expect me to stay and finish the deal with them. I would walk out now, just to stagger them, but I'd only have to see these buffoons again tomorrow morning if I did. I'm afraid I'll be at least another hour."

"Oh. Well, maybe another time, then."

"No. You must be starving. Please, go ahead and have dinner. I recommend the boeuf bourguignon; it's the house specialty. Enjoy it and pity me with my cardboard Chinese takeout." His voice fell a note. "I won't stand you up, Elizabeth. I promise."

"Good luck with the deal."

"Thank you. I'll see you soon."

"'Bye."

Thursday, 24 June 1999, 8:23 PM
Near Abingdon Square, Greenwich Village, Manhattan
New York City, New York

"Yes, Thompson?"

"Janet calling for you, sir. The agency came through with the report on Miss Dimitros," said Thompson, as the car emerged from the garage to street level. One eye was on the traffic ahead, the other on a blinking light on his console.

"Put her through."

"Good evening, sir. Would you like the highlights, or should I fax it to you?"

"Both, please. Go ahead."

"Full name, Elizabeth Ariadne Dimitros. Born September 28, 1970, to Christopher and Melissa Dimitros. One sibling; an elder brother, Paul Theodore Dimitros. The family is mostly Greek; the Dimitros children are the third or fourth generation in America, depending on which side you count from. 'Dimitros' is the Anglicized version of 'Dimitrouleas'. I'll spare you the rest of the genealogy."

"Thank you."

"Curriculum vita included in the fax; basically, she's an art historian with the practical skills of a museum restorer—she worked as an intern at the Met several summers running—and special interests in anthropology, semiotics, symbolism, and half a dozen other things. Her master's thesis and professional publications are also attached to the report. She's nearly completed her doctorate; her dissertation proposal was not available for copy at time of investigation. She's worked for Rutherford for four years as sales assistant, art restorer, appraiser and buyer. The older generation of Rutherfords seem to think she's still in training; the younger partners regard her as an equal associate—or as near as possible for an outsider. The agency didn't dig too deeply there; I presented the job as a full check for potential employee, current employers not to be alerted. I hope that's all right?"

"Fine."

"Now: There were a few...zingers."

"Zingers, Janet?"

"She has no permanent place of residence. Her mail goes directly to Rutherford House. Her driver's license expired two years ago; the address given on it is now occupied by a jazz musician with three cats and a drinking problem. Her passport was issued at about that time, so the agency expects it to be just as out-of-date.

"Second: Your note mentioned her father's displeasure with her career choice? Brace yourself. He really *did* have a fit. Christopher Dimitros died of a stroke two months after Elizabeth took her master's degree. His wife blamed their daughter for his death, and moved to California to live with her son's family almost immediately after the funeral. Paul Dimitros stays in touch with his sister, but the rest of her relatives won't talk to her—even the ones who still live in New York and Jersey."

"I see." Hesha stretched his legs, and regarded the speaker with calculation. "Other relations?"

Janet cleared her throat, and her employer could see, in his mind's eye, the exact look of disapproval on the woman's face. Janet Lindbergh was an efficient secretary and a model of discretion, but past middle-age, and of a generation that simply hadn't discussed these things over the phone. "She's not seeing anyone at the moment, sir."

"Go on."

"Three serious boyfriends; brief descriptions of the... affairs...are included in the dossier. The last liaison broke off two and a half years ago; the agency suggests a connection between her father's death and her change in habits."

"Thank you, Janet." Hesha tapped his fingernails on the

armrest thoughtfully. "Commend the agency on their speed and thoroughness; laser letter on company stationery, but with the puppet president's signature in person. And be sure their investigation halts with this; I want her files and all hard copy removed from their offices.

"Will do." She paused. Just before the connection went cold he heard her mutter, "And have a nice date, sir."

Thursday, 24 June 1999, 9:57 PM
Charles's Fifth, Upper East Side, Manhattan
New York City, New York

"Good evening, Elizabeth." His voice carried clearly through the restaurant's refined din—deep as a river and closer than her heartbeat.

"Good evening, Hesha." She smiled ruefully up at her host. "Won't you join me? They're just bringing dessert."

He sat down in the other chair, and waved a swarm of waiters away. "You look lovely."

"Thank you."

An awkward silence grew, broken by the arrival of the maître d'—himself carrying the tray—with an outrage of chocolate and cup of hot tea for the lady, and a small, steaming, silver liqueur glass for his patron.

"Dinner was wonderful," Elizabeth remarked when the entourage had departed.

"I'm glad to hear it. I wish I could have been here. You weren't too bored?"

"No. It was fun, in a way." He raised an eyebrow, and she continued. "A lady sitting alone in a place like this attracts... attention. I've had four rescue attempts from sympathetic gentlemen shocked to see me stranded. One family party tried to adopt the lonely wallflower. The waiters *would* keep dancing attendance—that was a new experience for me. And half a dozen tourists thought, because of the celebrity treatment, that I was someone they should recognize. They kept sending people past the table to get a better look."

Hesha chuckled lowly. He sipped from the silver cup, and watched as she slipped a fork into the chocolate confection.

"Oh. This is fantastic." Elizabeth closed her eyes and took another bite. She offered the clean teaspoon to her companion, with a flourish that indicated the dessert plate. "Would you like some?"

"Thank you, but the caffeine…"

"Even in chocolate? How terrible for you. I tried to give it up once—" she whittled away at the pastry parts—"but decided that skipping rope was less painful than skipping dessert."

Hesha watched her finish. She relaxed with the teacup into the depths of the comfortable chair, and seemed willing to sit quietly if he cared for it. He let the cup of tea pass by in silence, and when she was done, he rose and offered his arm to her. She knew how to walk escorted, and they made stately progress through Charles's Fifth to the exit. A low, black sedan pulled up to the curb within seconds of Hesha's arrival on the sidewalk, and he smiled down at the woman by his side.

"May I offer you a lift?"

She bit her lip, doubtful. "I don't want to take you out of your way. My house isn't exactly on the beaten path."

"Please," said Hesha, holding the car door open for her, "get in. We'll take you home."

The heat of the June air was enough to give his fingers a little warmth, and so he steadied her shoulder, too, as she nestled into the lush upholstery. Thompson came around to his master's side of the sedan, and Hesha joined his guest in the back seat. Elizabeth gave her address, and the car started off.

Hesha glanced at the driver and pushed a button. Dark glass slid smoothly up to give them privacy, and he gazed at his companion as if distracted before he spoke. "This wasn't quite the evening I had planned, Elizabeth," he said softly, confidentially—though in truth, of course, it was. He had arrived as soon as the summer sun would let him, and had hardly hurried to her side.

She looked at him, and shook her head slightly. "What *did* you have in mind when you asked me?"

"On Monday? Recompense for first aid. You tried to do me

a favor. I don't care to be indebted, particularly to strangers."
His eyes flickered over her face. "After last night, I was looking
forward to the experience. You're a rather unusual person."
Elizabeth let the statement pass without comment, though
the tone of his voice suggested a profound compliment. She felt
a flush start at her shoulders, and hoped it wouldn't show in the
darkness of the car.

"I was also planning to show you a little mystery of my
own," he said. She frowned slightly, not understanding, and
he continued. "There's a piece I've been working on; a small
statue that came into my hands without a great deal of history
or background. I have some idea, now, where it might have been
carved, but I thought I'd see if you could tell me anything about
it."

"I doubt there'd be anything I could see that you couldn't."
Elizabeth hesitated. "Amy told me you were something of an
expert on antiquities."

Hesha gestured vaguely, modestly. "It was really 'Sleipnir'
that convinced me you might have an insight. You might have
thought of it as silly, but I was…impressed. What you did was
an in-depth *forensic* study of a common typewriter desk…. The
point, really, was to let you in on a tantalizing puzzle I thought
you might enjoy."

"It sounds like fun. What period is the piece from?"

"That would be telling, wouldn't it?"

"I get no clues?"

"It's not with me," he explained, in mild disappointment.
"The lawyers took too long."

"Oh."

"I don't suppose… I have more business tomorrow, *and* a
formal dinner…would it be too much trouble to ask you to meet
me somewhere, around ten or eleven or so? I'll bring the statue
with me, and we can talk without all the waiters and tourists
and gallants trying to rescue you."

"No trouble at all." Elizabeth swallowed a rush of hope, and
brought out some of her business manner to bolster her courage.
"But this time," she said, facing him with determination, "I'll be
the host. I can't say that my place is anything like so nice as

Charles's, but it is quiet, and comfortable, and it sounds like I'll need my full arsenal of experts' books behind me to cope with your puzzle."

"And if you're tied up by lawyers again," she finished wickedly, "I'll at least be able to get some work done while I wait for you."

And Hesha, who had had layers of subtle hints ready to persuade her to bring him into her home, allowed himself to be argued into agreeing humbly to her suggestion.

"Thompson? You heard the number and the directions to her door? Arrange to have the apartment searched. Maximum discretion; no traces left to trouble her. In fact, I'd be obliged if you'd see to it yourself." Thompson kept his eyes on the road, but his attention wavered. "Yes, sir," he said, but his reply had less than its accustomed crispness. "May I say something, sir?

"If I didn't value your opinion, Thompson, I would have made it clear at the beginning of our association.

"You know I'd never stand in your way, sir, but...she seems like a nice girl."

"I am sure that she is, Thompson." Hesha reflected for a moment on the tone of his retainer's statement, and went on carefully. "Vegel and all that went with him are dead, Thompson. You are looking for replacements for his team—a driver, a plane, a pilot and crew. *I* am in need of an art historian...as well as a replacement for Vegel's other capacities."

"*Which* other capacities...sir?

"I'm not sure yet, Thompson. There are weaknesses to her; under the right circumstances, they could be made...strengths our organization does not currently possess. But she need know no more of our real business than Alex, or the agency, or Patterson's." They drove in silence for a time, and the master spoke again, speculatively. "For that matter, Thompson, you might wish to consider whether you would care to replace Vegel in that capacity yourself." Thompson said nothing. "Think it over carefully, of course. You have been with me long enough to know that it is hardly an unmixed blessing; and you have seen firsthand what it can do to others. Of course you would have to change the nature of your activities, and I know you enjoy your work at the head of the security team as it is. But do think, and let me know whether and when you might wish it."

"Thank you, sir."

"And soon, Thompson. Keep in mind what happened in Atlanta. We are passing through dangerous times, and a 'living will' might be a good idea."

Friday, 25 June 1999, 11:12 PM
A studio apartment in Red Hook, Brooklyn
New York City, New York

The black sedan glided smoothly to a halt at the entrance to the old warehouse. Streetlights were rare, there was little traffic, and though a few lit windows shone in buildings on both sides of the street, the rooms were sterile. Blue-tinged fluorescent bulbs burnt late and coldly for janitors and night guards; desk lamps warmed small patches of overtime for corporate slaves.

A tall, broad, grizzled figure in a loose-fitting raincoat left the shadows of a fire escape. He approached the right rear door of the car, waited for the locks to click open, and climbed in without a word. The locks clicked back, and a touch of the tension left his creased, red face.

"Good evening, sir," Thompson said. He nodded acknowledgment to the man behind the wheel, and added, "How're you doing, Asp?"

"Never better, Ron," said the driver.

"Report, Thompson."

Ronald Thompson took a small flip-over notebook from his raincoat pocket. It was a habit, from his time as a cop; from a memory of what an ideal policeman was supposed to be. A younger Ron Thompson had found that, in this world, the reality was less than ideal, and walked away from a dirty job in search of something...cleaner. Now he sat in the back seat of a monster's car and felt no remorse as he laid a young woman's home bare before his master's eyes.

"Here's the layout. Door, a little closet and walk-in space. Open kitchen; counter and stools here—but it doesn't look like she does much entertaining. Library starts here; there's an iron rolling-door behind the bookshelves; probably from the warehouse era, probably why she keeps her books over it. Library runs into office, which runs into living room—there are books everywhere, though. This area is raised up a step, and full of your kind of stuff—antiques, I mean, sir. Her workshop, I assume. Bathroom facilities walled off here. Bedroom curtained off here." He stopped, and said meaningfully, "This entire outer wall is windows, sir."

From the front seat came a sniggering chuckle. "I guess you won't be staying the night, then, boss."

Thompson shot a scornful glare into the rear-view mirror. Hesha ignored the Asp completely, and the detective went on: "Weapons check: Usual assortment of kitchen knives. Further collection of little blades and awls in the workshop. Lots of small, heavy grenadables. No real guns; there's a flintlock in the shop next to a xeroxed article on stabilizing wood found buried in peaty soil. Non-operative.

"There are," he sighed, "a hell of a lot of spray cans and flammables. She's not a smoker, though; no lighters anywhere. Electric stove. Matches, candles and that sort of thing on a bookshelf in the office area, but not many. Fire shouldn't become a problem.

"I found out why she has no address; she sublets the loft from Rutherford House. The paper on the place was a little convoluted. I snapped a photo for Janet, on the off chance you'd be interested."

"Thank you, Thompson."

Hesha flicked the latches open, and as one, the three men left the vehicle. Thompson kept watch on the street; the Asp took a bottle, a package, and a raincoat from the trunk; Hesha accepted the items and turned to go inside the old building.

"Your time is temporarily your own. I anticipate being here at least two hours, but less than five. I will call. If your phone rings, Asp, you both should come back immediately, expecting trouble. If yours rings, Thompson, it's a straight pick-up."

Thompson took the keys and the driver's seat; the Asp took the passenger side. Neither took themselves off guard until the intercom buzzer sounded, the little door to the warehouse opened, and the steel bolts had snapped safely into place behind their master.

Hesha paced slowly along the dimly lit corridor. His steps slowed at each door, and he read the names taped, tacked, or painted on them: Kelvin Photographic; Herlin, Inc.; Malay Imports; a row of ten doors labeled with the name of a law firm he knew, and marked "File Stores, 7" A-C, D-G, and so on.

He climbed stairs and made turns; he passed by the rest of the law firm's alphabet. At the end of a bare metal catwalk he came to her door. A faded notice on the wall beside it informed him that these premises were owned by Rutherford House, and gave him a number to call in case of emergency or accident. There was no trace of light from within, and no sound. He tested the air before knocking—rust, turpentine, old paint, and grime surrounded him, but through the cracks around the jamb he could detect a trace of smoke. It was good sandalwood and frankincense, complex and not cheaply come by.

He rapped on the door with one knuckle.

On the other side, there was light—warm and relaxing light—and sound—faint strains of something Celtic—and Elizabeth, waiting for him in a dark-blue denim dress and a nervous smile.

She took the wine with thanks and exclamations at the vintage; to his instructions she propped it on the counter to breathe and to settle. She offered him a drink or something to eat; he declined politely, and drifted into what Thompson called the living room. He draped his raincoat strategically—near the center of the loft, easily reached from the sofa or the workshop but out of the way—over an old, walnut office chair, and put the package down on its seat. He made a point of gazing around him, to check his retainer's report, to make his own assay of dangers and exits, and to seem to admire.

The windows that bothered Thompson by day were concealed by night; the same floor-to-ceiling curtains that walled her bedroom rolled down from the joists and kept the bleak city at bay. Hesha tendered his compliments on the apartment, and found opening to ask for a tour.

"No, wait." Hesha laughed, and twirled a finger clockwise. "You have it upside down. Now it's only backwards. There."

Elizabeth steadied the package on what felt like its base, and slit open the packing tape with a razor blade. She peeled paper and bubble-wrap away like layers of onion, and was rewarded by a misshapen, unwieldy mystery still swathed in black velvet.

"Close your eyes," said Hesha, and he slipped the shroud away from his prize. "All right, open them."

It was inky-blue, and red, and jet black. It was perhaps sixteen inches tall, and might have been larger had it retained all its limbs, weapons, and trappings over the years. It was fierce, and it seemed to writhe in anger, and it defied with a monstrous grimace those who looked upon it.

Elizabeth stared at it, and Hesha watched her face change as she took in the details. First, there was the frank appreciation of an expert in the presence of the unusual. Her mouth corners twitched as her eyes flickered over the grotesqueries. She reached forward to touch the chipped tip of a broken ax, and her brows furrowed in doubt. Suddenly, her hand darted to the workbench's side. A halogen light blazed into Hesha's eyes, and he flinched away. "Sorry," said the historian, distractedly. She swung the lamp and its attached magnifying lens into position over the raw edge. The Setite blinked back rage—the light stung him, and he lost sight of her face in the red miasma that hovered before his eyes.

Her voice spun through the fiery void: "Is this a trick question?"

He left her there, and walked to the kitchenette. The microwave blinked 12:01 just as he passed it. "No. You were thinking forgery?"

"I wanted to eliminate the possibility." Elizabeth took up a pad, and began making notes. "Particularly after the spectacular build-up you gave the 'puzzle.' One of my professors tried that on me. Bet me lunch over it. I made him pony up steak and cocktails."

Hesha browsed through the cabinets. "Good for you. This coloring is amazing." She frowned down at the enlarged ax and arm in the lens. "Made me think it was art glass, to begin with. The carver was a real master.

"And why do you say that?"

"Aside from the fact that the physical surface of the piece is exquisite? Wine glasses are under the island. Rather dusty, I'm afraid. It's the red. Look where he's chosen to leave the red...it's like an optical illusion. Seen from below—the figure is a warrior lording it over the viewer. He's come home from the battlefield absolutely *dripping* blood from weapons, hands, and teeth. Seen from above—it's a demon rising from the fires of hell. His arms and armor ripple with the flame, but the fight hasn't started yet. It's fascinating. And where the black is bluest, that's where he's designed metal trappings. I can't understand how..."

Hesha washed the glasses, and poured for two. "What are the rules, Professor Ruhadze?"

"The rules?" He set her wine before her, and pressed his own glass to his lips. "For the puzzle...just tell me what you see. Make statements, and I'll tell you if I know them to be true or false. Think of questions I've already looked into, and I'll tell you the answers. Think of questions I haven't looked into...and you get an A for the course."

"It is carved from a solid piece of stone, except for this—" and she pointed to the white of the creature's sole remaining eye. It had begun with three; two empty sockets beneath it attested to their former occupants' existence.

"Yes." Hesha pulled a soft chair into the workshop.

"The stone is chalcedony. Specifically, the kind of agate the jewelers call 'apache flame.'"

"Yes."

She sipped her wine, and said sharply, "It isn't a modern artifact."

"How are you sure?"

"Because," she began, and went on decisively. He granted her the arguments, and the game continued for hours.

"Oh, damn." Elizabeth held her head in her hands, and shook it.

"What's wrong?"

"I had a theory," she moaned, letting him refill her glass. "I had a perfectly lovely theory. And then I went and made putty casts of the sockets. And my theory's ruined. I'm no expert, Hesha. I can't place this blasted thing in a civilization, let alone a time or site."

He put an arm over her shoulders, and pulled his chair closer. "What happened to the casts?"

"Look at this," she said. "I used polymer putty—stable enough to get the shape of the holes and flexible enough to pop out of the sockets without damaging your friend here. And I didn't need to." She handed him half a putty eyeball. There was a small plastic dowel rooted in it as a handle. "Watch this."

With thumb and forefinger, she twisted the remaining cast out of its seating.

"And I'll bet you anything you like," she said, touching the third socket gingerly, "that the last one—yes." She handed him a small, pale stone—the white of the demon's sole preserved eye. There was a hole in the center for the iris, which remained in the statue's head.

"The whites screw into the sockets. There's the stumps of irises broken off in these two. You can see the 'negatives' in the casts. The bases were black; I'd imagine that the 'whites' were red. Yours is the spirit eye; white with a red iris."

She laid her head down on the workbench, cushioned by her left arm, and looked up at the inexplicable marauder.

"Find me a near-Indian civilization with the belief structure to give this thing three eyes and four arms, the warcraft to put those styles of weapons in his hands, the mechanical knowledge of even primitive screw threads like these as *fasteners*, and the tools to work carnelian like *that*—and I'll tell you where he came from. I'm sorry, Hesha. I can't even think of lost civilizations this poor devil could be from. Did the little man who sold him to you come from a spaceship?"

Hesha turned the burning lamp off. "No." He stroked her hair away from her face, and pulled her to her feet.

"Have you had him carbon-dated? There's black grime stuck in his mane and tail."

"You wouldn't believe me if I told you what happened when I tried."

"Inconclusive?" she mumbled, drowsily.

"Something like that."

Elizabeth stumbled down the step into the living room. She leaned heavily against the almond-painted column in the center of the apartment, and began to fall. He caught her, held her, and carried her behind the curtains into her room. Along the way, she tried to speak, and he closed her mouth by kissing her. She kissed back with a kind of sleepy surprise, and then he laid her out on the bed.

He took her sandals off, and untied the sash of the dark-blue dress. She made no noise; the hour and the strong, drug-laced wine had overcome her. Hesha looked down at the quiet body, and studied her intently. After a moment's deliberation, he lifted her up again, turned down the quilt, and covered her with it. Satisfied by the effect, he toed off his own shoes and strode noiselessly back through the apartment.

He took putty and made casts of the demon's eye sockets for himself. He wrapped the statue into its velvet, plastic, and paper, and set the package by the door.

He went next to her desk—a modern creation of particle-board and laminates, not the heavy antique that stood empty in the studio area—and went through her papers. He pored over her dissertation notes, her address book, her finances. He found a box of old letters, and read with interest the sympathy cards on the death of her father; the venomous words of Elizabeth's mother; the friendly correspondence of brother Paul and his wife, and nodded as the tone grew terse and strained over time. There were what passed for love letters; he gleaned what he could from them as well.

A small silver clock on the desk told him about the sun, and he collected the bottle and glasses. He rinsed the dregs and drugs from them in the sink. He took a flask from his pocket and poured away what little wine he had had to pretend to drink himself.

He found a small blue juice glass in the cabinets; a rubber band, pen, and scrap paper in a drawer; and plastic wrap in a rack on the pantry door. He flexed his left index finger. The claw hidden there slid forward in its scaly sheath, and with it he sliced open the topmost vein of his right wrist. A slow drop of red-black ichor welled up from the cut. Hesha forced his blood forward, and the thin stream filled the little glass quickly. The wound closed over.

He tore a sheet of plastic loose and covered the draught. In fine, small handwriting, he wrote *Hangover cure* on the scrap of paper and snapped it to the glass with the rubber band. He placed his blood on the top shelf of the refrigerator.

From his raincoat, he took a notebook. On a torn-out page he constructed a note. When he had finished, he brought it to the bedroom and propped it against the mirror. Elizabeth lay motionless, in precisely the position he had left her.

Hesha sat on the edge of the low mattress. He took her fingers in his, and watched her face to be sure she knew nothing. He lifted her hand to his lips, and bit.

He drank from her quite slowly. He had hunted earlier, to sate the hunger, but this was better. Her blood coursed gently into him, and the warmth was sweet. He closed his eyes, and let himself enjoy the taste. It was a wonder...the difference in savor between mortals...that the blood should never pall...

The Beast stirred slightly, curiously strong. Hesha had long practice wrestling it, and was well fed—he fought it down. It twisted and turned on him; for an instant the surprise allowed a second duel; rare for the Setite. He knew it was too much to expect truce, but decades of disciplined tending and watchfulness had given him a little slack with the thing. Hesha beat it back again.

Uneasily, he took Elizabeth's life from between his teeth, and licked the tiny wounds closed.

Something light touched his cheek, and his eyes snapped open—it was her other hand, reaching up to caress him. He dropped her wrist, startled, and stared at her as she moved— and kept moving, despite wine, drug, weariness, and the Kiss. She was asleep; she couldn't possibly be conscious. He relaxed as she began to turn. She *was* only moving in her sleep, but she rolled into the sole sliver of light that came through the curtains, and her neck lay bare and pale against her dark hair.

The Beast stretched and roared, and Hesha scrambled to find his shoes in the dark.

He snatched up his overcoat and the statue, slammed the door behind him, and ran down the hall dialing the phone.

"Thompson."

"Sir."

"Baltimore."

"Yes, sir."

Saturday, 26 June 1999, 1:16 PM
A studio apartment in Red Hook, Brooklyn
New York City, New York

Elizabeth woke to the uncomfortable warmth of clothes in bed. Groggily, she threw off the quilt and sat up. Her mouth tasted terrible, her hair hung into her eyes, her dress was twisted around her, and her bra poked into her ribs. She planted both feet on the floor, stood up, and started toward the shower, shucking her dress and the rest of it along the way.

Thirty minutes later she poked her head back out of the bathroom—cautiously. It had occurred to her that she didn't remember the end of the evening. The apartment *felt* empty, sounded empty…she crept to the edge of the curtains, and looked out. No sign of Hesha, she saw with relief. She shrugged into an old, comfortable T-shirt and sweats, and reached for a hair band from a pile on the dresser. The note lay next to them.

Dear Elizabeth—

Good morning—I hope you slept well. The wine was apparently a stronger vintage than expected. I brought you in here—I hope you don't mind—you looked rather crumpled in the living room. I'm afraid you'll feel rather crumpled in the morning, too. My father's secret hangover cure is waiting in the fridge for you. Whatever you do, don't sip it. It tastes worse than it smells.

Thank you for the 'consultation' on the statue. You get the 'A' and I owe you steak dinner and cocktails, if you like. I'm not sure how

much longer I'll be in town, but 202-555-7831 will catch up with me
eventually, no matter where I go.
Hope to see you again soon.

—Hesha

Elizabeth stuck the note by magnet to the freezer door.
She stacked a hangover-friendly breakfast on a tray, added the
blue juice glass, and balanced the lot across the room. Sleipnir's
broad back took breakfast from her.

She nibbled absent-mindedly at a muffin and started
drawing the long curtains up to the ceiling. Her reflection stared
back at her, paler and more fey than in her mirror. She cranked
open the windows, and the images slanted away, disapproving
crookedly of her slothfulness. Elizabeth turned on the fans,
plopped down on a stool in the workshop, and turned to her
assignment for the day, an American Colonial painting that had
been, unfortunately, varnished for its own protection several
times.

Most of the afternoon later, picking out another solvent took
her past the bench where the putty casts lay, and on the way back
she took them with her. She stared at the little eyes, and tried to
remember where she had seen their like before. She abandoned
the easel to search her office desk. It was a journal article, she
was sure now—something the statue had reminded her of—but
she couldn't put her finger on the issue or even the year in which
she'd read it. She thought of a place in the bedroom shelves that
held a bundle of old xeroxed references. She flew to them, and
spent half an hour eliminating the possibilities of the shelves,
the magazine rack, the bedside table.

"Damn."

Then she saw *it*—just a corner sticking out of a pile of
magazines—the cadet-blue paper cover of *The Southern California*
Archaeological Digest. Elizabeth leaped for the couch, sent the
stack sprawling, and seized the journal.

The article, entitled "Further notes on the Sur-Amech burial
site," was 'further' notes because the digs had been disrupted

by border wars and travel sanctions to the nation that laid claim to the patch of desert the old necropolis occupied, and because the grave under study was set apart from the main cemetery. Elizabeth looked at the atlas and the dates given for the research—the author had to have returned to his excavations under threat of fire, if he'd worked when and where he claimed to.

There were photographs of the grave, and diagrams in three angles of the location of each artifact uncovered. Two pieces merited their own diagrams: a beautiful, unbroken example of the pottery native to the time and region, and a carnelian bead the corpse had worn on a thong around her neck.

Elizabeth pored over the writer's description of the little jewel, and walked over to the workbench. She measured the putty casts with calipers, string, and a ruler. The left eye was a perfect match. She grinned, propped her elbow on the bench, and bit her thumb in satisfaction.

Flipping the blue-gray journal over to its cover and contents page, she found the author's name: Dr. Jordan Kettridge, Professor of Archaeology, University of California, Berkeley.

Of course. Kettridge was the kind of man who would rather dig during war than peace; she'd heard of his exploits in Iraq. She'd heard complaints, too, from her own professors and the staff at the museum. Kettridge wouldn't specialize properly. Kettridge wouldn't stay with an expedition, not the way real archaeologists worked the field. Kettridge would waltz in after someone else had been carefully running test trenches and stratification holes for ten years to establish culture and diet and timeline and everything that was *important*, get permission to do a foundation study on some farmer's outhouse, and immediately stumble across the high priests' personal quarters. Some said it was luck, some said it was instinct, but everyone agreed it was goddamn annoying.

Elizabeth found UC-Berkeley on the net, ran through the faculty e-mail to Kettridge, and shot off a query.

Dear Professor Kettridge,

I recently had occasion to review your article on Sur-Amech in the Fall 96 SCAD. I was particularly interested in the pattern of striations found on the carnelian bead from grave d-24. Do they, as they seem to in the diagram on page 138, spiral counterclockwise in relation to the flatter side of the bead?

If so, I believe I have a client interested in purchasing this artifact. The piece is not described as a part of Berkeley's museum collection in the article; I assume that, being a minor item compared to the pottery found during the expedition, it has passed into a private collection. Could you inform me of the final disposition of the bead? Thank you for your time.

Sincerely,

Elizabeth A. Dimitros
Associate, Rutherford House Antiques

That done, she took to the kitchen phone, and punched Hesha's number in from the note he'd left.

"Hello?" It was a machine; eventually it beeped. "Hesha, this is Elizabeth. It's Saturday evening. Thanks for, um, carting me to bed. Anyway. I found something in one of my journals about your statue, I think. Give me a call when you can. Take care. Bye."

She set down the phone, and began scavenging her cupboards for dinner, clearing the remains of breakfast away as she went.

The forgotten contents of the little juice glass went swirling down the sink.

Saturday, 26 June 1999, 9:14 PM
Laurel Ridge Farm
Near Columbia, Maryland

Hesha woke to darkness and the silence of the tomb. Lethargy lifted from him, and he felt the last light of day leave the earth. He wondered if the face of the sun had changed in the centuries since the curse had been laid on him. He wondered if Set fled Ra's glory as he traveled the underworld, or whether the dead god were forced by the curse to attack his grandfather's barge every night, or if Set slept, as Hesha himself did, and fought the curse in the land of the living.

Hesha, childe in the seventh degree from Set, the son of Geb, the son of Ra, stirred in his chamber, and lights hidden in the ceiling glowed dimly at his first movement. They threw the carved walls into deep shadow; shallow relief stood forth like sculpture in the round. Farmers, fishers, hunters, artisans, scribes, priests, nobles, and royalty performed their daily tasks in the friezes. Beneath the arched body of the sky, they marked the hours with ritual, work, prayer, and pleasure. They were copies of the most beautiful art of Egypt, blended into a single masterpiece by modern hands. Hesha ran his night-black fingers over the smooth stone, and traced the outline of the cartouche in the wall to his right: a rope, bound into a loop by thinner cords, filled with the signs of Set's name and the simple title, "Lord of the Northern Skies."

Set's descendant rose and paced the walls, admiring the work. He touched his own cartouche above the lintel of a door, and walked on. In a crooked corner of the irregular cave, he came to the only unfinished section of the work. Chisel, hammer, brush, and charcoal lay neatly in a box at the base of the stone. He picked up the stick of charcoal and drew a last cartouche on the gray rock. Within the oval, he scribed a horned viper, an open tent, a vulture, a man, and an ankh—VGH—Vegel, the artist. His work was over. Hesha chiseled the rock away from the sign and laid the tools down again. The unfinished panel would remain that way forever.

"Thompson," Hesha said into the dimness.

A small speaker among the lights clicked on. "You called, sir?"

"Conference. Half an hour. You and the Asp in person. Have Janet and the doctor call in on secure lines." Hesha pushed lightly on a papyrus plant carved into the rock, and a door opened to more mundane apartments. He returned clean and clad in a simple robe, the gallahbeyah of his native North Africa. The amulets that had been hidden by western garb swung freely from cords at his neck and waist.

Thompson was waiting for him. A door to the upper areas of the house swung open as he entered, and the Asp made his way into the room. Hesha sat at the foot of the stone bench on which he had spent the day.

"Janet? Doctor? Are you with us?" Hesha asked.

"Yes, sir."

"I'm here, Hesha."

"Let's begin, then. Reports. Thompson?"

"The bodies of Vegel's team are all accounted for, sir. Transportation arrangements are under way; and we've made funeral provisions for their families. I'd like tomorrow and Monday afternoon free to attend services." Hesha nodded approval. "There wasn't much left of the car, but Atlanta police identified it yesterday as a wreck left in Cabbagetown early Tuesday morning. In their opinion, it was stolen for a joyride and then deliberately crashed.

Probably true," said Hesha, "as far as it goes. Asp?

Six of the Family have come to the townhouse looking for shelter—one from D.C., two each from Charleston, Richmond, and Atlanta, all separately, all in a hell of a hurry. I found them crash space here and there, and put them on field rations, per your orders. I gave them your number here; calls have been piling up, but so far they've lain low like good boys and girls.

"That won't last much longer."

"I'm afraid you're right, Hesha," said Doctor Oxenti from her office. "D.C. hospitals and the Red Cross were on our backs for rare types before the riots, and now we're low on everything. Plasma's cleaned out completely; whole blood is in short supply."

"I see." Hesha placed his hands flat on the stone beneath him. "It's going to get worse," he began. "By now you all will have gathered that these riots are Family business. My own branch is neutral, but that won't make a difference to either faction. We support both sides against the middle, and they will take any opportunity they can to use us, to trap us into allegiances we can't afford, or to rend us in the general slaughter.

"Washington, D.C. is now under attack." He drove on, ignoring the expressions on the faces before him, and the gasp— Janet's—that whistled through the speakers. "Assume, based on the war's progress so far, that Baltimore is not only a target, but the next target in a line north up the East Coast.

"Our open business and the townhouse are almost certain to be ransacked or firebombed. Begin removing the most valuable and portable pieces, slowly. Fake buys, arrange shoplifting, send things out for recycling, and make small shipments, but don't let it be too obvious that we're withdrawing. Warehouse the goods in the deep country—the Appalachians would be best, I think.

"I want the staff out of the buildings well before sundown every day until further notice. If we don't have more information by autumn, we'll keep later morning hours as the day gets shorter.

"Janet, you're coming out of the city center. Choose whatever files and equipment you want to bring with you, but hurry. You move to new quarters at dawn tomorrow. Asp, you're moving her yourself. We'll pick a safe zone after this meeting, and the location doesn't go beyond the three of us."

"Doctor?"

"Still here, sir."

"Can you leave your research at this time?"

"No." Hesha heard the tapping of Yasmine Oxenti's long, manicured nails on the phone receiver, and then, "A week. I need a week, at least."

"We'll try to give you the week. After that, I want you to take a holiday. Janet, book passage for the doctor to Alaska, one week from tomorrow."

"Alaska?!"

"The sun isn't setting there. I'd send you all if I could afford to do without your aid, but blood banks are particular targets, and you are particularly resistant to efforts by Thompson's people to protect you."

"But—"

"In the meantime, order the usual shipments for the next month. Have your second-in-command coordinate emergency blood drives with the Red Cross. Start at our own open offices, in fact. And put your staff on daylight hours, same as the other businesses."

"How in hell am I going to rationalize that?"

"Convincingly," Hesha frowned, "if you want to save their lives. Should the enemy take the clinic while the staff are still there, our people will be massacred. Understood?"

There was a pause. "Yes, sir."

"And all of you: Cut communications between branches of the organization to a minimum. Close what channels you can. I want our holdings concealed from onlookers as much as possible. I want the four of you speaking to each other as little as possible. Thompson has briefed you all on the emergency procedures; start using them.

"Any questions?" Silence fell. "Further business?"

"Yes, sir." Thompson darted up the stairs and back again, holding several plastic-wrapped bundles on a tray. He wore gloves to handle them. "Family letters for you, and a few others that Mrs. Lindbergh had a feeling about."

"There are messages waiting on your private line, as well," said Janet. "And I show a call from Miss Dimitros's number."

The Asp snickered.

Monday, 28 June 1999, 9:15 AM
Rutherford House, Upper East Side, Manhattan
New York City, New York

Elizabeth let herself in by the alley entrance, and found Amy Rutherford waiting for her on the stairs. She held two cups of coffee and very little patience.

"Good morning, Miss Golightly. Here's your coffee." Amy waited until the younger woman had had a good gulp of the hot, black brew, and then developed a cat-and-canary smile. "Tell Mama all about it."

"About what?" Elizabeth slipped past, hugging the well-wrapped package tightly under one arm. She waggled the package at her boss. "This?"

Amy ran after her, and caught the door to the offices open with a deft foot. "You scamp. You know exactly what I'm talking about. About the *date*."

Liz sat down. "Thursday night didn't go well at all. He had a business meeting beforehand, it dragged on, and he was three hours late." She shrugged. "Dinner was good, though. He and his chauffeur drove me home, and he asked if I could meet him the next night. So he came over Friday after dinner, and we talked antiques and things."

Amy's mouth fell open. "And?"

"What do you mean, 'And?'"

"Good God, Liz. Do you realize you've made fire-irons sound more exciting than that? You sell a cheap Roman bracelet to one of the Miller sisters, and it's all romance and the story of how the glass went from hand to hand along the silk road, and the wedding it was bought for, and the...well, you go on and on, you know you do, and it sells the thing. Here you have not one, but two nights with one of the most interesting men I've ever met, and all you have to say about it is, 'He was late. Dinner was good. We drove home. He came over. We talked.'" She ran the sentences together in singsong mockery. "Do you know what I did Friday?"

"You attended an estate sale in Massachusetts." Elizabeth got up and started down the carpeted stairs to the display floor. "How did it go for us?"

"I—well, it went fine. Four good pieces of Philadelphia cabinetry, a nearly complete set of Spode china, a—damn it, you changed the subject. I spent Friday wondering what happened to you Thursday night."

"That was sweet of you, but he was quite the gentleman. Brought me home safe, sound, and with my virtue unassailed."

"Liz—" Amy began seriously, and looked at her. An eight-day clock on the wall beside them chimed the half-hour, galvanizing her into movement. "Oh, Lord. Do you realize we open in thirty minutes? Hurry. The Totiros took the floral, but they also cleaned out all the Nouveau we had in the showroom. We've got to reorganize before ten.... Call Antonio and the boys in to help us with the heavy things, would you, Liz?"

In fifteen minutes, the front room was ready enough to start the day with. The two women tramped upstairs to brush dust from their dresses and jackets, comb Amy's flyaway hair, and make themselves, as Miss Agnes would have put it, "decently presentable." They stole a moment for more coffee and gossip, until the phone rang. Amy reached for it with one hand, but kept her eyes on Liz. "Hold that thought, dear."

"Rutherford House Antiques," she answered, in excruciatingly well-bred tones. "How may I be of assistance to you today? Yes. Yes." Her brows waggled at Elizabeth, and she mouthed 'asking for you.' "She is here with me now, as a matter of fact. Would you like to speak with her?" There was a pause. "In about five minutes. Our hours begin at ten, Mr... Yes, that is the street. Three blocks from...that is correct. Well, we will see you then, sir."

"Another gentleman caller for you, Lizzie." Amy shrugged and waved away Liz's questions. "Didn't leave his name. Didn't state his business." She glanced at her wristwatch. "Time to unlock."

The elegant smoked-glass-and-chromed-steel doors opened for the first customer of the day. Amy Rutherford drifted unobtrusively forward, neither putting herself in the man's way, nor giving the slightest appearance of neglect, should he be looking for assistance.

His eyes flickered over her, but he said nothing. He started a circuit of the room, examining it silently. From time to time, he would look over at the two women, but his attention seemed absorbed by the antiquities. His hair was a graying ash-blond, his face dark in a way that suggested layers of honest sunburn, not trips to a tanning bed. He wore a wrinkled, khaki button-down shirt with too many pockets, and blue jeans that seemed to have come across the idea of "threadbare" in ages past and liked it. Neither woman judged him on the clothes; enough VIPs took pride in shabby casuals that he might have been anyone.

"Mrs. Dimitros?" he began at last, addressing Amy. Up close, his carriage seemed younger than the gray hair suggested. His face was a mess of wrinkles, but beneath the lines hid the face of a young man. He could have been thirty-five, she thought... or fifty-five.

"Mrs. Rutherford—I'm Amy Rutherford." Her eyes narrowed as she checked his voice against a memory.

"Good morning, ma'am. My name is Jordan Kettridge."

"Lizzie—" Amy pulled Elizabeth across the room with the tone of her voice. She said to Kettridge, "You called us half an hour ago?"

"Yes, ma'am."

"Jordan Kettridge, Elizabeth," said Amy, informatively. Liz nodded and extended her hand to shake.

"Good morning, Professor Kettridge. I...was hardly expecting to see you here in New York."

"You're Elizabeth Dimitros?" He stared hard at her, and let her hand go a moment later than was entirely comfortable or polite, cocking his head to one side as he studied her. "You don't look like you write." Elizabeth said nothing, but her gaze was as frank and open as the stranger's was blunt and suspicious. Amy glanced from one to the other, and decided to stay close by.

"Well, Ms. Dimitros. The bead in my article does have striations running counterclockwise in relation to the flatter side." His eyes were gray-green and piercing, and they locked with hers. "Though I would have thought, looking at the diagram in SCAD," he said sharply, and threw the words down like a challenge, "that it would be impossible to determine that from the angle at which it was drawn."

"Nevertheless," said the young woman smoothly, "I'm glad to hear that the design, at least, matches the bead I'm seeking. Can you tell me who is currently in possession of the bead, Doctor?"

"The artifact is in my private collection, Ms. Dimitros." Kettridge spoke with an inexplicable emphasis—his tone would have suited a death threat better.

Elizabeth kept her shock out of her face, and was glad to see Amy wearing her best Rutherford business expression as a mask.

"I see," Liz said, though she was almost certain that she didn't. "And are you willing to sell?"

"That would depend entirely on the circumstances, Ms. Dimitros." Kettridge rubbed his chin thoughtfully. "Who's the buyer?"

"Rutherford House," said Elizabeth, hoping like hell that Amy's face wouldn't betray surprise and give her the lie.

Kettridge chuckled. "I'm sorry. I don't believe for one minute that you pick your antiques out of archaeological journals at random—who put you up to this?"

Amy broke in. "Doctor Kettridge," she said slowly, "when we represent a client, we do not make a habit of giving their name away to simply anyone who asks for it. Confidentiality is a watchword here. And when the buyer specifically requests us not to divulge their identity, it is a point of honor with us to respect their wishes."

He said, "Honor, is it?" and smiled. His wrinkles wrapped around his mouth and eyes readily enough; the lines had come there smiling in the first place. Elizabeth rallied, and sat on the edge of the center table. "It's far too early, at any rate, to begin discussing terms, Dr. Kettridge. We haven't any idea whether your find is the piece our client wants—we'll need to see your bead to verify that, and match the data on it to the data on the item being sought. After that, we'll contact our client. It is possible, I suppose, that he or she will be willing to make an exception to their confidential status this one time, as a concession to you."

"And just how much data do you have, Ms. Dimitros, on the 'item' being sought?"

Amy cut in. "*Is* the bead for sale, Dr. Kettridge?"

He looked at the two women—Amy Rutherford, clad in iron-gray, her arms folded, her chin held high— Elizabeth Dimitros, perched on the table's edge, chic and trim in burgundy, following him casually with her eyes—and found his way to the door without quite turning his back on either of them. "I'll think about it," said the professor, and then he left.

Elizabeth let out a sigh, and some of the backbone dropped out of her posture. Behind her, she could hear Amy walk to the viewing table, pick up her coffee cup, and finish it.

"All right," said Amy Rutherford. "What the hell was that all about?"

"I don't know."

"Tell me another one, Lizzie."

"I'll tell you the whole damned story. If it makes any more sense to you than it does to me—I'll—I'll probably die of apoplexy. Look," she said, and told her boss the story of the "puzzle" Hesha had brought with him. She dug the casts and the journal out of the tote bag she'd brought with her, and the recitation ended with Amy wearing a jeweler's loupe, scrutinizing the tiny bits of putty as if they were the crown jewels of Ruritania.

"I just don't see it," she said, trading the loupe for her bifocals.

"Good. I felt like a blasted idiot. On the other hand, I was hoping you'd know something about the statue, or Kettridge, or Ruhadze that would make that—" Elizabeth gestured toward the display floor with a wild hand "—make some sort of sense."

"And all you did was ask what collection the bead was in?"

"Yes. I signed as Rutherford House staff—you said yourself that Ruhadze was a VIP even to Agnes and your—

"Don't mention her, please."

"Mrs. Rutherford," finished the younger woman, hopelessly. They stared at each other across the viewing table.

"So what do we do now?" asked Elizabeth.

"We wait and see if Kettridge comes back, and we wait to hear from your beau. In the meantime...I'll make some phone calls. I always wanted to be a sleuth."

"*Everyone* I know is turning into a detective, these days."

"You mind the store, dear, and don't worry. I can't see how even...Mother...could possibly *blame* you for any of this. It could be a very nice deal. And if we pull it off, I'll see that you get a cut, even if it has to come out of my share." Amy tromped up the stairs, leaving Elizabeth alone in the shop to wonder.

"You have reached 202-555-7831. At the tone, please leave your name, your number, the time you called, and your message."

"Hesha? This is Liz. Look...well...all right. To start with, the article I found was in the *Southern California Archaeological Digest* for Fall 96. If you can't get a copy, I'll fax pages from mine.... the article is by Kettridge, Jordan Kettridge; he's a professor at Berkeley. As far as I could make out from the article, he's got one of the missing eyes of your statue. So I e-mailed him to see if he would sell. That was Saturday. He turned up in our showroom this morning, acting as if he was about to... I don't know, start a fight. Punch Amy in the mouth. Damn it. I don't even know why I'm calling. He was hostile, I doubt he'll sell. Do you want Rutherford House to pursue it? Give me a call when you can. Bye."

Tuesday, 29 June 1999, 2:14 AM
A studio apartment in Red Hook, Brooklyn
New York City, New York

Elizabeth staggered through the door and into her apartment. It locked behind her, and she shuffled, exhausted, to the living room and threw herself on the big sofa. For ten minutes, she vegetated in absolute stillness. Only when the standing-up aches from her day at Rutherford House had been replaced by face-down-on-the-couch aches did she move.

Her hand reached out and tapped at a blinking red light, and presently it spoke to her.

"Elizabeth? Hesha. I found the article; I think you're right. You're very quick. Thank you for looking out for me—or at least, gnawing away at my puzzles for me. I'd love to acquire the piece, of course. Put the Rutherfords on the track. They'll finagle it out of him if anyone can. Do look after yourself, though. I've met Kettridge once or twice, and he's a touch...eccentric. The scene today sounds typical of him. I'd hesitate to use the word 'unstable' about such a prominent and capable scholar...." The tinny copy of Hesha's voice slowed, and a note of concern crept into it. "Please, be careful, Elizabeth. I'll talk to you again soon."

Wednesday, 30 June 1999, 11:58 AM
Victor's Authentic Mediterranean Cafe,
Upper West Side, Manhattan
New York City, New York

Elizabeth sat in a tiny booth of her favorite, very small restaurant, reading a heavy volume on the prehistory of Persia. From time to time, she remembered the salad in front of her, and took a few bites. She turned a page. Without warning, a man slid into the seat facing her. She looked up, ready to scream bloody murder—she was enough of a regular that, even in New York, one of the waitstaff would care—and closed her hand over her keyring on the seat beside her. The tube of pepper spray provided an iota of confidence.

Jordan Kettridge greeted her with an apologetic grimace. "Hi."

She said nothing, but kept her hand on the keys.

"I just wanted to say, I'm sorry about the scene at the gallery yesterday."

Elizabeth, stony-faced, waited.

"I'd just flown in from Turkey, I was jetlagged, I confess to a terrible temper, and I have been having the weirdest time with this damn bead. There have been some really...strange things happening in connection with it." He smiled ruefully, and the lopsided effect was actually very appealing. Liz still said nothing, but the hand with the pepper relaxed the slightest bit.

"I had a second offer for it, yesterday. Sight unseen," he said, stressing the two words as if they were unspeakable possibilities. "I don't have the faintest idea why." He leaned forward, hands open as though begging her. "Can't you tell me anything about it?"

"Professor Kettridge, I haven't seen the bead," said Elizabeth wearily. "So far as I know, you have a rock with a hole through it."

He nodded. "That's exactly what it looks like. It's not a work of art, it's of no particular archaeological significance, it's not even *made* of anything intrinsically valuable." He searched her face in some desperation. "So why am I being offered ridiculous sums of money to part with it?"

"How ridiculous?" He told her. She put down her book, and stared at him. "Now can you see why I'm worried?"

Elizabeth frowned. "I can see why you're worried today. That's a frightening amount of money for one bead. I still don't understand the scene you caused at Rutherford House, Professor."

"Please, call me Jordan."

"No." She shook her head vigorously. "Why the hell should I?"

"Damn it!" he snarled. "Look I came here—"

"You *followed* me here—it's called stalking, Professor."

"To tell you," he shouted her down, "that I'm willing to consider your client's offer."

Elizabeth waited, and slowly the attention of the staff and other lunchers drifted away from the spectacle.

"I can't say whether he'd be willing to pay such an extravagant price for a lump of rock with a hole through it, Professor."

"The money doesn't matter."

Elizabeth raised both eyebrows, and he relented. His gray-green eyes locked with hers, and he continued levelly.

"The money doesn't matter that much, Ms. Dimitros. But I want to know who I'm dealing with. I don't dig for or sell to thieves, to collectors who deal with thieves, to idiots who want to 'invest' in things they're incapable of appreciating, or to blood-sucking corporate art-buyers." Kettridge was good at reading faces, and he watched the woman across from him carefully as he said each word. On "blood-sucking," her expression didn't change in the least.

"Well," said Elizabeth. "I suppose I can thank you for your apology about the scene you made in front of my boss. And I'll remember that you hold a certain code in your dealings; we'll note it in the company's file on the item. If I were you, though, I'd be less concerned about dealing with Rutherford House— which if you know anything about the market, you know is as clean as it gets—than about dealing with someone willing to pay so much, blindly, for your find. Most of our clients are connoisseurs. Sometimes we work for families trying to recover their heritage or build one. As for corporations…well, museums incorporate these days, and corporations build museums. I hope you don't consider building the Getty a sin? We certainly don't deal on the black market. I can't say we check to see whether our clients do; it would be an invasion of privacy."

Kettridge listened. "Ms. Dimitros, I believe in your sincerity. But I'm not sure whether you really know who you're fronting for. Be careful. Be damn careful. There are *dangerous* people mixed up in this business."

"In antiques?"

"No!" He struck the table with a closed fist. "Sorry." He whispered, "In *this*—wrapped up in the bead and whatever goes with it.

"Look." Kettridge stared at the speckled Formica tabletop as if for answers, leaned his head on his hands, and spoke softly. "You read the article. The bead was found in a grave. I excavated that grave from the natural surface down to the cemetery level. As I dug, I found broken pieces of clay with amulet-signs baked into them. They were scattered around in stratum after stratum. The placement suggested that the people of Sur-Amech put one or two a decade onto the grave for *generations* after the body was interred. The writing degenerates after a century or two, but the symbol stays the same.

"When I reached the original surface of the grave, I found the same sign scratched onto a large flat rock, facing downward. When I found the body, it was surrounded by the same kind of stone, with the same rough drawing of the amulet sign—again, facing toward the body. Literally surrounded, Ms. Dimitros— lying on a bed of them, walled in by them, and covered with them. The body was in the worst preservation of any found in the area. We pull desiccated, brittle bones from the sand there. This was just the dusty outline of a skeleton.

"There's no other grave like it in Sur-Amech.

"And the most interesting thing, Ms. Dimitros, is that the symbol carved into the rocks in that grave is still in use as a protective sign among the nomads who live in the area." He whipped out a pen, took a napkin from the dispenser, and drew a little glyph on the flimsy paper. "It's a ward against the Evil Eye, Ms. Dimitros." Elizabeth caught the eye of her waitress, and signaled for the check. "Thank you for the lecture, Professor. What's your point?"

"The people of Sur-Amech wouldn't bury this corpse with their own dead. They hauled the body and the stones into virtual wilderness to get rid of it, and they protected themselves against the power of that corpse as well as they could, for as long as they could. They were afraid, Ms. Dimitros. And so am I."

"You believe in curses, Professor?" Elizabeth asked, incredulously. "Is the Smithsonian going to wrack and ruin because the Hope diamond is on display there? Did the Carter expedition really die because they violated Tutankhamen's tomb?" She paid her bill, and stood to leave.

"I wanted to warn you. But I can see that you're blind to it all, Ms. Dimitros. I'm terribly sorry. I hope you'll be all right."

"Thank you." Liz picked up her book and turned toward the door. Kettridge didn't rise. She had to speak to the back of his head. "And the bead?"

"I'll be in touch," said Kettridge.

Wednesday, 30 June 1999, 12:53 PM
Rutherford House, Upper East Side, Manhattan
New York City, New York

Amy found Liz in the bindery. The younger woman was pale, but her eyes weren't red. As she worked, very slowly, but with her usual care and precision, she brushed her hair away from her face, and the hand that moved trembled, just the faintest bit. Amy pushed the door open. "Lizzie?" she asked softly. "What's wrong?"

Elizabeth jumped in her chair. "Sorry, Amy. You scared me."

Amy shut the door behind her. "You were fine two hours ago. Now you're spookier than a cat with its head in a bag. Are you sleeping all right? You aren't walking again?" Starkly suspicious, she asked, "Did your mother call and upset you?" The girl shook her head, and Amy insisted: "Tell me what's happened, dear heart."

"Kettridge...came after me."

"Oh, Lord. What do you mean?"

"I was eating lunch at Victor's, and he sat down at my table. He was trying to...warn me, or threaten me, or something. There's something terribly wrong with this bead, I think..."

In bits and pieces, Amy gleaned the whole story from her friend.

"First thing we do," said Amy seriously, "is insulate you from this whole affair. If Kettridge shows up again, you tell him you're not at liberty to discuss Rutherford business. Tell him to contact the partners. Then you leave as fast as you can, okay?"

Elizabeth nodded.

"Second, I'm calling your Mr. Ruhadze and telling him to do his own negotiations. We'll ask for a finder's fee, but if there's trouble, it's his. Not ours, and certainly not yours, Liz.

"Third, we're going to pin down the mysterious Professor Kettridge. He comes in and out of here without so much as a contact number, fine and dandy. I've been asking after him around our mutual associates already—I'll find out where he's staying, or I'll find him through Berkeley, and I'll get him off your back."

Elizabeth smiled uncertainly.

Amy smiled back. "I'm sure there's a reason for all this. Damned if I can say it'll be a logical one, though. Everyone I talked to Monday said Kettridge was 'a nice guy'—which means nothing, of course—neither 'nice' nor 'good' mean anything nowadays. Kettridge is not supposed to be off his rocker. He can get a little insistent over his favorite theory, but I've never known a scientist who didn't, at least a little. We'll deal with this." She got up and opened the door. "You stick to the diary, Lizzie, and I'll go tackle the madmen."

Hesha stirred in his sleep.

"Sir?"

Hesha forced his eyes open. He tasted the cool air of the tomb, dusky with the scent of his pets. He was alone…as his mind cleared, he knew the voice. "Janet?

"Yes, sir. I'm sorry to disturb you so early, but there's been a development I think you should know about."

"Give me a moment." Hesha stood and found his way to the door unerringly. In Vegel's chamber, he let the lights come up. The stone door swung silently shut behind him. "All right."

"We had a call today from Rutherford House…through ordinary channels, but undeniably concerned with your projects there. It seems that Kettridge has seized on Miss Dimitros as a potential source of information. Mrs. Rutherford didn't put it like that, of course."

"Which Mrs. Rutherford?"

"Amaryllis. She expressed concern that you had exposed Miss Dimitros to some sort of danger…and frankly, laid down an ultimatum; if there is trouble between you and the professor, Miss Dimitros must be kept out of it." Janet paused, and speculated, "I got the impression, sir, that she thinks your statue is a stolen item, and that there are black-market forces beneath the mystery."

"That's harmless enough. Don't encourage it, however." Hesha pulled the loose, white eye out of his robes. Ever since the night Elizabeth had discovered how to remove it, he'd kept it on a thong around his neck. He scrutinized it as if for the first time, and made a decision.

"Janet, we're going to take Miss Dimitros out of the professor's way. Start making arrangements for an appropriate Friday flight."

Thursday, 1 July 1999, 11:20 AM
Rutherford House, Upper East Side, Manhattan
New York City, New York

Agnes Rutherford strode stiffly through the front doors of her establishment, and her sharp eyes took in every inch of the display floor with no sign whatever of approval. She looked down at her nephew James's wife—they were nearly the same height, but Agnes could look down at people who were head and shoulders taller than herself without straining.

"Good morning, Aunt Agnes," said Amy. She leaned forward and exchanged dry pecks on the cheek with her elderly relative. "How was your flight?"

"No worse than usual, for this time of year. I look forward to the end of the tourist season, however." The senior partner took a few steps farther into the shop and looked down at Amy from even greater heights than before. "Have we any important appointments scheduled for today? No? A pity, but it will at least leave us time to review the figures for the last week."

Agnes took a moment to view the display again. Her glance came to Elizabeth—and if Amy was dwarfed by the old lady's eyes, Elizabeth was less than an ant. "Miss Dimitros."

"Welcome back, Miss Rutherford."

"Carry on down here." Agnes started for the stairs to the offices, and turned back halfway. "You attended to Mr. Ruhadze last Wednesday? Were you able to sell the collar to him?"

"Yes, ma'am."

Agnes said nothing, but continued up the stairs.

That night, Thompson brought the sedan to a perfect, parallel halt at the curbside. The walls of both tires grazed cement. Between his master's door and the doors of Rutherford House there could be no shorter distance, but he worried anyway. "Careful, sir."

"Relax a little, Thompson. It really is too much to hope that the professor would have staked out the store."

"And if he did?"

"Then you are here, the Asp is...waiting in the wings, and I am not entirely without defenses of my own." Hesha slipped into his suit coat, picked up a shining black alligator briefcase and a brass-topped cane, and stepped out of the car.

Amy Rutherford welcomed him inside. "Good evening, Mr. Ruhadze." He looked at her through earnest eyes, and shook her hand. Her manner was as polished as ever, but beneath the gloss, she was not pleased with him. "Aunt Agnes is waiting for you in her office. Shall we?" She led him through the dim and empty display floor to the office stairs. The workroom was dark. At the end of the corridor, she stopped, knocked once, and ushered him into the throne room, as she thought of it.

"Mr. Ruhadze, Aunt Agnes."

"Punctual as ever, Hesha." Agnes Rutherford looked neither down on him, nor up, but she gave Hesha Ruhadze the gaze of an equal, and half-rose to greet him.

"I would never willingly waste your time, Miss Agnes," he said courteously. "It would be an insult to keep a lady waiting, particularly one with such demanding responsibilities."

Agnes half-smiled. "Sit down, Hesha, and tell us how we can be of assistance to you today."

Amy drew the door shut behind them, and sat respectfully in a corner chair to watch the giants meet. Her aunt—Jim's aunt, she reminded herself, grateful that her own family was less...everything—sat behind a stately, massive desk. Her thin, frail body dwindled in the equally impressive, red leather-upholstered chair.

Ruhadze, on the other hand, fitted the matching seat as if it had been built around him. He was a vision in monochrome—the red leather, in shadow, was the warm, brown-black color of his skin. His suit—of an outdated cut, she realized suddenly, almost contemporary with Agnes's father's days—was the color of coal. The old fabric devoured the light, but his shoes, his bag, the ebon cane he held across his knees, and his bright eyes shone with it.

"I have an unusual request, Miss Agnes." He hesitated, and seemed to pick his words carefully. "I'm afraid that I have inadvertently endangered one of your employees."

Agnes lifted her fine gray brows. "Miss Dimitros," she said quietly. He nodded. "Please explain yourself, Hesha."

"I own a particular item—"

"A statue?" interjected Amy.

"Yes." Hesha half-turned in his chair to include her in the conversation. "It is not, I assure you, 'hot' or 'black market' or anything of the kind. On the other hand, as with many antiquities, the country of its origin disapproves of any entity other than itself possessing the piece. Just as the Greeks want the treasures of Athens returned from England, a certain nation wants my little treasure returned to native soil. I have no more intention of giving it to them than I have of handing the collar I bought last week over to Cairo—less, in fact. Egypt and Greece at least have democracies, museums, and relative peace. They bring their heritage back through treaties, special funds, the United Nations...diplomatic means.

"The government in question, however, has abandoned diplomacy in almost every matter, and is a known haven for terrorists. The ruling party has made it clear that they will hide and back even the most radical of organizations, provided their demands are met and policies adhered to...one of which is the recovery of 'cultural artifacts' that, in fact, they have little claim to.

"I showed Miss Dimitros the statue as a challenge—I wanted to test her skills. Unfortunately for all of us, she was more clever than I could have hoped. Not only did she find some details previous experts had missed, she recognized a piece of the statue in a diagram in a professional publication, and contacted the author."

"Professor Kettridge," murmured Agnes.

"Yes. And Kettridge came to New York to find her." Amy clicked her tongue against the back of her teeth, and said, "I've looked into Jordan Kettridge's background. He's a fine scholar and no more a terrorist than I am."

"I don't mean to suggest that he is. I suspect that the terrorists recognized the bead, and tried to steal it. They were obviously unsuccessful. From his point of view, I suppose, Elizabeth's message was just another tactic of the thieves. When that failed, there came the extreme bid for the piece...

"I don't know what they may try next, but Kettridge has had two contacts with Elizabeth, and the terrorists are likely to think that she knows more than she does, or can lead them to the professor. For her own safety, I want to take her out of New York and away from Kettridge, the terrorists, and Rutherford House."

Agnes's eyes narrowed. Her thin, pale lips twisted into a speculative frown. "And that's why you asked me to keep her here tonight. Well, Ruhadze, what do you intend to do with our Miss Dimitros?"

Hesha stroked the harsh line of his cheekbone. "My own collection," he began, "is in need of some restoration. From what I've seen of her work, Elizabeth would be the ideal candidate to work on it." He lifted his briefcase to his lap, opened it, and slid a small sheaf of paper across the desk to Agnes. "I would make up your losses, of course, and supplement Miss Dimitros's salary while she was contracted out to me." He waited while the old lady examined the numbers. "These are figured on a week-by-week basis. I doubt that her absence would be prolonged... though there is certainly work enough in Baltimore to keep her busy for months, if need be." Amy watched her aunt's ice-blue eyes scan the bottom line, and knew what Agnes's answer would be. "Mr. Ruhadze," asked Amy, "Isn't this a matter for the police? Or," she continued sharply, "if all you're suggesting is true, a matter for the CIA *and* the FBI *and* Interpol?"

"It is," said Hesha. "And I have gone to them," he lied. "That's how I came by what information I know. We could arrange to have them take care of her. But Amy," he said, trying to meet her gaze in the shadowy corner, "do you know what the phrase 'protective custody' actually means? It means jail, and isolation, and little hotel rooms with no one to speak to but police officers and nothing to do but wait. I'd rather not inflict that on Elizabeth. She'll be safe in Baltimore, and she will be working at what she likes best. Unless one of *us* tells her about the danger, she won't even need to know it exists until after it's already passed." He looked away again, down at the thick Persian carpet. "I'd offer the same protection to Kettridge, if I could find him."

"Hesha," said Miss Agnes. "I concur with your appraisal of Miss Dimitros's value to us as a shop assistant, but I believe you are underestimating the restoration costs we will be subject to in her absence..."

And Amy listened in vague disbelief as Jim's aunt proceeded to dicker over Elizabeth Dimitros as though she were a French Provincial chair or a Ming vase. Mr. Ruhadze, at least, had the grace to be embarrassed—their eyes met once, as Agnes pulled a rate list of out-of-house fabric workers from the files. He put up very little fight; he seemed genuinely more interested in the merchandise than in the price. At least Lizzie was going where she was...highly valued. Amy stood up, suddenly unable to take any more of the haggling, and Agnes's piercing voice split though the growing headache.

"Amy, where are you going?"

"I need an aspirin, Aunt Agnes. Excuse me."

Amy fled into her own office, downed the aspirin, and sank into her big, overstuffed sofa. She tried to think straight. Terrorists and fugitives and contacts...it sounded like a spy movie, and a poorly constructed one. Ruhadze had explained everything, but...there had to be simpler ways to protect Lizzie. Was he going to all this trouble to protect her because the danger was real and he cared for her? Or was he trying to entice her away for nefarious purposes? *Oh Lord*, she thought, *Lizzie's well over the age of consent*.... She argued herself into circles and corners for another half hour or so, until she heard the door open to Agnes's room. Speech spilled into the hallway.

"I'd like to speak with her myself, of course." Hesha's

baritone came clearly through the walls.

"Of course," answered Agnes. "She's in the bindery...the third door on your left, Hesha."

Amy left the couch for the door, and opened it just as Ruhadze approached. "Mr. Ruhadze? I have some more questions for you."

He came in and sat.

"Why doesn't Kettridge go to the police? Why shouldn't we simply transfer Elizabeth to our London offices for a month, or a year, or however long this takes? What gives you the idea that there will be an end to it, if terrorists are the enemy? You're moving Elizabeth to Baltimore at a great deal of trouble and expense. Now, if you weren't telling the truth to Aunt Agnes, I doubt you'll tell it to me. Please let me make one thing clear to you. I want you to take good care of Lizzie."

Hesha smiled. He stood up, took her by the hand, and stared deep into her eyes. "Trust me," he told her, overwhelmingly serious, and compassionate, and sure. He waited for the command to sink in. Satisfied that she believed, he released her.

She sighed. "I'm sorry to have gone on like that...but I'm all she has, and I can't just let her disappear. Oh, Lord, do you realize Lizzie's been here since nine? Let's go talk to her, and send her packing. Promise me you'll keep the poor child working only eight-hour days. She'll think it's Christmas. Agnes is just a slave-driver, really."

"I've noticed," said Hesha, as he picked up his things. She smiled, and led him down the hall to the bindery.

Elizabeth looked up as she came in. "The diary's finished, Amy. If I never read another word about Elizabethan shipping businesses, it will be too soon." She flicked a hand toward the work table with contempt. "I went ahead and started the blasted papyrus—" Hesha followed Amy into the room, and Elizabeth stopped short.

Amy took up her favorite chair, and watched as their visitor came around the table to examine Lizzie's work.

"A tourist piece," he said, and the same contempt filled his voice. "Nineteenth-century souvenir." He leant over the beginnings of the repair work, and nodded approval. "But you know how to restore papyri properly. Good."

"Lizzie, Mr. Ruhadze has asked Rutherford House to lend him one of our most prized assets. How would you like to go to Baltimore and do restoration work on his private collection?"

Elizabeth sat quietly, her hands folded on the desk in front of her. She tried to catch Hesha's gaze, and did, but there was nothing there for her to read. She stared at a beaming Amy, and though the smile was luminous, the eyes were tight and worried. Slowly, the rays of confidence faded in that smile, and the older woman's anxieties revealed themselves in the lines around her mouth, too.

"You don't have to go, of course," said Amy. "And it isn't a permanent post. Your job here will be secure; we'll look after the loft for you. But Mr. Ruhadze needs someone to do the work, and Aunt Agnes is simply putty in his hands. It's all arranged—if you want it."

Elizabeth's glance appealed to Hesha again—and though there was still no sign on his face, his hand grasped her shoulder reassuringly.

"When?"

"Tomorrow afternoon?" he suggested. "You can settle in over the weekend and start work on Monday."

"That's fast."

"I know."

Elizabeth covered the crude cartouche in its protective wrappings. After the papyrus, there would be another diary, perhaps, or deed papers with "New Amsterdam" at the top instead of "New York," or a Renaissance floral with no merit besides age. Hesha's collection would be different. And Hesha himself...but she cut the thought off there.

"I'll go."

Inside the black sedan, it was unsettlingly quiet.

Elizabeth sat with her tote bag at her feet. The tickets to Baltimore were tucked into her sketchbook. She watched the lights of the city speed by, tinted blue-purple by the windows.

Introductions had been made between herself and Ronald Thompson, but Thompson wasn't one to chatter. There were streets to watch, and other cars ever to be suspected of holding the Enemy in one form or another. Hesha sensed, too, that Thompson was unsettled by the "collection" of Miss Dimitros. Hesha held his tongue. A kind word to Elizabeth would have soothed her fears and apprehension...but Thompson wasn't ready to hear his master whisper sweet nothings to a "nice" girl. A curt, businesslike discussion with the girl would have put her in her place as a curator, and nothing more, and satisfied Thompson entirely...but Hesha wasn't ready to relinquish the hold that a feigned romance might have over Elizabeth, and wasn't sure that she would let herself be railroaded to Baltimore with that enticement taken away. He would take a moment with each, separately, soon. If the drive to her apartment was silent as the grave, so much the better for his concentration.

They dropped her off at the old warehouse. She wished them good night, and faded into the darkness of the front door. A loitering figure signaled to Thompson, and the driver confirmed the watchmen's orders. The sedan pulled back onto the main roads, and Thompson looked for Hesha's eye in the rearview mirror.

"Sir..."

"Not now, Thompson. Take us back to Rutherford House. Kettridge has been there recently, and I know now how to find him."

"How well do you know New York?" Hesha asked, unexpectedly.

Thompson considered. "The main roads, the places *you* go, some of those neighborhoods in depth, and a little more, maybe."

"We're going to follow Kettridge with this." said Hesha, dangling the milk-white bead from its cord. "Its power is very low, and I will have to shut out as much of the world as I can while I use it. I will close my eyes and direct you as well as possible. Take turns to follow my line whenever the roads allow. Remember exactly where we are each time I speak to you; if we lose the trail you will have to drive back to that spot as quickly as possible, and we will try again. Do you understand?"

"No," admitted the driver, "but I think I can follow the orders."

Hesha lay down on the back seat, holding the little eye between both hands.

"North from here," he said. Thompson checked for cops, made an illegal U-turn, and drove slowly up the street.

"Stop."

Thompson eased the sedan into place next to a fire hydrant, and waited for the still form in the back seat to say further.

"He spent a long time here...but he isn't here now. Are we near a hotel?"

Thompson blinked in surprise. "We're on the doorstep of a big one."

Hesha felt for the trail through the bead. "Southwest," he said. The car rolled on, and within half a block, he knew the traces were colder than those he'd followed. "Back again. East from the hotel." Again, there was a trail, but a stale one. "Stop. Back again."

"Sir?"

"What is it?" asked Hesha, wearily.

"Let me drive around the block a few times. When you find a good lead, tell me. His 'footprints' are going to be a hell of a mess right in front of where he's staying."

"Do it."

"Stop." Hesha opened his eyes. "He's here." Thompson looked into the back seat. "Sir, I think maybe you'd better hurry."

Hesha stepped onto the curb, and understood. They had pulled up outside Grand Central Station. Hesha very nearly ran to the entrance. He hurtled into the crowds on the main floor, his quick senses devouring the faces of the travelers he brushed past. He scanned the forms of the passengers and pick-ups waiting in the long rows of seats as his footsteps took him instinctively to the walls.

Kettridge was not, now, buying a ticket at the counters or eating at any of the stalls, but he had been to both. He had not, though Hesha's search was taking time, left the building. The Setite drew slowly to a halt. It ill befitted him to run around the platforms and into the subways. He sought the solitude of an empty bank of phones, and pulled his own sleek model from his coat.

Behind him, one of the pay machines rang. He ignored it, and began dialing for Thompson, but it rang and rang until he grabbed it, checked the receiver reflexively, and put it to his ear.

"Hello, Ruhadze. How's death treating you?"

"Professor Kettridge," acknowledged Hesha.

"It's been a long time since Syria, hasn't it?"

"For you."

"Yes," said Kettridge. "for me. You haven't changed, a bit, of course. No scars from that last firefight at Baalbek, I notice. I imagine *I* look like hell, though."

"I couldn't say."

"I don't intend for you to be able to." The mortal's voice held a sharper edge than before, and he continued, "You're getting sloppy in your old age. Using a girl you were seen with so publicly to make the contact—hardly your usual finesse, is it?" Hesha said nothing. "Or were you behind the burglary attempt?"

"That might be a better guess."

"I'll give you credit, though, you weren't behind the high bid."

"I'd double it, if I thought you were interested."

"We both know I'm not…. How about a trade, instead?" Kettridge inquired, thoughtfully.

"What would you take for the bead?"

"I'm not bartering beads today," said the professor. "I'll trade you information."

Hesha considered. "I'm listening."

"I'll tell you where the high bid came from, if you'll tell me why every dead man in the world seems interested in my little lucky charm."

"Not good enough. There are probably five or more intermediaries between you and the bidder."

"No, not this time. Someone was in an awful hurry." Temptation brushed by Hesha, and she was smiling. "Tell me where the high bid came from, and I'll answer three questions about your bead. Specific questions. How helpful the answers are will depend, of course, on how intelligently you put your questions."

For nearly a full minute—which Hesha spent in efforts to pinpoint Kettridge and his "lucky charm"—the line gave up nothing but static.

"Harlem. What *is* the bead?"

"It's the eye of a statue."

Kettridge named a street. "Why does it pull me toward Atlanta?"

"It's a subsidiary item to a more powerful artifact. Your eye can locate the main artifact. The main artifact is or was in Atlanta."

"2417A. Basement entrance. How did you find me here tonight?"

"I have another eye of the statue. It can locate your eye. I can follow you anywhere you go, Kettridge," said Hesha, and the mortal could hear the smile in the creature's voice.

The professor, from his own booth deep within the maze of the station, felt a chill run down his spine. He hefted a duffel bag onto his shoulder, and felt the comforting metal lumps of his weapons within. "I wouldn't recommend that, Ruhadze," he said evenly. "I've learned a lot since Baalbek."

"Good. Let me offer you some advice." Hesha whispered into the phone. "Get out of New York as fast as you can. I won't come after you—yet—but if the address you gave me is correct, you have half the hounds of hell on your tail."

"I know. I've singed some. Your kind don't like crowds or fire, do they?"

"Don't assume anything. Don't call *them* my kind," hissed Hesha. "And if you want to rely on crowds for protection, don't go to Atlanta or the other riot zones."

Kettridge looked down at his tickets: Amtrak to Atlanta— through D.C. and Raleigh. He was suddenly afraid. "Damn it, Hesha—your telling me not to is a good reason to go! Why should I trust you? Why warn me? Why all these mindgames? God, I can't believe we're having this conversation—give me a reason why I should believe a single fucking thing you've said, from start to finish?"

"I would rather that you kept the bead, Jordan, than have it fall into the hands of the high bidder. In the riot zones, they won't care about witnesses. Understand?" He waited. "Jordan?"

The line was dead, and though Hesha quickly found a phone still warm from his rival's hand, he felt the red eye speeding away south. In ten minutes, he could no longer sense it at all.

part two

maryland

Friday, 2 July 1999, 6:20 PM
Laurel Ridge Farm
Columbia, Maryland

Elizabeth strained to see through the twilight. The woods around them looked much like the woods they'd been traveling through for the past ten minutes, and the road was the same nearly unmarked, two-lane affair it had been. She knew that Columbia was a large, built-up suburb. Logically, there should be houses, shops, lights, and larger streets nearby, but she hadn't seen any since the last stop sign.

The sedan passed a yellow diamond with the most elaborate squiggle on it that Elizabeth had ever seen. She grasped the armrest tightly, and they took a series of curves like a drunken roller coaster. Thompson flicked up the headlights halfway through a sweeping arc, and gray tree-trunks flashed by in a blur. They sped around one last corner and turned up a driveway. It clung to a creekside and then edged its way up the side of a hill, passing a mailbox, unmarked. They bumped gently and slowly over gravelly macadam, crested the shoulder of the hill, and Elizabeth had her first sight of the house of Hesha Ruhadze.

In the center, facing the drive, was a solid massif—a majestically proportioned old house with tall, mullioned windows, grand double-doors under a neoclassical lintel, and perfect symmetry. As the car pulled around, she saw a later addition, tacked on by a lesser architect for a larger family. The back wing tried to echo the front, but it was cluttered with odd side-roofs, long eaves, dormer rooms, and gables that projected at impossible angles. The whole mess was painted white—not recently, and not for the first time. Good red brick showed at the corners, where the winds had had the best chance to knock the flakes away. The roof was verdigris-green copper in excellent repair, and behind a morass of bracken and wildflowers, Elizabeth could see a real fieldstone foundation running underneath it all. It was shabby. It wasn't what she had expected. It did have charm.

Thompson eased the car over the weed-eaten drive and pulled up to a slightly more modern-looking barn. He touched a button on his console and the broad doors slid open. The black sedan rolled gingerly into place beside a car that might have been its twin, and stopped.

Elizabeth stepped onto the clean-swept brick floor. She dragged her carry-on, her purse, and satchel out with her. Thompson walked around, pulled her checked bags from the trunk, and groaned.

"What do you have in here, bricks?"

"They're books. I'm working on my doctorate in Art History. That one rolls, by the way. We can pile everything else on top of it."

"What's your concentration?" he asked, as he swung the lighter suitcase into place and clipped it down.

"It's rather obscure…call it comparative symbology."

"What does that mean?" Thompson began trolling the double-decker baggage along a moss-covered path of slate flagstones.

"Um. Take a bull in a painting—a painting you don't have captions for because you can't read the script the people wrote in. Does it represent fertility? A sacrifice? An amount of goods for barter? A god? If it is a god, which god is it, and why did the painter use the allegory of 'god as bull'? And did it represent that god before or after an invasion from another culture that happened to have a thing for cattle?"

Thompson manhandled the cases up three wooden steps to the porch. "Why can't it just be a bull?" He punched a code into a keypad next to a wasps' nest and opened the door to let her through.

"Sometimes it is. But my specialty is very primitive motifs. The farther back in history you go, the less plain doodling you get, and the more each symbol *means* something important to the person who made it."

Elizabeth turned to look around her. They'd come into the long, narrow kitchen. The appliances were ultra-modem, but the cabinets and table looked, to her experienced eye, as if they were original to the house. She drifted a little into the working end of things, and fiddled idly with a white enamel drawer pull.

"Just set your stuff down here," said Thompson. "You have your choice of rooms, so I'll show you around and let you pick before I take your bag of bricks anywhere. Come on."

He led her through a wide hall into the older half of the building and up a dark and creaking staircase.

"My room is down that way," he said, inclining his graying head to the back of the house. "And the cook's, too; you'll meet him later. The guest rooms are in the front." Thompson leaned into an open doorway, turned a lamp on inside, and stepped away for Elizabeth to have a look. "Or, if you aren't claustrophobic, you can come downstairs. Some people don't like the idea of basements...."

"No, that's fine. I worked under the Met four summers running, and you feel the traffic through the tabletops down there."

The cellar door from the kitchen still led down to the cellar—but where the original inhabitants had left packed earth floors, Hesha Ruhadze had laid shining planks stained nearly black. The fieldstone foundations formed the walls, and support pillars four feet square stood in carefully cut gaps in the dark wood.

The main room was filled with display cases and glass-fronted shelves. Here and there a couch and table, a chair and desk, or stool and workbench were grouped near the exhibits. Several huge tables held binding supplies, pieces of pottery in reconstruction, and other temptations for the historian. Elizabeth dragged her feet past a long, low table full of *things* that needed her ministrations, and only when Thompson cleared his throat and called her could she turn away. On the other side of the long hall—at what she thought must be the outer edge of the house upstairs—he waited at the bottom of short flight of wide, slate steps, holding open a door made in the same style as the floor.

"This was Mr. Vegel's room," he said.

"Mr. Vegel?" The little apartment was richly furnished in a very Victorian, masculine fashion. Three walls were paneled and the fourth was wood only to waist height; above the chair rail it was covered in white satin fabric, and discreet silver pins held papers, photographs, and pieces of fabric to it as if to a huge bulletin board.

"Mr. Ruhadze didn't mention him?" Thompson asked. She shook her head but didn't show much curiosity. He let the subject go. "Books and so forth here," he said, unnecessarily. The entire wall was shelves, not full, but comfortably crowded. He and the Asp had had a rough day going through Vegel's apartment. Hesha's list of items forbidden to the newcomer was long, and there weren't many safe places to store the really dangerous things. After the clean-out, Thompson's practiced hands had massaged the gaps in the shelves. Unless you knew how full Vegel had kept his office, you'd never realize anything was missing. Thompson watched the girl react to the room, her fingers wandering along the rows of rare and expensive editions, and decided that the boss's guess had been correct. It always was.

"Mr. Vegel was the previous curator. He lived down here, mostly. Of course, you're the only guest. You could turn this room into office space, work area, whatever you need, and actually sleep upstairs. The guest rooms do have nice views, particularly in the summer."

"Oh, no," said Elizabeth, looking at the desk and the library. "This will be perfect."

"I'll bring down your things." As he left, Thompson smiled in satisfaction. Trust Hesha to know what was catnip, and for which kitties…. He pressed a code on the kitchen intercom, and spoke into it. "Sir?"

"Yes, Thompson?"

"Miss Dimitros is here. She's chosen Vegel's room. I'll bring her things down in a moment. I've left the impression that you won't be available for at least an hour yet."

"Thank you. I'll see her when Janet and I have finished."

Thompson cut the connection. He picked up Elizabeth's carry-on, and took from the closest drawer an object that manifestly did not belong in a kitchen—a hand-held metal scanner. All the bags were clean.

He looked longingly at the hall leading into the old house. In the space between the walls, there was a hidden elevator. But Elizabeth might not be in her room when the car opened in the first basement, and so he slung her bag full of books over his broad shoulders, and used the stairs. The girl was deep in a book when he brought the luggage in, but she smiled and offered to help.

"No thanks," said Thompson. He put the heavy case in a convenient corner—blocking her off, he hoped, from finding the door hidden there—and in two more trips all her things were with her.

"Well, if you'll excuse me, I have some chores to see to, and business arrangements to make for Mr. Ruhadze's townhouse. If you need anything, there's an intercom here by the door," he said, sliding open a wooden panel. "Just press the green button and speak into it." He closed the tiny cabinet again, walked out, and shut the door softly behind him.

Elizabeth looked up from her unpacking. Was that a knock? She closed the drawer on her socks, crossed the room—now rather cluttered with open suitcases and boxes of notes—and opened the door.

"Good evening, Elizabeth."

"Hello, Hesha."

They wavered on the threshold. "Come on in," she said, smiling. "I'm still in the messy stages of the explosion, I'm afraid." She backed into the room, and gestured vaguely.

Hesha lowered himself into Vegel's chair, stretched his legs out, and watched her move. She rattled off expressions of gratitude, compliments for Thompson, and amazement at the house. She had questions about the building, and he answered them with his connoisseur's voice and attitude...a stock character, a mask held up for her to look at while he studied her. She was nervous, but comfortable with the surroundings. It was he himself who made her fingers restless and the tiny muscles of her face unsettled. Every time she looked to him, a question was in her eyes, and he made sure to keep all the answers out of his own.

He found himself relieved that the Beast remained calm in her presence...and was shocked to realize that he had been worried unawares. What was it that had given the thing so much strength in her apartment? The statue? His worries about the Sabbat's machinations? Vegel's disappearance? He determined to watch the Beast and his own mind more closely—the weakness could not be allowed to remain.

"Are you tired?" he asked, changing the subject.

Elizabeth stopped in mid-fold. "No."

"But you had to think about it?"

"It's nearly ten, isn't it? I suppose that I should be—I had to be up early to pack—but I'm too excited about the work. I caught a glimpse of some of the pieces coming down here."

He nodded understandingly. "Would you like a tour?"

Absolutely." Halfway to the door she stopped and faced him earnestly. "Unless you're tired. I don't want to keep you from your schedule...."

"I confess that I succumbed to temptation earlier. West Coast lawyers are the worst, I think. I had the cook bring down some coffee...Turkish coffee. I'll be awake all night," he sighed, "but it was the only way I could deal with the fools who were chattering at me. Besides, tomorrow is Saturday. Only my international affiliates will try to get at me, and my secretary can say 'No' in forty languages."

Elizabeth chuckled and followed him out.

"...And the ventilation system is fully labeled...if you have any problems, do let Thompson know," said Hesha. He turned to another corner of the workshop.

"This flat file is full of paper that needs acid-balance treatment. The vertical stores contain ten or twelve paintings that need work of one kind or another, and I have all kinds of stabilization projects, of course. I know that painting restoration is a specialty of yours. If you'll finish just that section during your stay here, I'd be amply compensated for your expenses. However, if you'd like to try your hand at more unusual things…" He paced back into the main room at a businesslike clip. "Here," he said, almost smiling, "is the emperor of all jigsaw puzzles."

It was under glass, on the longest, narrowest table in the entire museum. On smooth fabric lay what once had been a scroll. "Papyrus," said Hesha. "Part of the grave goods of a pharaoh. Thieves robbed the tomb but the left the 'rubbish' behind—baskets, clay pots, food. This was in a plain wooden case, and they ignored it. More literate thieves picked it up later. Unfortunately, it has been shaken and jarred, and some fool tried to unroll it."

He turned and asked of her, "Do you read the hieroglyphs?"

"No."

"Vegel left notes of the script in use at the period," he said, opening a small drawer built into the table. He offered her a sheaf of hand-made sketches. "Also, the tweezers…" He held up a bizarre-looking pair of tongs. "To keep the dust and the air currents from playing havoc with the shards, we had to cover the whole piece with glass. These slip into the gaps at the edges." He demonstrated, setting two halves of a glyph closer together. Gingerly, he tilted the tweezers up and away from the scraps, and slowly drew the tool back out of the danger zone. "You might want to practice with the sections at the top of the scroll first. The damage is less extensive, and the pieces are easier to read."

He whisked her away from the long table, and continued. "Vegel's particular hobby horse—" he led her to an area carpeted in canvas. An unfinished wooden frame ten feet square and one foot high hemmed in the dusty white cloth. On low shelves on three sides, fragments of jars and bowls freed from the matrix reposed in little trays; one half-reconstructed amphora-like vessel stood above the detritus. In the midst of it, a small boulder of dried clay lay at a resentful tilt. Edges of pottery shards stuck out of it from every angle.

"What is it?" asked Elizabeth.

"We—I'm not sure. Vegel collected it from someone; no provenance available." Hesha thought of the haven the thing had originally occupied. They'd never found out why the Malkavian had treasured the boulder, or where it had come from. But Vegel insisted that it hid something unusual, and the elder Setite had agreed—after certain tests and precautions— to let the archaeologist bring the boulder home. "I don't know whether Erich expected to find anything particularly interesting in it. He had been an archaeologist earlier in his career, and I think he simply liked to keep in practice."

Hesha stepped back, regretfully. "That's all for now. If I'm going to sleep in tomorrow, I have to work tonight, and I'm sure you'll want to finish settling yourself. I can spare the time to show you our finished pieces Monday, perhaps."

"Thank you."

He shook his head. "Thank you for coming on such short notice."

She laughed. "Thank you for rescuing me from Aunt Agnes." Her eyes sought out his. Hesha felt the glance coming, avoided it so deftly that she never knew he'd shunned her, and began the walk back to his office. Behind him, her footsteps tapped a trail across the floor—not toward Vegel's room, but to the long table.

"You're not thinking of starting on that tonight, are you?" he asked without looking.

"I thought I'd just go over it to see what's been done so far."

"Well," he said, nodding to himself. "Try not to stay up too late. If you get hungry, there are all kinds of things in the kitchen…just be careful not to wake the cook."

Hesha left his new protégée hard at work, and joined his other servants in the crypt. Even the Asp was shocked to see the smile on their master's face.

Saturday, 3 July 1999, 11:42 AM
Laurel Ridge Farm
Columbia, Maryland

Feeling late and guilty, Elizabeth trundled up the stairs to the kitchen and found herself confronted by a small, unexpected man in an apron, washing dishes. His hair was very dark, and slightly curly. His skin was a shade or two deeper than her own—a clean, tanned, Mediterranean olive color. His rolled-up shirt sleeves exposed arms thick with wiry black hair. He reached for another bowl, and smiled at her.

"Good morning. I'm sorry I'm up so late," Liz said.

"Why are you sorry? It's Saturday, isn't it?"

"I'm sorry for missing breakfast," she began, then hesitated. "Aren't you the cook?"

"Oh. That's just Ron and the Man being polite. I can cook, but mostly I just buy the groceries. Are you hungry? Of course you're hungry. You just woke up, right? Want an omelet?" He gave her no chance to protest. "I was only washing up from breakfast so I could start lunch. We'll call it brunch. I make the best Italian-American French cooking you've ever had." His twinkling black eyes gave her the once-over. "A big omelet. You're too skinny, as my Mamma would've said." He dried a hand on the dishcloth and extended it. They shook vigorously. "I'm Angelo Mercurio. But just call me the Asp; everybody does."

"Elizabeth Dimitros. Liz," she said back. Then, "The Asp?"

"I bite," said Mercurio with a conspiratorial wink, thoroughly enjoying himself in the role of colorful, harmless houseboy. "Anyway. Noon is fine. Ron Thompson's the only early riser I know, and he cheats. Naps from about five to eight. Hesha—Mr. Ruhadze—well, the boss just comes and goes as he pleases. Jetlagged half the time, working himself to a frazzle the other. I can't remember the last time he had anything like a good night's sleep," said the Asp, in total honesty.

"How many other people live here?" asked Liz, watching as the Asp cracked eight eggs into a bowl one-handed.

"Just Ron and the boss and me, since Vegel's gone. House guests, of course. And occasionally the boss will have some of his assistants in for a working party. We're not precisely 'Lifestyles of the Rich and Famous' here."

"What happened to Mr. Vegel?"

The Asp's bright eyes dimmed for a moment. "Heart attack. Very sudden. Just a few weeks ago...and he was a young man, too. Mid-thirties." He picked up a spatula and began to do clever things to the cholesterol-laden omelet. "Maybe we'll have salad for lunch tomorrow, huh?"

Hesha came down the stairs from the kitchen holding a briefcase and a *Wall Street Journal*. He passed the papyrus table on the way to his own study and broke his slightly weary stride to look over Elizabeth's shoulder as he went by. It was only a moment's pause; long enough for the woman to expect comment, short enough that the lack thereof would not seem dismissive or curt. In his study, he laid down the props. In his apartment, he shed the suit and shoes, pulling on khakis and a worn-looking linen shirt. Quick change complete, he stepped back into the basement hall.

"Nice work," he said over his guest's shoulder.

Elizabeth nearly dropped the tweezers into the papyrus. "Lord. You'd think you'd make some noise, walking across a wooden floor, Hesha."

"Sorry."

"Can you take a look at the text near the topmost illustration? I'm sure the painted parts go together, but I can't tell a faded ibis from a faded owl from a faded vulture."

He pulled a chair up the table's edge, and fixed a monocle

into his left eye. "Tweezers?" Elizabeth handed him hers and fetched another pair from the drawer. They worked quietly for some time. "It's a falcon," he said eventually. "That would explain the confusion."

Silence reigned once more, though Hesha could feel that the woman's attention strayed to his face quite often. He kept his eyes on the text, and his conversation on the work. At length, Hesha peered into the scraps directly beneath him. "I think there's another illustration coming here. See if you can fill that in." He stood up. "But don't wear yourself out. I hear you were up past four last night." Elizabeth smiled, shrugged, and nodded. "Well, do as you choose. But if you find yourself keeping owl's hours, don't blame me." He started to leave.

Reminded, Liz looked up and asked, "Is there an alarm clock I could borrow?"

"You might talk to the Asp or Thompson," said Hesha, watching her. "I don't use one." He added, "Have a nice night," and was pleased to see her distress as she realized he was going for good.

Sunday, 4 July 1999, 7:56 PM
Laurel Ridge Farm
Columbia, Maryland

"Thompson? Report."

"The Asp has two new refugees. Three of the originals have found havens with closer kin under Prince Garlotte. Miss Dimitros took a walk earlier and tripped the perimeter alarm, but otherwise not so much as a raccoon."

"How did she spend her day?"

"She began on one of those modern things…the bluish one… did some more work on the painting she'd already started; some reading in her room; dinner with the Asp and me. I believe she's on the papyrus at the moment."

"Did she get her alarm clock?"

"I lent her mine. It 'mysteriously' shorted out when we plugged it into the socket."

"Good." Hesha thought for a few moments. "Have my car ready."

"Your car, sir?"

"Yes. Follow if you like, but I think Miss Dimitros needs a night away from work. Today is a holiday, you know." The old cop looked at him blankly, and he went on. "Independence Day, Thompson. In fact, take the night off. Tell the Asp the same thing."

"Both of them, sir?" Hesha's man's voice was incredulous.

"Yes."

Sunday, 4 July 1999, 10:00 PM
Aboard the sailboat Lotus, Baltimore Harbor
Baltimore, Maryland

Over the water, the last strains of "The Star-Spangled Banner" could be heard—confusingly mixed with the orchestral finish that came, a second and a half sooner, over the radio. The diva's voice gave way to the master of ceremonies, and Hesha switched off the channel.

In total silence, the first fireworks went up...and by the time the second round had risen, the popping, crackling noises of the bright red, white, and blue rockets came to Elizabeth's waiting ears. She slid a little deeper into the deck chair, happier at that moment than she could remember being for years...since her father died. Dad had taken her to Atlantic City once, to see the fireworks fly off a decrepit old pier. Her eyes filled with the shooting stars and she forgot her troubles.

Hesha closed his eyes to slits, and enjoyed the flashing colors through the shield of long lashes. But eventually, as at his age, he supposed was inevitable, the charms of the celebration faded. He let his dark eyes roll toward the woman beside him. Elizabeth, still entranced by the spectacle, didn't notice his attention, and he took full advantage of the opportunity to see her in this secret way. The colors above them reflected off of the water around the boat, off the night-pale skin of his guest, in the spheres of her eyes, and from a tear on her cheek, which he didn't understand. Red and gold burst above them, and the water, the girl, and her eyes turned to flame...blue and white and yellow together, and they were tarnished silver... in green and blue, she'd risen from the ocean, and the streaking tears were only seawater falling from the naiad.... The Beast began to stir. Hesha shook himself mentally, and retreated in his mind to the icy core of his nature. This was the opportunity he had looked for to analyze the weakness that had touched him in her loft.

She was not beautiful. That might have tempted what few urges of the flesh remained to him, but in the circles with which the millionaire Ruhadze mingled, beauty—of kine or Cainite or his own kin—was common enough, and had not bothered him in such a way for centuries.

She was not brilliant. Intelligent, yes. Perceptive in an unusual manner, perhaps. But again, he surrounded himself with geniuses of one kind or another—Thompson and the Asp both in their way, Janet a wizard in hers, and Yasmine Oxenti... who *was* beautiful, though he had never considered the fact before except as an asset to her utility.... Vegel had been brilliant. Kettridge was brilliant.

She was not devious. He had a deep admiration for that twist of mind in others, of course.

Was it because he had placed her off limits to the Beast? In the sheer perversity of the thing's instincts, the forbidden nature of the girl—too valuable to be swallowed whole, not yet controlled enough to be kept for food, too unknown to be Embraced—could be enough to drive the creature to frenzy. But again, Doctor Oxenti should be the more tempting. Beautiful, brilliant, devious, and so valuable a retainer that he could never hope to bring her to Set until an equal pawn arose to replace her...if he sought a childe, a victim, a companion, or a—he laughed to himself—a mate, Yasmine should be the kine that took the Beast's attentions.

Elizabeth stirred in her chair, and curled her bare legs beneath her. Her gaze was still on the sparks and the stars, but one hand moved toward her cheeks.

Hesha reached out and wiped the tears away for her. The woman's grateful, troubled face turned to meet his. From within the ice, he directed his face to show a little kindness. He pulled a clean handkerchief from his trouser pocket and handed it to her silently, as though there were genuine sympathy behind the act. "I'm sorry," she began, but he shook his head. Elizabeth persevered. "No, I really have been enjoying myself. Thank you for bringing me here. It's just…" she started to sob, quite quietly and without losing control.

And Hesha pulled her closer to him, held the shaking girl in his arms—warm arms, in the Baltimore summer—and let her tell him about her father, about everything he'd learned from reading her papers. He listened, and he contemplated cold-bloodedly how best to repair her wounds, and what weaknesses he would leave to control her by, and how soon she could be the equal of the Mercurio twins and Janet Lindbergh and Yasmine Oxenti and Ronald Thompson.

Monday, 5 July 1999, 8:06 PM
Laurel Ridge Farm
Columbia, Maryland

Hesha emerged from his resting place to find Thompson already waiting for him. "Good evening, sir," said the retainer, obviously nervous. "I've...I've made up my mind, sir. About the 'living will' we were discussing." Hesha sat down on the edge of the stone bench. "I would like to become one of the Family, sir."

Hesha nodded, and in his least human tones, asked, "You have decided to become accursed, damned, forbidden the sun, forbidden a heart, bound to the service of Set and through him bound to the service of Apep?"

Thompson faltered. "Sir?"

"You have a purpose in your mind that will fill centuries and drive you forth every night without despair?"

Thompson said nothing. Hesha stood, and advanced on his servant. They stood face to face, within inches of each other, and the mortal could feel the chill of the other's robes—the temperature of the rocks around them—cave-cold.

"You accept the risk that you may lose your mind, like the Cainite we destroyed in Mexico?" Hesha took his man by the jaw. The Setite lifted until the feet no longer touched the ground, and stared golden-irised and slit-pupiled into Thompson's blue-gray eyes. They remained locked together for nearly two minutes...and then Hesha set his servant gently down.

"You have thought about what you know," he said. "Tonight I have told you things you did not know. Think about them. Ask me questions. Consider that your education has begun, and start looking through your men for a replacement for your position. If, after you have learned a little more of the consequences, you still desire Set's blessings, we will need a security man as good as you yourself.

Hesha threw a glance back at the mortal. "And do relax, Thompson. You passed a test just now. There will be others, but if you change your mind at any time, you may turn off the path. There is no *necessity* to 'graduate.'"

"Now," he resumed, in his accustomed tones, "Report, please."

Half an hour later, Hesha and Thompson sat at a horseshoe-shaped console, watching the records of the day. In black and white, color, and heat-register, the various views from the farmhouse's security system surrounded the main display. Outside, a stiff wind created a confusion of swaying trees and bracken. The interior shots were calmer. The Asp moved from one screen to the next—leaving the kitchen for the main staircase and his upstairs room. Elizabeth sat in the center of another, motionless except for one hand and arm and the long tweezers they held. Her precise movements went on without hurry or hesitation, but she might have been a statue otherwise.

"Elizabeth Dimitros," murmured Hesha, "is, for all practical purposes, an orphan. You've read her dossier?"

"Of course."

"Good. She needs a family, Thompson. We are going to provide one." He paused, and met the eye of his prospective heir. "It is my intention that she come to see me as a father figure. I would like you to use what talents you possess to put yourself in the role of an older brother or an uncle, whichever you prefer. Consider this your first assignment on your new path. Don't act, but bring the parts of your personality that will be more useful into play. Tell no direct lies, if you can help it. Imply what you will. Less is more, Thompson. Understood?"

"Yes, sir."

"Excellent. Get the car ready. I'll make a token appearance to our guest and join you in the garage in twenty minutes."

Tuesday, 6 July 1999, 3:41 PM
Laurel Ridge Farm
Columbia, Maryland

Ron Thompson loped easily in through the workshop's open door and called out. "Liz? Liz?" He rounded a corner, and found her dabbing slowly at the surface of a painting. "There you are," he said unnecessarily. "Wait—is that the little square thing you started on last week?"

Elizabeth nodded, and carefully brought the cleanser away from the canvas. "The genre painting."

"Genre?" Thompson put a friendly, interested spin on the single word, and was pleased to see her reaction; she smiled and turned the picture to him, explained it in a manner neither patronizing nor dry.

"Norman Rockwell circa 1630. Life as lived by the simple folk in the Benelux."

"Wow." He stepped up to see it better, carefully not looming over her. "That looked just like mud before you came. What are they doing?"

"Farm chores. There'll be more detail tomorrow." She dabbed at it again.

Thompson watched for a while longer, waiting. "I was wondering if you wanted to run some errands with me. I need to do a hardware run for the house and some shopping for myself—I don't know if you need anything, but if you want to give me a list or come along yourself, there's a mall and an art-supply store Vegel used to go to."

"Can you wait half an hour? This is almost done."

"Sure."

Wednesday, 7 July 1999, 2:03 PM
Laurel Ridge Farm
Columbia, Maryland

"Morning, Asp." Elizabeth leaned over the central island of the kitchen, and watched the cook work on some kind of pinky-gray mixture in a steel bowl. She raised an eyebrow.

"Tuna-fish Pâté," he said. "We're playing 'guess that meal' again. It's breakfast for you, isn't it? The boss is having early lunch—or late lunch, I'm not sure, and good old Ron hasn't made an appearance yet. So the plan is sandwiches."

In the bowl's mirror-like finish, he watched the woman sit down at the table with her book and soda. He concentrated on the ingredients his brother had left ready for lunch. He wished Gabriel had a less professional hand in the kitchen....

"Relish?" he asked, when the bread was sliced and ready.

"Relish what?" she punned shamelessly, but the Asp didn't catch the joke. "Sorry. Yes, please. Sweet relish—provided it's pickles and nothing weird like okra or guava or something."

Raphael laughed again. Elizabeth looked up, startled.

"You have something against nouvelle cuisine?" He frowned into the condiments; he wasn't paying much attention to her.

"Don't you?" she inquired, watching him.

"Well, I'm with Ron. If it's such a bad idea that you have to say it in French, he's against it...with," snickered Raphael, "*a few* exceptions...." He brandished his wide knife over the various mixtures in front of him and began pasting relish onto slices of bread. Elizabeth took the food with a smile, fled down the stairs, and looked back toward the kitchen with something like fear. Silly, she knew, to suddenly shun a man because his laughter was…a little…different. Had she misjudged his sense of humor? She'd come to think of Angelo as a—not yet a friend, but certainly as a potential friend. She was afraid, now that she knew him better, that he would be someone to be tolerated rather than liked.

"Thompson," said Hesha. "Your new assignment?" The old cop closed his notebook. "Miss Dimitros and I are completely Liz and Ron now, sir. She likes baseball, chocolate, mysteries, and drama. She thinks Vegel had wonderful taste in adventure stories and whodunits, and we dropped in at a bookstore on the way home. She's started me on Shakespeare, and I found a police-procedural series that she wasn't familiar with. She's the little sister I never had—"

"Yes." Hesha said dryly. "Very well. Look to business. I'm intending a long session with her this evening." He walked to his apartment door, disappeared within, and came back out wearing his most elderly-looking spectacles. "They add ten years, sir."

"Good. I hope that's enough."

During conversation over the papyrus, Hesha turned the subject toward his goal. "What's all this I hear about your dissertation?"

"I'm sorry?"

"Thompson's been going on about bulls and eyes and fish for almost a week now. Somehow," he smiled, "I have the feeling he's gotten things a bit garbled."

Thompson, listening in from the security bunker, snorted. He'd reported the bull story in total accuracy, and understood every word. Still, if it took the boss where they needed to go…. Yes. There she went.

Elizabeth brought out a sturdy manuscript box, and Hesha pointed to the largest empty table. Talking with the speed and enthusiasm displayed only by graduate students in mid-theory, she spread notes, drawings, and timelines across the polished surface. She pulled up a straight-backed chair and sat in it cock-eyed, one leg tucked beneath her, passing diagrams and summaries to Hesha as fast as he could read them. The glasses came out of their case, and his best professorial, fatherly manner came out with them.

Thompson, taking a rest from his own work, turned up the sound on the central screen again. Elizabeth's notes completely covered the surface of the huge table, and there were open books—some of them Vegel's—scattered on top of them. Light blue sticky-notes nearly hid the edges of the largest volume, and he recognized it as one she'd fastened onto the moment she was shown the dead man's room.

"...Good. Strong argument, strong defense." He settled back into the big chair. "But you'll never make a dissertation of it."

Elizabeth went red, and started to speak. Hesha cut her off with an open hand.

"How long have you been trying?" The girl's face grew angry-white. "There's too much here, Elizabeth. You have an entire book, possibly a multiple volume work in this. Take five percent of it, limit the scope, and write that. Take the degree and start publishing pieces in the journals. But this...this is too much."

Relieved, resentful, but generally pleased, Elizabeth relaxed a little into the straight-back. Hesha patted her hand reassuringly.

The debate went on, but Thompson wasn't listening anymore. He'd seen what happened to the girl's eyes when Hesha touched her. Ten-year glasses weren't going to be enough. He hoped that Hesha had noticed the look on Elizabeth's face—and he prayed that Hesha had expected it.

Thursday, 8 July 1999, 9:14 AM
Laurel Ridge Farm
Columbia, Maryland

Ronald Thompson awoke with a jolt.

An alarm—somewhere *inside* the house, by the tone. He threw off the covers and opened a panel by his bed— the perimeter lights were green—the house itself secure, according to the system—but an intruder had made it so far as Vegel's vault. The sun streaming in through the windows reminded him that Hesha would be asleep—sound asleep....

Thompson ran down the hall and jumped most of the stairs to the first floor, bellowing for the Asp as he went. Thank god it was Raphael here—if they had to fight, that murderous little creature was the better of the twins.

He whipped the elevator door aside and took the car down to the second basement as fast as it would go. His stomach objected to the drop, and he cursed Liz for the charade they all had to play. He belonged in his room off the security bunker, not upstairs in that draughty relic of a house. Thompson swore, and snatched one of the guns from the rack by the shaft doors. His eyes scanned the light codes as he ran through the surveillance station, and he swore again. No need to curse Liz. The intruder's entry point was from her room; the damned Cainite would have taken care of her before cracking the door open. Vegel must have been captured, not killed....

The door from Vegel's vault into Hesha's was still closed. Good. There might be time to see who or what had found its way inside. He brought the lights and the camera into full play in the carved stone room, and stopped cold. Elizabeth Dimitros, clad in light-blue striped pajamas, was stumbling aimlessly around the crypt. The door into her room—Vegel's room—hung ajar behind her. No light shone from the apartment. Thompson set down his gun. He hit the intercom to his ally, and called the killer off. "It's only Liz, Asp. Looks like she's sleepwalking." "You're shitting me." "No. The catch on the door must be faulty. I'll go up and put her back to bed before she knocks her head on a rock and wakes up." Thompson turned the lights in the vault down to a candle's power, replaced the automatic, and set about putting the house in order.

Hesha emerged from his resting place to the outer chamber. He was mildly surprised to see Thompson already in the room, and still more put off by the fact that his servant was not waiting for him. The door to Vegel's apartment was open, and Thompson's hands were busy with the delicate mechanisms that held it shut.

"Thompson?" Hesha lifted an ebon eyebrow, and his man rose to speak.

"The catch was loose, sir." He opened his mouth to go on, but Hesha cut in.

"Where is Elizabeth?"

"I asked her to pick up the mail. It's all right—I set up the box with only the kinds of things she ought to see there. But I had to get her out of the house to work on this."

"And we absolutely must fix this catch today because—?"

Thompson clenched his teeth at the Setite's tone, but answered calmly enough. "Because our Liz sleepwalks, and this morning she stumbled through Vegel's door without realizing it. I thought you'd like the secure areas *secure*, sir."

Hesha nodded. "Of course." He looked at the door's lock edge and scrutinized the work. "Thank you, Thompson."

After the sundown conference, Hesha followed Thompson to the bunker, and the mortal pulled the morning's tapes for his employer.

Elizabeth, they saw through the cameras, was working on the boulder, steadily whittling down a previously untouched area of the mud. Hesha dismissed Thompson to double-check all the concealed doors, panels, drop chutes, and caches in the other parts of the house.

Hesha sat down at the console and popped video after video into the machines. He set the counters to start the entire bank of recordings at the same time—roughly an hour before Thompson's frantic morning dash. He waited with the patience of death, and eventually movement began in the view of Vegel's room.

The woman's sleeping form tossed uncomfortably on the massive bed. The sheets tangled around her legs, and her pajama top had slid up until the first button nearly choked her. In another ten minutes, her jerking, unconscious movements had freed her legs, but now they dangled over the side of the mattress. A toe touched the floor, and she sat up. She slipped off the bed and wandered to the closets. Uncertain hands opened a drawer, and she pulled apart a pair of socks. The socks were then set on the bed, and apparently forgotten.

Elizabeth, her eyes half open, shuffled to the desk now. With the eraser end of a pencil, she wrote nothing—partly on the pad of paper that sat cockeyed on the desk, partly on the wood and leather of the desktop. She followed the pin-cushion wall back to the closet end of the room, playing vaguely with the tacked-up notes and articles. Her body hid the spring-latch from the camera's eye, so he couldn't see how the accident happened, but the door opened a crack, and the woman walked through onto the cold stone floor of the crypt.

Hesha observed idly as the other cameras began to show action—half-clad Thompson running about the house like a jumping jack—the Asp gliding sinuously down the stairs from the kitchen, weapons ready—Thompson in the elevator, in the bunker, in the room with the sleepwalker, plucking her sleeve, closing the door, and nudging her gently toward the bed.

Hesha watched Thompson watching Elizabeth as she slid back into real sleep. The old cop stood still as a statue for eight minutes, then turned and went out by the visible door. For the full eight minutes the Setite watched the mortals captured on camera, and then his finger jabbed the off button.

"Secure?" Hesha asked Thompson, who was just returning from his rounds.

"Yes, sir."

Their eyes leapt at the same moment to the center monitor. With the players off, the settings had reverted to Thompson's last arrangement, and Elizabeth and the boulder were displayed in soundless color. The Asp had just entered the view.

Raphael Mercurio carried a tray—chili, which Thompson knew gratefully was the reheated work of the other twin. Elizabeth smiled politely, but moved to the farthest corner of the work zone.

The Asp dusted off a little table. He set his burden down upon it, just outside the canvas, with a graceful flourish, smile, and jest. Elizabeth smiled again, but her eyes shivered and she stayed where she was. A dusty finger pointed to the mud, and she said something—Hesha leaned forward and called up the sound.

"—This last inch beforehand." Her thin smile came out again. "But thanks for bringing it down. It's very nice of you."

"No, no. It's my job—I got to make sure you don't starve, Liz. You're a pretty girl—you should keep the skin on your bones and the roses in your cheeks, you know? It's not just me here; you're dealing with generations of Mercurio grandmothers standing over my left shoulder, and they keep going on about it." He laughed, and she tried to smile.

The Asp left Elizabeth to her dinner. She didn't leave the safety of her canvas carpet until his foot was off the top stair cleat, and the relief in her face was patently obvious.

"Holy shit…" whispered Thompson. "She knows?"

Hesha watched his guest wipe her hands clean and sit down to eat. She sniffed at the food suspiciously, and took up the spoon without enthusiasm. "No," said Hesha. "I think not. Merely good instincts. She's afraid of him…and that's interesting." He swiveled in the console chair, and faced his protege.

"Should I call Gabe in from town?"

"I think that would be for the best. Fear can induce restless sleep. Keep Raphael out of her way until we can make the switch."

"Would you care to do the honors?" asked Elizabeth, steadying a nearly freed fragment of shard and mud between her gloved hands.

"Thank you," Hesha said evenly. He took up the dentist's pick and, with professional skill, scraped away the thin ridges of clay that supported the jug-side and handle in the boulder. In less than a minute, the fragile pottery piece shifted in the matrix, and he took up the receiving tray.

Elizabeth tipped the leaf-shaped fragment gently into the little bin, taking time to select a position that kept the shard's own weight from endangering it. "Down," she said.

"Down," confirmed Hesha, and he set the tray aside.

They leaned back against the canvas steps and regarded their hard-won treasure. Still covered with dirt and dust from its prison, it was an unimpressive, crumbly brown.

"It's not much, is it?" mourned Elizabeth.

Hesha shook his head and smiled. "It's older than we are. That's enough, for the moment. And it may match some of Vegel's shards."

"It's still not much. I'm sorry I dragged you out here for this, but at that last stage...two hands weren't enough, and I couldn't find Ron."

Hesha nodded, but ventured, "Mercurio's in the kitchen...."

Elizabeth turned pink and dove back into the boulder.

Hesha read the flush, keeping Thompson's briefing in mind. It might be fear of the Asp that brought her color up, but he suspected she hadn't even looked for either man...a loose fragment was a fine excuse for seeing him, Hesha, personally. He determined to keep the footing businesslike for the evening. Perching on the edge of the canvas box, he silently examined the progress of the work. The woman had given up entirely on what Vegel had always thought were the most promising sections, and her hands were busy inside a large crater below them.

Elizabeth grimaced inwardly. So the Asp, now that she

knew him better, made her back hairs rise and her fists itch—
she still should have gone to him, rather than bothering her
employer. Self-consciously, she tucked a few loose strands of
hair behind her ears. Foolishness had its advantages, however.
She confessed to herself she was glad that Hesha had come out
of his office. He was sitting not three feet from her. His perfect
white shirt-sleeves were rolled up, creased, and dirty from
the work; his jetty eyes were smoldering... intent on the rock,
completely oblivious to her, of course.

"What are you doing?" Hesha asked. He used the scholarly
voice she'd responded well to over her dissertation. Elizabeth
stuffed cloth wadding into the deepest part of the hole and
tested the top section with two fingers. She cleared her throat.

"Well, Professor," she began, playing (as he had hoped) the
earnest young student, "it occurred to me that the layer Mr.
Vegel had exposed was far too cluttered for real progress to go
on. I intend to isolate the shard-laden projection and remove
it from the body of the excavation. I expect that it will then be
easier to separate the shards...working from the rear, as it were."

"Go on, Miss Dimitros."

"That's it." She laughed self-consciously. "If Vegel's guess as
to the sedimentation order of this thing is correct, I'm probably
going to have to go back to doing it the hard way. But I think he
was only mostly right." Hesha studied the rock. "And the rock
is just 'this thing'?" She stared blankly back at him. "It's not
a he, or a she, or..." Elizabeth reddened, and Hesha grinned.
"What is it?"

"Oh, Lord." She kicked resentfully at the canvas draping. "I
tell you a story once...."

"Go on."

"This is an it. This is the rock of Sisyphus. It's big, and
bulky, and whenever you get to the goal with it—" she gestured
at the leaf-shaped shard in the bin, "—you wind up back where
you started, horrendously disappointed that there was nothing
beyond the goal but another goal, exactly the same as the first."
She scowled into the hole. "How long did Vegel work on this
thing?"

Hesha frowned. "A long time."

"And Sisyphus is probably still heaving his misery and guilt and shame up that mountain. He's supposed to have been a smart guy; you'd think he'd do something about it." She caught Hesha's inquisitive gaze, and went on. "There must be other rocks in hell. If he picked up one and gave the boulder a good whack in the same place every time, eventually he'd have a crack started...and one of these millennia, the whole thing would break open as it bounded down the mountain. Sorry; I'm babbling. They probably rolled up his wisdom somewhere in the rock...it's an allegory, after all."

Hesha said nothing, and Elizabeth returned to the crater she was boring into metaphor. *Sisyphus...futility...how appropriate... keep your mind on the job, Lizzie...and keep away from him. Resolutely, she kept scraping away at the rock. Best to go home to the Rutherfords without making a fool of yourself. Important client...strong business relationship...give you one up on Miss Agnes...he wants paintings done, you're damn good with conservation...*

"What next?" Hesha asked.

"Stabilization of the inner surface. It's glazed..." she tapered off, looking at the rock. *And maybe you'll find something decent in this thing...unbroken...or finely decorated...or bones...or even... metal....*

"Your next *project*," Hesha clarified.

"Sorry. I was planning to keep plugging away at this for a few hours more, then begin swabbing down another canvas."

"No papyrus tonight?"

Liz stretched herself, and regarded the huge mass in puzzlement. "I see hieroglyphs in my sleep, at this point. I need a change...and there's just something *satisfying* about digging into this. Put something together over there," she gestured at the long table, "take something apart over here." Elizabeth clicked her tools lightly into one hand, and shrugged a little. "I can work on the papyrus, if that's what you'd prefer?"

"Please, do what you like. The paintings are coming along well enough." He waited, half-expecting her to draw the encounter out longer. For the moment, though, she seemed more interested in Vegel's boulder than in him. *Good*, he thought.

Thompson must have been mistaken. He rose abruptly, slapped the dust off of his clothes and skin, and turned to go to his study. Elizabeth didn't even look up, and Hesha stalked out of the room in a perversely dissatisfied mood.

Friday, 9 July 1999, 10:43 PM
Laurel Ridge Farm
Columbia, Maryland

"Hesha?" Liz asked without looking up from the papyrus. The Setite stopped in surprise, glanced at his silent, stocking feet, and replied, "Yes." He sat down across the table from her, and picked up his own set of tongs. "You're making good progress tonight," he remarked.

"It's an easy section, I think."

Hesha compared her several nights' work—this piece was no simpler than the others; it must be that she had begun to memorize the hieroglyphs. And she'd slept more soundly the night before, though she could hardly be expected to know that. But Elizabeth seemed rather elated—pleased with herself to an incomprehensible degree.

He watched her deftly lay five scraps together to make a single feather sign, and though the next glyph was uncommon, her eyes looked to the notes spread out over the glass for only the briefest instant before finding it. There was something odd about the way she was sitting, as well...he began manipulating shards on his own half to disguise his curiosity.

Chair angle as normal...her hips curved into the seat in the same way...slight twist of her back to keep her long neck and delicate shoulders positioned comfortably over the work...but her shoulders were wrong. Hand with the tweezers—no, the other hand—instead of loose, relaxed fingers flipping through Vegel's transliterations, her fingers were closed in a near-fist, flattened against the table top. Her pulse was quickening the longer he sat with her…what was in her hand? He felt Elizabeth's eyes on him, and bent earnestly over the work.

"I have a present for you," she said eventually. Hesha looked up into the sweetest cat-canary smile he'd ever seen, and the amber lights in her eyes were absolute sparks. "Open your hand, and close your eyes, et cetera, et cetera."

"Pardon?"

"Here."

She turned her left hand over, and lying on the palm was a metal ring. It was a shining dark brown, completely untarnished, and Hesha had never seen it before. He took it warm from her body and peered at the sculpted surface through his old-man glasses.

"It's the crackerjack prize out of Mr. Vegel's rock," said Elizabeth. "The wisdom of Sisyphus, so to speak."

"Ourobouros," whispered Hesha.

"Bronze," she said eagerly, "Though why it hasn't greened away completely I can't imagine. I intend a pH study of the surrounding material."

Hesha hardly heard her.

Bronze, yes, though he had a better guess as to why the metal had been preserved. No inscription…no marks on the interior of any kind. He turned his attention to the design—two snakes, both self-devourers, twined around each other in opposite directions. The heads and tails met together on what must be the top of the piece, and the interweaving bodies formed a tight knot.

"Beautiful," he whispered.

She laughed. "If you like snakes." She leaned back in her chair. "Seriously, though, I agree with you." Elizabeth watched him stare at the little ring and decided to let him alone with it. She reached for her tongs again and began picking at the scattered scraps.

The Setite ran his fingers around and around the outside of the ring.

"Have you tried this on?" he murmured to his companion.

"Yes," she admitted. "Briefly, to see what the approximate size was. I've full measurements and excavation data written down in the 'boulder log' that Mr. Vegel had been keeping."

No traps, then. Still, he would have to examine it more carefully to make sure it was truly safe. He'd keep a close watch on the woman, too…there was a chance the thing was active in some way, and any after-effects would be informative.

"Greek, don't you think?" she said, noticing that his close scan of the prize was finished. "I can't remember any identical designs, but I thought that the two-snake motif might be helpful in tracking down the period and the purpose. Herculean cult object, or perhaps prophetic paraphernalia. Teresias and the snakes in the stable, you know. There's an outside chance of medical symbology, but I think that if the sculptor had meant a caduceus, he'd have made a caduceus."

Hesha slipped the ring into his breast pocket. "Good work," he said abruptly.

"Just luck," replied Elizabeth, modestly.

Hesha wondered.

Saturday, 10 July 1999, 9:28 AM
Laurel Ridge Farm
Columbia, Maryland

Ronald Thompson woke with his jaw clenched tight. Damn good dream, ruined. Didn't dream often. Forgetting it already…

Goddamn alarm.

He flicked open the panel without quite leaving the soft cocoon of his bed. It was an interior breach; Vegel's apartment to Vegel's crypt again. He swore in the foulest language he could think of, and tossed a robe over his grizzled chest. The door was fixed… yes, the door was fixed…she must have subconsciously triggered the actual latch…probably the door had never been loose in the first place…well, this time he'd wedge it shut from the stone side, and no matter how much her sleepy fingers played with the catch, there'd be no more midnight—mid-morning, curse it—alarms.

He pounded down the old house stairs, down the basement stairs, and across the wood floors of the basement rooms. His step grew lighter as he approached Elizabeth's end of the complex, and he laid his hand gently on the knob of her door.

Instantly, the alarm's tone changed. From a persistent, low G, it rose and clamored an octave higher—his earplug throbbed with the shuddering note. He drew back his grasping fingers, as if to stop the noise, but he knew the sound. There had been a second breach somewhere. Hand and knob were coincidence; he threw the door open and found Vegel's apartment abandoned. He switched on the lights, and saw that the door into the crypt was shut.

"Asp," he whispered into Elizabeth's intercom. "Turn on the mike and follow me." Thompson stepped quietly to the secret panel, disengaged the alarm, and opened the way to the crypt. The tone in his ears died completely and unexpectedly.

"Where is she?" he asked the empty room.

"She's not on your damn screens," said his earplug.

Thompson finished looking through the irregular curves and obstacles in the vault, and his stomach turned. There was only one room in the complex that couldn't be seen from the security bunker.

"Run the log back, Asp."

There came a series of keyboard sounds, a low whistle, and Raphael's voice, soft and purring over the circuit. "Her door at 9:28:17. It shut at 9:28:39. She probably…bumped into it. *His* door at 9:29:27. It shut automatically ten seconds later. Sorry, Ron. I know you liked her."

Thompson sat down heavily on the end of the stone bench. "Damn." He looked at his bare feet, his flimsy, plaid flannel robe, and repeated, "Damn. Damn. Asp, pick up the hook, the light, my fire boots, and the kit. Bring 'em down here."

Raphael Mercurio opened his mouth to object, but the sight of Thompson's broad back and clenched jaw on the monitor shut him up. He reached for the kit.

Ronald Thompson stood on the threshold of his master's tomb. He was shod in thick, thigh-high boots. His pajama bottoms were tucked tightly into the boot- tops, and the tightly belted, cut-down remnants of his robe had been tied down around his waist. He held a long, hooked stick in his left hand, and his right index finger was poised above a palette carved in the hands of a scribe. Behind him, the Asp stood ready and silent.

Thompson pressed the latch, and the door to Hesha's sanctum swung open. He pressed a second carving, and the door settled slightly on its hinges. It would stay open now, as it had not for Elizabeth.

The Asp turned on the floodlight. It was curiously baffled and shielded; only dim illumination shone through its cloudy lens. It was enough for the two men watching; their eyes were accustomed by now to the semidarkness of Vegel's chamber. When the sluggish head of the snake nearest the door began to move, Thompson prodded it gently with the blunt end of the hook, and the viper slithered away into a hole in the wall, seeking its den in sulky temper.

Thompson stepped forward, and the Asp nudged the lamp along behind him. There were two short corridors ahead of them. They took the left, and trod gently along the right edge of it. At the first turn, they passed around a shallow pit, and seven sleepy sets of double-lidded eyes watched them from its depths. At the second turn, for no apparent reason, they waited a full minute, standing close together on the same solid stone.

"Ron," began the Asp, "She's dead by now."

"If she's dead, where is she?"

"In the right-hand passage."

"I didn't hear anything from there. Did you?" Raphael subsided. He drew forth his own hook-and-loop without comment, and dislodged a curious neighbor from a ledge close by.

They started forward again and arrived safely at the last landing of a narrow, winding stair. The Asp put the lamp into his partner's outstretched hand, and turned to watch the steps behind them. He didn't see into the chamber; the ceiling of the stairs was low and steep, and he was on rear guard before the opening door finished its slow arc.

Thompson saw.

He saw the faint, tall curves of barely lit paintings fading into blackness. He saw the shadows of nearer mysteries, ranged along the walls. He saw, at the edge of the light, the closed sarcophagus. He saw his master's still, night-dark form stretched out upon it, bare to the waist. He saw a woman, draped in folded white cloth that clung tightly to her body. He saw her dark hair, plaited and knotted into a thick headdress. He saw shining gold flash dully at her neck, her wrists, and ankles. The girl—the queen—the goddess—she took up the black hand of the man before her, and wordlessly bid him rise.

Thompson stood in the doorway in shock; it was so much a scene from a painting of Vegel's—and he knew it was a trick of the light. The illusion faded—the chance resemblance died as the woman went on moving, and he saw the truth.

Elizabeth stood over Hesha's dead, cold corpse, holding a lifeless hand to her cheek. She was crying in half-formed sobs, quietly, but as if her heart would break. Her eyes were closed, and if there were words in her mourning Thompson could not hear them.

He took a step down, and the lamp came with him. The linen gown was a plain white nightshirt, wrinkled and twisted until the creases looked like pleats from a distance. Her hair was tangled. As he moved, it looked less and less like the high-born lady's wig and more like fever-locks. Her jewelry was not gold, but living copper....

And the floor was covered—covered so thickly that the light gray stone showed through only in tiny patches—with the same deadly, molten metal: hundreds upon hundreds of copperhead snakes. Thompson looked out across the sea of brazen backs and shuddered. "How many shots are there in the kit, Asp?"

"Two."

"You stay here, then."

"That was *my* plan."

Thompson crept slowly across the stone floor of the crypt, making a clear path before himself with the hook. The Asp moved onto the bottom step and adjusted the lamp to help the walking man—Thompson could sense the assassin's eyes on his back. The light did odd things to the shadows, and the edges of the darkness moved with the bodies of its inhabitants. The old cop could feel, instinctively, the closing of the way behind, and wondered how in hell he could ever bring a body out with him— whether dead, sleeping, or in the panic and shock of snakebite.

"Wait, Ron."

Thompson swiveled through his shoulders, hips, and knees. He didn't dare move his feet. Uncomfortably, he looked up at his partner. Raphael's hands held a thin cord: the drop line for the lamp. A tiny knife cut it free.

"Here, catch. Tie it to your waist." He knotted his end to the kit and anchored the plastic box behind the door's slack hinges.

"I'll bring down stronger rope and some gloves. You're going to need them." And the Asp disappeared up the stairs.

Thompson watched him go resignedly. He made a neat bowline around his hips and concentrated his attention on the floor.

Hook, clear, step. Step.

Hook, nudge, angle, hook again. Clear. Step.

Step. Halfway, now.

Step wide. Hook away the heavy body that blocked the straight way.

Step again. Step—

—and Thompson's boot slipped on an old, flattened, silvery skin. It rasped silkily under the rubber cleats and threw him. He jerked wildly to catch his balance—the hook swung free from his right hand, and it clattered against the stone. The other foot slammed down near the head of a small, skittish creature, and the vibrations of the whole incident traveled throughout the room. When the frantic movements stopped, there were hardly any snakes in sight, but three adults had their bodies coiled ready. Thompson left his feet and the hook where they were, and dropped into breathing that almost wasn't—tight, shallow motions of the ribs that made the head and sides ache but which caused very, *very* little noise. One by one, the challengers relaxed and laid themselves down. Thompson straightened his legs and ankles, raised the hook with the smallest, weakest fingers of his left hand—the only two that had kept the tool from crashing altogether—and began again.

Step.

Step, hook, clear, step.

He was at the sarcophagus. He touched her shoulder, and she muttered something incomprehensible. She slept still, somehow, and her color was healthy—she hadn't been bitten. Thompson hoped the miracle would go on, and prayed that miracles were contagious.

"Ron."

Thompson looked to the stairwell. "Yeah."

"Pull in your line."

Thompson took the straight end of the cord and began to

draw it after him. A cardboard box sledged along behind it. More rope trailed from the box. It made a godawful racket, and more snakes fled from the monster. He grinned maniacally as his three opponents struck at and then scattered from the strange and hideous thing that hurt their teeth.

There were gloves in the box, and Thompson put them on. He clipped a strong rope around his waist, and would have hooked Elizabeth into it....

But when Thompson looked down into the eyes of the old, old copperhead that had draped itself around the woman's neck and chest, he knew that the creature would never willingly let him do it. Where his gut had turned before at the danger, his mind turned now at the knowledge that the ancient reptile *thought* and fought in the same idiom that he did.

With one eye on the "collar," he reached for the young, slender, gleaming form of a bracelet. In the blink of an eye, he had the little one behind the neck, and he threw it far into the dark places of the tomb. He shuffled his feet to bring himself closer, and the hatchling from her other wrist joined its cousin. The head of the collar turned toward him, and it blinked golden eyes resentfully.

Thompson sighed. He hooked clear a large space on the floor around them, and bent—slowly—to kneel at Elizabeth's feet. The anklets were larger, older yearlings. He took a deep breath and reached for the left one. Above him, the collar hissed, and he stopped in mid-motion. Nerve lost, he leaned back on his haunches and flexed his hands inside the gloves.

When he—and the collar, too, he hoped—least expected it, his right hand darted out of its own accord. The instinct was good. He could feel the delicate jawbones clamped between his fingers, and he unwound it from her leg in a quick, smooth motion. He leaned back to throw, and the other anklet struck him just beneath the knee.

"Fuck," he cried, and nearly dropped the serpent he was holding. Impatiently, he flicked his wrist and sent the thin body flying into space. He heard it land, too close and audibly angry.

Thompson fairly tore the second anklet away. As he stood, he felt Elizabeth's legs for other snakes, and found one curled like a garter about her thigh. It fled higher, and he had to raise her gown to the level of her hips to catch the thing—it would have bitten her belly, but his thumb got in the way. The leather wasn't thick enough, and this time he could feel the extra sting of venom in the wound.

The collar hissed again. From his awkward crouch, Thompson strained to see what it was doing. His head rose above the level of the sarcophagus just as something struck him in the side—from its markings, he knew it to be the first anklet, the one he hadn't thrown far enough. He stopped cursing. Nothing seemed adequate.

In a frenzy, Thompson hooked the space around them clear again. Without trying to dislodge the giant snake, he took Elizabeth's arm and began leading her away from Hesha. The collar hissed a warning.

Thompson kept walking.

The collar hovered over Elizabeth's jugular, wavering challengingly. Elizabeth herself stumbled. She was still weeping, and the pale streaks ran down her face, her neck, and onto the dull body of the snake.

Thompson took a firmer, higher grip on her arm.

The collar, blindingly quickly, moved to take the open target. Thompson was ready, and he threw himself away from the girl the moment he was sure the copperhead was really coming for him, not for her. Thompson felt the huge, curved fangs enter the meat of his forearm, well above the glove. His arm tore open. Blood flowed freely onto the stones. The old serpent lost a tooth inside its victim, but the momentum of its strike and Thompson's lunge wrested its grip from Elizabeth's neck. Thompson regained his feet, tossed the unconscious woman over his shoulder, and ran headlong for the stairs.

Saturday, 10 July 1999, 7:48 PM
Laurel Ridge Farm
Columbia, Maryland

Hesha woke to a crowded and unexpected press of heavy bodies. The copperheads lay coiled over him in excessive, weighty numbers, and the Eldest had curled protectively around his shoulders. As he began to move, he felt the flickering whisper of the patriarch's tongue on his ear. "Light," he said softly, and the hidden bulbs glowed.

Hesha locked eyes with the old snake, and hissed back.

The Eldest was wounded. He bared his broken fang and arched his neck, the better to display a replacement descending from the roof of his mouth. He complained. He coiled and recoiled, disturbing the lesser snakes. He was fretful. The nest was not safe. The guardians were halved. Those that could had found sanctuary on the body of their ally; those that could not had left for their winter dens in the fields around Laurel Ridge.

Hesha soothed the old and faithful servant. He ran his hands along the slim backs of the copperhead's descendants. In time, they found their necks and bellies secure on the floor again, and the stones did nothing unexpected. The Setite's bare feet slid smoothly among them without causing alarm; he was family, and his scent was theirs.

He satisfied himself that the intrusion had been limited— his treasures and projects were untouched—and made his way, though the center passage, to Vegel's crypt. He noticed with interest that Elizabeth's door was wedged shut with the chisel.

"Thompson."

There was, for the first time in fifteen years, no response. "Thompson," he said again, with force.

"Sir." It was the Asp's voice. "Sir, Thompson's a little ill just now."

"Ill."

"Yes, sir. Could you—could you come help me with him?"

Thompson's quarters were comfortable but sparsely furnished. They ran to bookshelves full of old magazines, tapes, tattered true-crime case studies, and a fine set of vinyl albums he never listened to. There were a few old certificates on the walls in thin, plain frames. There was one good rug; he'd bought it in Afghanistan. It was beautiful, and it was valuable, but it had attracted him chiefly because the design—though traditional in every other way—had substituted for random decoration the simplified shapes of machine guns and helicopters.

Hesha Ruhadze's chief security man sat in an old, battered recliner with a small trash bin in his lap. His face was unhealthily blue, his eyes swollen half shut. His right arm lay in a jury-rigged basin of newspaper, plastic bags, and blood-soaked towels. Similar wadding covered the lower left half of his ribs.

As Hesha entered the room, the Asp had just come from the bathroom with a double armload of fresh towels. He lifted Thompson's swollen arm and exchanged red cloth for white and beige; the trash bin filled with the dressings, and Mercurio swapped the little can for a mixing bowl. Acidic fumes from the kitchen testified that some receptacle was necessary. The two men looked up at him with weary, resentful, smug expressions. Hesha took the whole scene in in a second, and then wiped the satisfied looks off his men's faces by turning on his heel and slamming the door behind him.

"Mercurio!" he shouted into the intercom.

"Boss, what the hell are you doing?" The Asp followed Hesha into the bunker, angry, annoyed, and afraid all at once. "Ron's sick, goddamn it. He's gonna die, and you just—"

Hesha turned on him. "Wash your hands, you fool!"

Raphael looked from his blood-soaked cuffs and dripping

hands to the animal eyes of his master. White with fear, he shrank away.

"Warm four bags and bring them here, quickly."

Raphael scuttled down the hall, running without turning his back on the bunker and the creature inside it.

Hesha sat down at the console to wait. The smell coming from Thompson's quarters was overpowering…old blood, new blood, fear, sickness, venom…fresh blood spilling, wasted on the floor, the cloth, the paper…fresh blood…his eyes drifted to the video display of Thompson's room.

He could not look away, but his hands obeyed his will. The monitor sparked off.

The curse fought him for control of his legs. The man's door was only five feet away. The man was too ill to fight. The man trusted him, and wouldn't flinch from the Beast; wouldn't know the difference between the slave of Apep and the ascetic, thoughtful, rational being that the Setite had fought to construct over the centuries. And the man's choice was made; he was in pain, he would end his life willingly to start the new one now.

Hesha let the waves of persuasion crash against the bastions of his sanity. From the cold center of the storm, he took exercise and amusement in analyzing the onslaught. The Beast surged forward in raw and willful attack, monstrously strong but poorly armed. Hesha thanked Set that his mind was yet clear, and that the voice of the curse spoke in clumsy shreds of logic.

A plastic bag landed in his lap, body-warm and shockingly heavy.

He picked it up and drained it quickly. The curse cried out for more—in perfect concert, Hesha and the Beast lifted their hand—and the Asp tossed them the second bag. The blood streamed down his cold gullet as fast as the first. Hesha braced himself and began to sip, slowly, the third bag. The Beast clamored still, infuriated by the scent of Thompson's life, by the wretched flavor of the bagged blood, by the failure of its fight…. Hesha finished his drink, and the unthinking creature within him seemed to loll over, still angry, but caged…not sated, not too drunk to rage for more supper, but understanding on some level that there would be more soon enough.

"Snakebite," said Hesha.

"Yes, sir." The Asp had retreated down the corridor. One foot was actually inside the elevator. "This morning."

"Antitoxin?"

"Yes, sir. Right after the bite."

"Why is he bleeding?"

"Convulsions, sir. He was puking in the john, and he just lost it. He broke the mirror when he went down, boss. Then he rolled around in it. I've been pulling glass out of him for over an hour."

"Warm three more bags. Knock before you come in," Hesha directed, moving from his chair, "leave them at the door, and get back out. Understood?"

Raphael nodded. He watched the creature walk into Thompson's rooms, and he fled back to the freezer chamber, glad to have the heavy, insulated doors between himself and his master.

"Thompson." Hesha knelt by his servant's side, clutching the fourth blood bag like a talisman between them.

"Sir." Ron's eyes fought crazily for focus. "Sir, were you here just now?"

"Yes."

"Thank god. Thought I'd imagined it." He leaned over the bowl and was sick in wracking, dry heaves that shook the old chair with him. Hesha patted him on the back, running his fingers along rents in the robe and open wounds in the skin beneath it. No glass was left there. The Asp seemed to have been thorough enough.

The Setite took Thompson's head in his hands, looked into his eyes, and said, "Be calm." The vomiting slowly stopped.

"Is it time, sir?" Ron croaked.

"No," answered Hesha, understanding his man's question perfectly. "Tonight you merely have an unscheduled lesson in the powers of Set's blood." Thompson stared dully at him from swollen eyes. "Let me check your arms, first." Minutes passed with forceps and scalpel. A few shards of mirror were added to the bowl the Asp had started, and from the snakebites came forth a broken fang or two. The bowl and the tools went into the kitchen sink, and Hesha returned from the drainboard with a knife and a large coffee mug in his hands.

"Drink this."

"I haven't been able to keep anything down, sir...."

"Drink *this*."

Thompson took a sip. His eyes flickered to the dark contents in apprehension, and Hesha could see the questions starting.

"Drink it all, Thompson."

When the mug was empty, Hesha filled it again from his wrist. Thompson took it back obediently, and they drank together...mortal from the cup, Setite from the bag. The Asp delivered the rest of the blood as ordered; it flowed into the cold body and trickled from it to fill the mug again.

"Enough." Hesha pulled up a chair opposite the wounded man. "Now burn that. Use it. Don't tell me that you don't know what I mean—keep listening. There is fire in your stomach...like fear..." said the Setite, softly. "Like anger...like adrenaline...like whisky..." his voice went on, hypnotically. "You've done a little drinking in your time, Detective Sergeant Thompson...take the fire, take the whisky, and force it out of your gut. Put it in your arm. The venom you were hit with today...that was fire in the veins, killing you. This is fire in the arteries, destroying the venom. Set your arm on fire...burn the venom away...torch out the glass and the cuts and the bruises.

"Look at your arm, Thompson."

Ronald Thompson moved his head painfully and saw his swollen, discolored limb changing. The streaks of white and red faded; the blue-purple that had begun to fester sweetly turned green-gold, then faint brown, then his own skin-tan. The sickly colors shrank from his fingers, his wrist....

"Concentrate. Don't let it stop."

"What am I doing?!"

"Healing yourself. Set's blood, even diluted, can heal the living. So, I understand, can Caine's...." Hesha looked into Thompson's eyes, lifted the shredded robe from his shoulders, and examined the knotted terrain of his back. "Move it away from your arm. Fix your feet. Then spread the fire to the back.

You're still bleeding there." The gashes mended themselves. "Good. You have control over it. Now stand up and be sure every wound is closed."

Thompson stood and tried to obey. He shook his head. "The fire's out, sir."

"Excellent. It was necessary to burn it all. There are side effects. Think about how you felt before and after you drank my blood. With one night's drink, you probably felt gratitude, friendship, nostalgia, tenderness, unreasoning trust...."

Thompson's expression held none of those fine feelings now. Hesha's list was far too accurate.

"Two nights, and you should come almost to love me."

Thompson's still-puffy face took on fear.

"Three nights' drinks form a kind of slavery between the drinker and the one whose blood is taken. It is called the Blood Bond, or the Vinculum, or the Coeur Vrai, or the Oath, or the Coils of Apep, or a hundred other names...and it lasts forever."

As the implications sank in, Hesha's bodyguard turned chalk white. "Forever?"

Hesha stared at the floor. With a long, thin hand, he dismissed *forever*. "Until you die, or until you die again. Long enough. There are said to be seven ways to break it; five are legendary, three are impossible, four are impractical...all of them are difficult, and only one is quick."

Thompson's face lost none of its horror. "So you could...you could use this on any one of us...."

Hesha's eyebrow twitched. "But I do not, obviously." He paused. "Or you wouldn't be in a position to ask the question, Thompson." Without haste, he collected the empty bags, the bloodied knife, the red-stained mug, and took them to the kitchen. He returned with a glass of juice and a new bowl. Setting them in Thompson's hands, he commented, "It is far, far better to *earn* the loyalty of the people you are forced to trust. I find that slaves make unreliable servants. Many of my enemies keep their retainers in bondage—and that, Thompson, is a very useful thing." He sat down again, and his manner changed.

"Lesson over," he said. "Report."

Elizabeth sat atop a tall, thin stool in the studio. She leant on her left elbow, holding a loose bundle of cotton swabs. Her right hand took one up, dipped it into a jar, and rolled it carefully over the fly-specked, smoke-stained surface of the painting. The swab, now a dirty yellow, she flicked into a waste tray by her side. Left hand fed right, the process was repeated, the clean path along the painting's edge growing steadily.

Hesha walked into the room. Where there were shadows, he wrapped himself inside them; where there was light, he merely slipped unnoticed within it. The woman heard nothing. There were new, weary lines around her eyes; the delicate skin was stained the color of old bruises; the lids were red-rimmed. He smelt salt on her cheeks.

Hesha walked back to the door and let the light strike him again.

"Elizabeth."

She looked up in surprise. "Hi." The swabs dropped to the tabletop. "I thought you'd all gone into town until tomorrow. Thompson left a note...."

"It was a lie."

Elizabeth's chin tilted up, her eyes narrowed defensively, and she turned on the stool to face him. She said nothing, but searched his face. It might as well have been carved from marble.

"Come here, please. I would like to talk to you." Hesha stepped back, leaving the way clear for her to go by. After a moment's hesitation, she rose and followed him. "In my study, if you don't mind." The Setite led her to a door she'd never been through. He held it open for her. Hesha paused at the precise distance into the study that would force the wall seat upon his guest, and she took it.

"Tell me about your dream last night," he began.

Elizabeth flushed. "Excuse me?"

"You walked and spoke in your sleep."

Her eyes shuttered against him. "Sleepwalkers don't necessarily remember their dreams, Hesha."

"But you do, Elizabeth, or you would have said: 'I don't remember.'" He almost smiled. "Yours is a very diplomatic dishonesty."

She clenched her jaw and said nothing. Hesha read the lines of her face—anger, caution, resentment, logic. Whatever harm the truth might do her, he had at least put her on her guard.

He went on, softly. "I expect that there are nightmares for you. I want to help." The stern note returned. "In fact, it is absolutely necessary that I intervene."

"I don't understand you."

"I intend to devote the remaining hours before sunrise ensuring that you do." Hesha paused. "Under ordinary circumstances I would never have brought you here. I picked you up in New York as a diversion—" she winced— "from more pressing matters. You were...you are...unique. Contrary. Fascinating. I suspected you had an uncommon gift for observation. I showed you a statue that puzzled me. You put your finger on the crux of the matter in one night. You removed the eye. I was impressed, and I decided that I would visit you often...in New York," he finished heavily.

"Within a day, you had destroyed my plans. There were..." He sought, visibly, for words, and spoke slowly: "...worse things following Kettridge, and I could not, in good conscience, leave you to be found by them. So I brought you here intending to protect you and keep the truth of the danger from troubling you. In time, I would have returned you safely to New York. Or—" his voice lowered. "Or in time, I hoped we might have had a different, less hurried, less disturbing version of this conversation."

"We aren't having a conversation," snapped Elizabeth. "This is a monologue, Hesha."

She takes the truth by the heart, he sighed to himself. His soft tones and feigned embarrassment dropped away. Curtly, he spelled out the essence of the problem. "In order to keep the reality of the situation from you, the Asp, Thompson, and I have constructed an elaborate charade. The events of this morning prove to me that you, whether you know it consciously or not, have seen through the acting and the stage set. Our little masquerade has put each of us in still greater danger." With the last word, his voice fell, and what came next from Hesha's throat was like thunder.

"Now tell me your dream, Elizabeth, before your gift of perception gets one of us killed."

Elizabeth stared back at him through wide, hard-rimmed eyes. Her face was pale, her mouth shut and voiceless. Her throat was tight with tears and anger, her gut knotted in fear. *He's insane.* Her mind churned frantically, but nothing helpful rose to the surface. *Whatever I'm supposed to have seen, God, why can't I see it now? He doesn't look crazy, he looks...every sentence makes less sense, not more...but he obviously thinks he's explaining something...paralogia...paranoia...but his face...* She turned her eyes away. Whether he was sane or mad, the sight of his face hurt her. His eyes, so near black, guarded by strong brows and cunning smiles...once or twice there had been a gentler look in them, something encouraging and open.... Elizabeth watched his hands instead. The bones were long and beautiful, like a sculpture some god had hidden under flesh...the color of his skin was so rich and deep and mellow a brown...*there isn't a word for it. Like horse chestnuts and old saddles and...he's mad, I think.*

Hesha studied the woman's reaction clinically. Despite himself, he was impressed that she could sit silent after the treatment he'd given her—either she had no will at all, which he knew was not true—or she was stronger than he'd guessed. *Set below,* he thought irritably. *What am I doing guessing?*

He held out his hands. "Come with me," he said.

Elizabeth let him pull her up from the chair, thinking how cold his fingertips were, how impossible he was.

Hesha opened the door to the main hall and drew her behind him. He strode to a full and solid-looking bookcase and slid it aside. The passage beyond was dark and narrow, but the walls were ordinary enough. They turned a corner into lighter, wider space, and a sturdy metal door blocked the way.

"Unlock."

He had kept tight hold of her right hand. As the door swung open, he let go.

Elizabeth walked ahead of him into a long, low room crowded with steel, glass and black plastic. The Asp was there, and the expression on his face was insufferable. Liz took it as astonishment mixed with malice; Hesha knew more of Raphael's moods. He knew the killer was savoring the wreck of the illusion, and why. Hesha smiled, and decided that the Asp was having enough fun. *Pride goeth before a fall*, he thought wickedly, and waited.

Elizabeth had drifted to the security station. The cameras were on—all of them—and the monitors up and working. She took a seat in one of the chairs. She looked at every screen in turn, coldly, and without comment. The front hall. The kitchen. An outdoor scene. The staircase. The front drive. A wall...part of the garage, she remembered. Views of the guest rooms; of Thompson's austere bed, of the Asp's den. A shot of the stairs to the basement. Every possible angle of the museum. Blank corridors. A room she didn't recognize, very messy. Another, rather cleaner. Hesha's study, and the two chairs empty there. Hesha's rooms from another angle, the back of the screen showing behind a large bed, a sliver of neatly kept dressing room to one side. More pictures of the woods, waving gently in night winds. Her own room, she saw without surprise. The bunker—a miniature Asp standing gaping over her shoulder, her own tiny figure motionless in the chair, Hesha looking up at her...into the camera, regretfully. Thompson lying in a chair in a room she didn't know. Stone hallways. Stone walls— carved walls.

Elizabeth leaned closer, staring at the reliefs. The picture was dim and the perspective was wrong, but there was a memory....

"Asp." Hesha's voice rang out. "Introduce yourself to Miss Dimitros."

Liz swiveled the chair. If the cook's face had been stunned before—which she doubted, realizing that anyone in this room would have known precisely who was coming—it was a grotesquely genuine mask of stupefaction now. The small, dark eyes narrowed with anger.

He said nothing, and Hesha filled in the silence. "Elizabeth, this is Raphael Mercurio."

"Not Angelo," she murmured tonelessly.

"There is no Angelo," said the Asp, in a voice clotted with

resentment. "Raphael. Gabriel. My brother, my twin, he was here when you arrived. Angelo is…our creation. Our masterwork. The great alibi," he finished, throwing back his head and raising one glossy, defiant eyebrow.

"For what?"

"For everything," said the Asp, menacingly. He glanced at Hesha's face, and backed away. With an air of pride and hatred, he swept out of sight.

Hesha touched Elizabeth lightly on the shoulder. She left the chair, and he steered her through the bunker to a plain, wooden door. Hesha knocked once, but opened it immediately.

"Thompson."

"Sir." Thompson grimaced apologetically. "Hey, Liz." He straightened the recliner, but remained seated. "Sorry about all this."

Hesha allowed no time for pleasantries. "Take off your shirt, Thompson."

Thompson and Elizabeth exchanged glances. He grimaced again. "Yes, sir. I'll need a hand, though. The cuts are closed, but the swelling's gone up…."

"Your right shoulder still?" Hesha frowned. "Help him," he ordered.

Liz bent over the chair and took the loose shirt up and away—gingerly, after she caught sight of the first gauze padding. Beneath the pullover, Thompson was a patchwork of cotton bandages and fresh scars.

"Unwrap his right shoulder. Look at it."

Elizabeth removed the gauze and a cold pack. The flesh of Thompson's arm was puffy and discolored. The fluids trapped within stretched tight two shiny, pink dimples of new skin at the center of the wound. She replaced the dressing with skill and without comment.

Sitting on the edge of the armchair, Elizabeth gazed searchingly into the old cop's eyes.

Thompson returned the stare unhappily. She loved the boss—or had, at least. And she'd trusted her "friend" Ron. For the first time in—decades—he was ashamed of something he'd done. And there she went, the gaze broken; finished with him, following Hesha out, walking in his footsteps through the maze. Thompson reached for the mixing bowl, feeling slightly ill.

Elizabeth stood nervously at the door. Light came from the corridor behind her, faint, but enough to throw her shadow far from her feet. Here, on the raised step of the threshold, she could hear Hesha ahead of her in the blackness, making soft noises... hissing, and a fragile rasp like a broom. The sounds stopped, there was a long pause, and then his voice said quietly: "Light."

And Hesha's sanctuary was revealed.

The far wall—all the walls—were covered in painted reliefs. In ochre, dun, black., brick red, and blue as dark as night, three tiers high, each section longer than her own body...there would be twelve sections, she realized. It was the Am Duat—the Book of the Dead for royalty—twelve hours of Ra's journey though the Underworld, each hour divided into three parts, each part depicting an event on the god's trip from dusk to dawn, from death to life. She stepped into the room, and turned to look at the whole:

A bare floor, blue-black walls to waist height, then banded colors: red, black, ochre, black, a strip of dun- colored hieroglyphs, and then drawings done on the bare stone in black. The Ninth Hour covered the wall beside her, and she stared in fascination at the precision of the work. She looked up. Above the highest tier, the artist had reproduced exactly—so far as she could remember from photographs—the decorations that belonged there. For the ceiling, the sky by night; five-pointed, spindly stars covered it in elegant regularity.

The room was enormous. She had felt that from the door. Now she saw that it was nearly empty. Scattered at intervals along the wall lay small chests, low tables and benches made for them, and narrow boxes. Some were golden, some were dusty and worm-eaten. The walls curved with strange irrelevance, as though the masons had chosen to take a walk and the chisel had happened to lead the way. Only the floor and ceiling were parallel to each other. Where the room snaked away, she could see other things, half-hidden behind the living rock.

The largest, most obvious thing to see lay directly before

her. Hesha watched in fascination as her gaze fluttered first to everything else in the room.

She was unwilling to notice it.

It was a plain box, simply made. The lid fitted tightly and squarely. It rose from the floor to a height of forty inches. It was forty inches wide, and a little over eight feet long. Elizabeth stared at the thing for a long moment, and at last she walked over to the sarcophagus.

"I was here, in my dream. In this room."

Hesha stayed where he was, and waited.

"But the floor was beaten bronze and there was no ceiling and no sky. The sun shone in, straight down like noon, and there were no shadows."

Her left hand strayed out and brushed the gray surface of the stone coffin with the edge of her palm.

"You were here, lying down. The light was on your face, and the rock and your clothes were brilliant white. I thought that you were asleep. I reached out to...to..." She stared at her hand, as if she didn't recognize it.

"I reached out to tell you something. To show you the sun, I think...but you wouldn't wake up." Her voice, trance-like until now, became a little desperate. "You wouldn't wake up. And I started to feel frost. The metal floor was cold; that was wrong, in the sunshine, and the bed...the mastaba?...was cold, and you were as cold and motionless as the stone.

"And suddenly I knew that you were dead." She choked back a sob. "You were dead, and I looked down at myself, and I wasn't Elizabeth anymore...."

Visibly, the spell broke. Her hands traced a line over her collarbone, where the Eldest had rested that morning, and her eyes cleared of the memories. Her skin reddened with anger.

"I don't have to tell you, Hesha." Her face was fire; her voice was ice. "You have your cameras and your spies. You can damn well watch my dreams from the outside." Elizabeth sprinted for the door.

Hesha was three times farther away from the exit; he reached it before she took her third step.

She didn't see him get there; her eyes were open but her

mind was too slow to catch the movement. Simply, suddenly, he was in the way, blocking the passage. The message came to her feet too late to stop the headlong rush. Elizabeth dashed into his arms, and the momentum carried her into the space between the monster and the wall. He caught her by the arm and spun her, gathered her in to face him, held her against his body. She didn't scream, and wondered, later, why not.

He said nothing. His vision was tainted red; his fangs slid down from their sheaths and forced his jaw apart; the only sound worth hearing was her heartbeat, her quick, wet breathing, the faint start of a cry in her throat...and his hands, taloned, reached for that throat. His hands buried themselves in her long, dark hair and tilted her face toward him. His head bent to her neck—he lunged for her, she twisted in his grasp at the last possible moment, and his open jaw met her lips, not her jugular. Blood filled his mouth—living blood—and he let it go on; the Beast took Hesha and the woman with him; his last thought was filled with the taste of her.... It *is a deceit; it is an illusion; she is nothing different...*

Elizabeth, shaking and unable to stand under the flames of the kiss, dropped away, and Hesha fell with her, following the blood to the ground. She sprawled on the third step of the tomb; he knelt above her. His hands, supporting her, scraped stone, and the tiny pain brought him—barely—to himself again. He tore his mouth away, wiped her lips clean with his tongue, and sat back. For long seconds he watched her body...at last she breathed...and again...and she opened her eyes and turned her head away from him, struggling to get up.

Hesha rubbed his scraped knuckles and knew in that instant that the Beast had nearly taken her life; that the taking of it would have given him more pleasure than the slaughter of any other living thing; that her murder would have caused him sorrow for the first time in centuries. And part of him wished that it had won.

Elizabeth, her feet not yet obeying her, had still managed to sit up. She pushed herself up to the fourth step with all four limbs, and she did not look toward him.

"Elizabeth. Wait." Hesha swarmed after her and hunted

for her hands. He placed her struggling fingers over his wrist. "Take my pulse," he demanded.

She stared up at him in fear. Dark, dark irises in the centers of wide-open white eyes...Hesha heard the roar of the Beast rising again, and he snatched her hands to his neck.

"Feel. Where is my heartbeat, Elizabeth? You won't find it."

She stopped fighting him. Her fingertips searched his jawline, the hollow beneath his ear, the curve of the neck into windpipe. "The first night we met," said Hesha, in a nearly normal voice, "when I fell, you were going to take my pulse. And I stopped you." Comprehension and denial rose in the dark eyes below him. She was trembling now.

"How many nightmares have you had since you met me?" She blinked, and the fighting flush drained from her face. "I think, Elizabeth, that I wasn't fast enough, keeping your fingers from my wrist that night. Without knowing, you knew...just as you knew that one Asp was frightening and the other friendly... as you knew how to reach the ring in the stone...you knew what I was."

"What are you?" she whispered.

Hesha paused. He licked his lips, and his hands tightened, involuntarily, over hers.

"Deathless."

Sunday, 11 July 1999, 4:13 AM
Laurel Ridge Farm
Columbia, Maryland

Ronald Thompson waited angrily. He was sick; he watched the scene in Vegel's apartment through narrowed, puffed-up slits of eyes. He was irritable. Inaction suited him badly; convalescence still worse. Patience he had, and he could have endured the night creditably well—if Hesha hadn't switched tactics in midstream. Thompson was puzzled, and so, instead of lying down and resting (as Janet had pleaded with him by phone to do) he sat at the center of his net and waited.

Hesha came out of Elizabeth's room backwards, bidding the girl good night and better dreams. Thompson nearly choked. As his master turned toward the door of his study, his room, and his sepulcher, Thompson flicked a switch with one swollen finger. Hesha looked up, waited, and then crossed the museum to the bookcase door.

Thompson straightened his abused body in the chair. He shot Hesha an expectant, a *challenging* glare.

Hesha regarded his servant impassively. "Yes, Thompson?"

"Sir," Thompson began. He ground rapidly to a halt. How to go on? "Sir, may I ask you a personal question?"

"You can ask me anything," said Hesha. The Setite's eyes clearly promised no answers.

"What happened," barked Thompson, "to the plan, sir?"

"Which plan?"

"The family plan," said the mortal harshly. Thompson bit his lip, and fought for the right opening—for words civil enough to keep peace with his employer, but strong enough to vent his wrath—and all that would come to him was the blasted, vitriolic curse that had begun the day.

Hesha watched as his prospective heir stumbled over his own ire. The man's eyes hunted the air, and he radiated disapproval. Hesha drew up a chair, sank sinuously into the seat, and said, "Put your thoughts in order, detective. Start again. You object to my handling of the Dimitros situation? Naturally, you have been listening ever since I brought her back to her own room...if you had not caught my performance live, I would have insisted on your review of the recorded version."

Thompson nearly exploded. A shout choked up his chest; his mouth opened—and he saw Hesha's lids twitch, lightly, in amusement. The old cop imploded, instead. So the boss was playing him. A *test*, he realized. *Another test. I wonder if I'm passing it or not.*

"I took her to the place where she felt most comfortable, Thompson. I told her what had really happened to her this morning. I gave you and the Asp hero's laurels, just as you deserve. In a few nights' time, she will recover from the shock of the—" his arcing arm indicated the bank of closed-circuit screens—"security arrangements, and I have no doubt that you and she will be fast friends again in a month or so. In fact, by Tuesday I expect that she will have thanked you for saving her life."

"I'm not talking about that."

"You don't care that she hated you tonight?"

"I do. And you say you've fixed that. And I believe you, because you're always right about people, and my gut tells me the same thing. But you said last week that we were going to be family to her—that you 'intended her to look on you as a father figure.'" He slammed his fist on the wide arm of the chair. "If you think those were paternal moves you put on her tonight—!"

"I think you have thrown yourself too deeply into the role of 'older brother,'" Hesha interrupted.

"Vampires are all very well, sir, but I wouldn't want my sister to marry one."

"A very Victorian older brother," commented Hesha, in a

dangerous voice he had never used on Thompson before. "I am not a vampire, and you've had time enough to learn that. I expect you never to use the word again unless you are referring to Stoker or Hollywood's creations. Do you understand me?"

Thompson nodded warily.

"Furthermore. Elizabeth is not your sister, and you'll do well to remember that. Fall too deeply into any role, and you put yourself in danger; fall too deeply into this one and you may get Miss Dimitros killed. She's a target to be guarded, Thompson. Don't let your emotions sway you. Just do your job. As for marriage..." Hesha indulged in near-silent laughter.

"Now. We were discussing my conversation with our guest. I told her she would have many questions. I promised to answer them. There will be answers Thompson; convincing ones. I told her that she was confused, vulnerable. I told her that I cared about her. I told her that I didn't want to say too much tonight, that I didn't want her to leave. I told her that there was more between us than I had realized. I told her that I had never met anyone else like her. I apologized, I confessed, I fell over my feet promising to make it all up to her."

"And did you mean any of that, sir?"

"What would you do if I didn't?" Hesha waited. "Did you believe it when you heard me say it?"

Thompson uttered "Yes," without tone or emotion.

"Good." Hesha paused and looked at Elizabeth on the monitor. She was getting ready for bed; conscious of the camera, she had decided to change clothes under the covers. "Then I trust that she believed it, too. You know me better. You have doubts. You should."

Drawing breath to speak with, he went out on a tangent. "How many times have you been in Vegel's chamber, Thompson? And in mine?"

"Sir?"

"In Vegel's room there are farmers and hunters and artisans, Thompson. Pharaoh's guards, lords and ladies, scribes, masons. They work at their stations in life, and the river flows past them, and the green fields support them, and the waters cool their thirst, and the fruits of their labor slake their hunger, and the sun beats down on them all, scribe and farmer, master and servant. And that is life.

"In my room, the king is dead, the souls of every man, woman and child are stripped apart and sent to judgment in pieces. They are defenseless as they wander without direction from their tomb to the Place of Ma'at. The world is forever dark, and cold, and once they leave the necropolis there is nothing. The desert is cold and full of monsters. The river cannot give them drink, the fields cannot feed them. Only what the living leave for them can sustain them. And that is death.

"Love can live in the sun. And it is said to flourish in the afterlife. But in the desert between them, Thompson... Neither my kind, nor the Cainites, nor any of the brood of Apep know the meaning of the word after their rebirth. Two of my souls may be here, but my heart lies in the dark underworld, between the jaws of Ammit, the Devourer of the Dead. Understand that. Accept it. And tell me again whether you want to join Set's children."

"*Damn* you, Hesha," whispered Thompson.

"As you say." The creature's voice held nothing.

They sat together in silence for a good five minutes. The main lights went out in Vegel's apartment. Elizabeth lay on her side, reading by the lamp on the bedside table.

"You still," said Thompson, "haven't told me why you changed the plan. I was under the impression, even tonight, that we were going to continue the family game. No changes."

"Miss Dimitros is a very perceptive woman. I knew as soon as I saw her with the Asp that Raphael had no hope of deceiving her. He is limited. Gabriel is much the better actor; that's why I prefer to keep him in the townhouse. My visitors there can look through brick walls, given time...." He trailed off. "Remind me, at sundown, to readjust our arrangements there. I'll need to speak to Janet about the Greywhethers Building."

"But Elizabeth?"

"Let her be. Give her time." He rose. "Gild the cage."

The bunker door shut behind him.

Elizabeth lay in bed, pretending to sleep. Her body remained in the position it had held when she regained consciousness. Her mind was busy taking stock of her situation. She visualized Baltimore on the map, and tried to remember the details of the drive out. She thought about the house, and the cameras, and the woods around the farm. She thought about Hesha, and she acknowledged the blind spot there—she absolutely could not analyze him; could not predict his reactions. She couldn't reach him unless he allowed her to.

But there were other things.

Elizabeth slid out of bed, weakly, and into the desk chair. She reached for the phone, picked it up, and listened. There was a dial tone. She punched in the number for Amy Rutherford's house and waited for the connection. The line opened...and closed with a click. A voice came to her clearly and crisply over far shorter wires.

"Good afternoon, Liz. Do you need something?" It was Thompson.

"I'd like to call New York. How do I get an outside line?" she asked, letting go the fact that she'd needed no extra codes to do so before.

"I'm sorry, Liz." He waited, holding the phone in his room, ready with prepared explanations, excuses, orders from above.

"I think I understand." She replaced the receiver. *Strike one, Dimitros,* she thought. Idly, she turned over the books and tools on her desk—Vegel's desk. One drawer held office supplies: pens, pencils, erasers, staples, cellophane tape.

Elizabeth unplugged the phone, set the roll of tape down thoughtfully, and began—maddeningly slow and inexplicably light-headed—to search her room.

Thompson dropped stiffly into the wide console chair. The lights were green, the cameras on and tracking well. The Asp was long gone, but a litter of crumbs and wrappers testified that he had, in fact, spent the day on duty. Ron swept the trash away, and settled in to make check-up calls on his agents.

He'd finished the last when Elizabeth came out of Vegel's apartment. She was empty-handed, but wearing a light jacket—a kind of photographer's vest—that had several large pockets.

With experienced eyes, he determined that she wasn't carrying anything in them.

The girl paused on the edge of the museum floor. She still held the doorknob; nervously, she looked around.

There was no one there, by order of the boss himself, but the little table the Asp had put her dinner on before had been moved to stand beside her door. The tray on top of it held breakfast...lunch by now. She lifted one of the covers away, scrutinized the food on the plate, and dropped the dome back over the sandwiches. After a moment, she lifted the tray and disappeared with it into her room.

Thompson shifted cameras and watched as she put it on the bed. The desktop was empty, he noticed. Why not put the food there?

Elizabeth came back out, closed the door behind her, and walked, with faltering steps, to the studio. She went through the drawers and bins quickly. Thompson put the workshop on the central monitor and zoomed in on her. Aha. That's what the jacket was for. She filled the pockets with her tools—Q-tips, bottles of solvent, masking tape, the discard tray, a magnifying glass, soft brushes, stiff brushes—and picked up the smallest of the paintings under restoration. She left the studio, returned to Vegel's apartment, and spread her loot out on the desk.

Thompson nodded to himself. Good. Work would take her mind off things. He rubbed his eyes, stretched, and went off in search of more of that remedy himself.

"Thompson."

"Sir." Ron stood up; he'd been waiting, not in his customary position by the door, but resting as well as he could on Vegel's stone bench.

"You're looking better."

"I feel better, sir."

"Where is the Asp?"

"On the desk. He's been filling Janet in on the situation."

"Good." Hesha sat down on the bench. "Janet."

"Here, sir. Shall I patch in Mr. Mercurio?"

"Yes, please." More white noise filtered in. "Report."

Thompson began. "The townhouse and the city holdings are secure. The Asp reports no visitors. He says he's bored, sir. Bored and healthy."

Janet Lindbergh cleared her throat. "The last refugee is off our hands, sir. Mr. Vargas departed his safe house this evening with tickets for Seattle. He left a note for you; I'm sending it by courier."

"Good."

His secretary went on: "Dr. Oxenti's clinic has received a small commendation for volunteer services from the local Red Cross. The Doctor would like to return to Baltimore for the ceremony."

"Tell her no." Hesha replied immediately. "And keep an eye on bookings for flights in and out of Anchorage until after the presentation. Freeze her accounts if necessary. Other business?"

"Miss Dimitros tried to call out this morning. New York number—"

"James and Amaryllis Rutherford, 6724 Lake Park Drive," Janet interjected—

"I told her she couldn't. She seemed to take it very well, sir. She took in lunch and one of her paintings at three o'clock; since then she's been quiet as a mouse and twice as well-behaved."

Over the intercom, there came the sound of snorting laughter.

"Asp?"

"You have a comment, Mr. Mercurio?"

The Asp laughed again. "She's taking it well, sir. Oh, she's behaving herself beautifully. Quiet as a mouse. But we're not going to be able to see her being quiet anymore, Ron. She's found all the cameras in Vegel's room, and she's sticking masking tape over every goddamn one of them. Found the microphone, too."

The conference broke up shortly after that.

The Asp lowered his tray onto the table outside Vegel's apartment and knocked once. With the family flair for stealth, he slipped away again.

After a long delay—two minutes, at least—the door to Vegel's room opened a crack. The woman inside peered out. A hand mirror poked through. Its reflection flashed around the basement. The door closed again.

After another five minutes, Elizabeth herself emerged, pale, thin, and nervous. Warily, she took up the tray. She backed into her hole like a badger, and the door shut immediately. The lock clicked after her, and through the thick wood came the sound of something heavy being dragged across the boards.

In his study, the master of the house watched his prisoner's movements.

In the bunker, Thompson saw Liz gather in her dinner, he saw the Asp wolf down his, and he saw Hesha—sitting perfectly, unnaturally still—watch Elizabeth.

Monday, 12 July 1999 3:18 AM
Laurel Ridge Farm
Columbia, Maryland

Elizabeth maneuvered the canvas through the barricade at her door. She set it down on the "room service" table and then locked the apartment behind her. She picked up the painting, headed for the studio, and puttered around inside the workroom for a few minutes. She pulled another piece, an oil panel, from the flat drawers. With that in hand, she walked back into the main room. Lunch had appeared on the table, but there was no one in sight. *Good,* she thought.

She propped the panel beside the little table and headed for the stairs. She checked the kitchen—empty—and tried the mudroom door. It was locked, and the deadbolt needed a key. She saw why. Even a novice housebreaker like herself could smash the glass above it and turn latches from the outside.

Elizabeth listened. The house was silent. She turned right, into the colonial wing and through the main hall. The front door had no windows set into it; there was just a chance that the bolt was simpler. She turned the knob. No luck. Perhaps she could find a spare key? Of course, this was hardly a house whose inmates would leave their spares lying around. Elizabeth bent to examine the shape of the keyhole and saw that it was parallel to the ground. Hadn't the kitchen door bolt been vertical?

She went back. After a minute, she found the problem; there were three bolts altogether. One turned with the handle and could be set by a spring catch. She'd fixed that. One was near the floor and turned with an odd-shaped knob—she hadn't noticed it the first time. The keyed bolt had been open when she tried it; in an instant the door was open, too. Liz double-checked the snap lock; if she couldn't find civilization in one hike (the word *escape* occurred to her and was promptly dismissed) she didn't want to have to ring the doorbell to get in the house.

The sun shone down through a bleached, thin blanket of clouds. The watery-gray ripples in the cover were moving quickly, but at ground level the air was stultifying: humid, thick, and still.

Elizabeth's eyes stung her. She'd forgotten how dark it was in the house. Through the faint blue afterimage, she set out up the hill. With slick fingers, she pulled open all the vent zippers in her photo jacket. It was bulky and uncomfortably hot inside it; already she was drenched with sweat. Still, she felt better—ludicrously better—knowing that every pocket was stuffed with something useful. The tools she'd gleaned from Vegel's desk and the studio weren't much, but...

In ten minutes she crested the ridge. It was a worn-out mountain, no longer even a foothill, but it was the backbone and a stump or two of rib from an old Appalachian. The granite spine of the giant lay exposed on the hilltop. Elizabeth rounded the curve of it and found a place to climb. The little wall's slope was too steep for the dirt to find much hold, and the blackberry brambles that grew solidly up the other sides were thinner here. She pulled herself up and looked around.

Damn. The landscape was beautiful; it was dark green, rolling country. It was full of trees, and between the contours of the country and the height of the trees, there wasn't much of what she had come to see...not even the house or the drive up to it.

She sat down on the highest point, pulled out a battered brass compass, and found northeast. Baltimore would, or should, lie in that direction anyway, and if she kept her eye out for the broadcast tower as she walked, she'd hit something sooner. She hoped she knew the road to the house well enough to know it if she came to it. The last thing she wanted was Thompson driving up beside her in the sedan just as she reached the mailbox.

Elizabeth set out cross-country.

In a shadowy niche among the brambles, the Eldest watched her go with lazy eyes.

Elizabeth came out of a rhododendron thicket covered in spider webs. She wiped away the strands and dislodged a few hitchhikers. Struggling a little with the thick carpet of old, shiny brown leaves underfoot, she reached out to a wrist-thick sapling for support. It helped her with the descent, and when she had crossed the damp patch at the bottom of the gully, she used the thick roots of the oak above her for a ladder.

The Asp waited on the other side of the tree. He let her pass, and then he broke a dry branch between his hands. It sounded like a shot in the still air.

"Hello, Lizzie." The words were friendly; the tone was not. "Going somewhere?"

Strike two, she thought. "Nice day for a walk," she said aloud.

"Has been." Raphael paused, pursing his lips. "Looks like a storm coming in now, though. You'd better go back to the house. Don't want you getting caught out in it."

"Thanks." She shifted her weight uphill, and took a step farther away from the Asp, his tree, and the farm behind them. He watched her from half-closed eyes. "Liz...you don't want to go that way."

She took another step. "I think I do, actually." Raphael reached out a hand for her wrist. He was quick, but she was jumpy enough to be quicker. She eluded his grasp and they stopped, facing each other, two yards farther from the creek.

"You're supposed to be a smart girl, Lizzie." He lunged again, and this time his trained reflexes won out over her nervous instinct. He pulled her down the slope and onto the slanting trunk of the oak, not gently. "You didn't think it was going to be easy, did you?" He pushed his face up to hers. There was an inch, no more, between them, and the tight, hard gaze of the Asp flickered from eye to eye...left, right...back again. Liz stared back. Her wrist hurt her; he was holding it in a tight twist.

"Come on," he said. "This way."

The pain rotated around her hand. Raphael pushed her

easily by the elbow along a path on the edge of the gully. The trees thinned out as they went. They descended into a hollow and began to cross the wetter ground at its base.

"Mercurio!" The shout came from the Asp's shoulder, as far as Liz could tell. "Goddamn it, Asp. Let her go." Static crackled around the voice. It was Thompson. "Let her go this minute. Fuck it, Raf. What if he checks these tapes tonight?"

Raphael released Elizabeth's wrist. She turned and put three yards between them, then stopped, chafing her burned skin. Neither of them displayed any expression. "She was trying to leave, Ron. I got a job to do."

"I know. I'm criticizing your style, not the performance. Hand me over to Liz for a second."

The Asp reached into his shirt pocket and retrieved a very small, flattish, black disc. He tossed it to her. The disc turned out to be a phone. "Hello, Liz," said Thompson's distant voice. "Do me a favor?"

"Maybe," she answered.

He sighed. "You know the path you were coming down? Get back on it and follow it to the drive. I'll pick you up in the car and bring you home."

"To Manhattan?"

Static. Then, "No."

"How far's the walk?"

"Fifteen minutes, twenty, tops."

"See you then."

"Thanks. Give me back to the maverick, there. He and I need to have a talk before the boss wakes up."

"Coffee?"

Elizabeth nodded. "If you're having some." Thompson clattered around the counter for a few minutes. With the steam rising and the pot filling, he leaned crookedly against the cabinets and watched the girl. She'd taken off her bulging jacket and hung it over the chair back. She sat with both elbows on the table, casually, and her hair was tucked behind her ears. Her hands traced the grain and scars of the battered wooden tabletop, stroking out the same patterns over and over.

Ron pulled two mugs off the rack and set them on a tray. Sugar, milk, the coffeepot, cookie tin. He scooped up the tray in one corrugated fist.

"Mind if we take these down to your room?

Why?" she snapped.

"Because I think you might enjoy a little privacy. It's against all my own regs, but hell—if something comes up through the floor, you run and sound the alarm." Liz said nothing. "I'm not kidding, girl. There's a *reason* we've got cameras every five feet. And the doors wired so we can keep track of the ones the cameras don't see." Elizabeth's eyebrows united in disbelief.

Thompson shook his head. "You've seen *him*. Let me start you out easy. Imagine…two of him. Twenty of him. Weaker breeds in six-packs like bad beer. The invisible man sneaking in to steal stuff. God only knows. Now can we go downstairs?"

She led the way. At the steps down to Vegel's apartment, she paused to fish a key out of her jacket. She opened the door and shifted the barricades aside.

"What the hell have you got in there? There wasn't that much loose furniture in the…" Ron ground to a halt. Awestruck, he laughed. "Good job, Liz. Damnation." Every one of the fancy cabinet doors—some floor-to-ceiling closet pieces, some as small as a medicine chest—had been removed from its hinges and piled up against the entrance. The heavy bathroom door leaned on the secret panel to Vegel's crypt, and its base was reinforced with pieces of the bed frame.

"The tray fits on the desk," Elizabeth directed. "Give me a minute and I'll liberate another chair."

They poured, and mixed, and sipped, and when she'd relaxed enough to explore the contents of Gabriel's cookie tin, he let her get through two chocolate monstrosities before he tried to talk.

Thompson cleared his throat. "Thanks for letting me come in here. I appreciate it."

"Thanks for pretending my carpentry would do a damn bit of good if you decided you wanted in."

"It would slow us down. And it was clever." He hesitated. "But really…I'm glad we're *here*, and not in the kitchen. I've got a few things to say I don't want the Asp—or the boss—listening to later."

Elizabeth gave him steady, stony, sphinx-like attention.

"First—let me say I'm sorry," he began slowly. "I know that doesn't mean a damn thing to you now...but I've got to say it because I do really mean that." He ruffled his grizzled hair, pushing on. "And I want you to know that I...well, I can't say that I—we—haven't all lied to you in one way or another, right from the start. But what I told you about my hometown, about my folks and my high school and why I joined the police and why I left the Force to start my own business—that was all true, every word of it." He paused, and a kind of hopeless look filled his face. "Believe it or not, I like you. And I've got to say I like you even better since this thing blew up in our faces. You've fought it, but you haven't panicked after that first night, and if you're feeling sorry for yourself I can't see it on the surface." He grinned. "Not even the boss was expecting the masking tape, Liz."

The faintest echo of a smile played across her lips. Thompson, uncertain how to keep a good thing going, took a long, hard look into his coffee cup. He shrugged with his hands, and reached for a cookie.

"And I want to apologize for Raphael. He's not a bad guy, once you get to know him, but he resents the boss telling you the Asp's names. The boss thinks—and I think, because I...well, I was watching you over the security system—that you knew the difference between the brothers. Raf doesn't believe it; he's too used to walking around as Angelo and feeling superior because of it. He doesn't know how to act around you, so he's playing the heavy. It'll wear off, I think. Gabe'll bring him around, anyway."

Elizabeth murmured, "You talk as if I'm going to be here a long time."

Thompson flushed a little. "I don't really know," he answered. His mouth twitched as if he'd tasted something rotten in the chocolate. "We're waiting for something on the outside to blow over. The boss is afraid if we let you go now you'd be killed by..."

"Killed by what?" Her voice was hard.

"Things," he finished inadequately. "Other people like him, but different; *other* things; a whole army of things tearing up the eastern seaboard. You saw the reports of riots in Atlanta, in D.C.? They're in the thick of it."

She said nothing, and Thompson could feel doubt pouring out of her.

"Look, Liz. You'll admit that he exists, I hope. If he exists, not breathing, not dying, what else is out there?"

"What else *is* out there?"

"The invisible man. Those six-packs. The late-late-late-show. I wish *I* didn't know," said Thompson, with such finality, with such weariness, that she let the matter rest. He freshened their mugs and took a sip. Minutes went by, and in each one, Ron nearly spoke. In each one, he thought better of it. After a dozen false starts, the words spilled out.

"About him, Liz."

"What about him?"

"About the two of you...don't look at me like that." Elizabeth's jaw had clamped shut. She was clearly unwilling even to listen to this. *Damn*, he thought. *He's really under her skin.* He took a long breath and prepared to risk deeper waters for Hesha's sake.

"Please, Elizabeth. I'm not blind. You're in love with him."

She almost laughed. "No. No, I'm not. I don't know him. You can't love someone you don't know." She set her jaw again. Her lips were abnormally pale and thin. "You can't love someone who locks you up," she said. "Someone who lies to you; someone who spies on you constantly; someone whose hired...guards... throw you around in the name of your own safety—and please don't be offended if I admit I still don't believe in the 'things' you say are waiting for me to set foot out there."

"No offense taken." He struggled to come up with more, and said, "But it sounds like you're working awfully hard to convince somebody."

"You," she insisted. "You're the one with the theory."

"Sure. But you don't have to convince me. You could just say no and stop the conversation. But you're willing—you're eager to keep talking about him, because you really did give a damn, and now he's hurt you. So you want to talk. Therefore—I don't believe you. I don't believe *him* when he denies it, either," he said, and realized that that, at least, was true.

"I've been married twice, Liz. I know the symptoms." He slouched back in his chair. "Let me tell you what's going to happen. Hesha will not come to see you. You think he scares you? You scare the hell out of him," said Thompson, crossing his fingers to ward off thunderbolts. Her eyes dropped—she believed that—*God help her*, thought Ron. And *God forgive me.*

"Now, if you don't care, or you can't get past the shock, or you're as scared as he is, you can stay here in this room for as long as the danger lasts, if that's what you really want. And then he'll send you home to New York, and you'll never see him again. But while you wait, each of you will know that the other is just on the other side of the wall—until *he* can't stand it and finds an excuse to run even farther away from you." Thompson, staggered by the size of the lie, foundered and reached for cliché. "I know it isn't fair that you have to make the next move." That was better. "What's wrong here is his…fault…because of what he is. But I can't go in there and talk to him like this. So I'm in here. And…I'm asking you." He shook his head. "Because I like you both." He played nervously with his empty coffee cup, and he sounded anything but sure. "Go see him. Talk to him. Maybe even let him try to explain."

Thompson checked his watch and stood up. "I've got to go now. Raf'll be looking for me." He looked over to her, but Liz had her eyes fixed firmly on the carpet. "Please, at least think about what I said. And don't…well, I'd rather you didn't tell the boss I was in here, meddling in his…personal…life…" He picked up the tray and took it out with him. After a few moments the lock clicked to and the sound of shifting barricades came from behind the door.

"Report."

"Miss Dimitros went for a walk this afternoon," said Thompson. "The Asp stopped her short of the interior fence and encouraged her to come back."

Hesha turned from his security chief to look at Raphael.

"*Encouraged*," he said evenly.

"Yeah." Raphael sounded slightly defensive even to himself. "I brought her back. And I handed her off to Ron. And then," he said, seeing a way out of his employer's uncomfortable attention, "they disappeared into her room for an hour."

Hesha focused his cool regard on Thompson again. "Into her room?"

"I wanted a look at her arrangements." Ron folded back the cover of his notebook. "The barricade, sir. You can hear her moving it around from the outside, even over the system microphones. As it turned out, she's constructed it from the cabinet fronts of Vegel's storage shelves. I have a sketch here— really, it's no more complicated a construction than a house of cards, but it's reasonably effective and—"

"Resourceful," murmured Hesha, glancing at the piece of paper. He handed it back.

"It didn't take you an hour to look at her room, Ron," interjected the Asp. "What else was going on in there?" Thompson ignored Raphael's leer and managed—by slow and careful folding of the sketch as he put it away—not to have to look Hesha directly in the eye, either. "After Raf's 'encouragement,'" he began, "I thought she needed a little normality." Ron flicked up the next page of his notebook and met his employer's eyes calmly. "A little metaphorical hand-holding. We had a nice, long talk, sir. Just consider the cage gilded."

Hesha took a long time to speak. "Very well. Other business?"

Elizabeth walked toward Hesha's study.

From the far end of the basement, there came a faint click. Hesha stood in the open doorway.

She held herself together, crossing the space between them at a slow pace that (she prayed) betrayed none of the anxiety she felt. "Good evening, Hesha," she said, taking his favorite greeting away from him. "I was hoping you would be in tonight. Do you have a few minutes to spare me?"

Her host stepped aside and invited her in with a gesture.

Elizabeth smiled. "Actually, if you don't mind…" She pointed with a careless hand toward her own room. "I was thinking of a slightly more private discussion."

Hesha didn't move. "I can override the system, if you wish."

Her upper lip twitched. "But I would have no way of telling whether you really did or not."

His sleek black head inclined toward her. "Very well, then, if you feel safer there."

"Marginally."

When both were seated, Elizabeth smiled as broadly as she could and extended her right hand. "Hello," she said. Hesha took his cue and shook with her. "My name is Elizabeth Dimitros. I was born in Brooklyn; I've lived in New York most of my life. I make my money restoring art for an antique gallery. I'm studying for my doctorate in an incredibly obscure field. I'm single and I'm twenty-nine and I'm not enjoying that very much." She finished with a shrug she'd inherited from her father; flourishing, Greek, and involving the entire arm.

"Twenty-eight," Hesha put in. "Twenty-eight until September."

"Strike three," murmured Elizabeth.

"Pardon?"

"I've never told you my age, let alone my birthday. Not Thompson or the twins, either." A little of her smile disappeared. "I suppose Amy might have mentioned it, but she didn't, did she?"

"No."

"So you know me," she said deliberately, "very well. And I know nothing—nothing, really—about you." She took a deep breath. "And I was wondering if you would care to introduce yourself." Elizabeth swallowed a nervous, choking reflex. "Please."

Hesha put his hands together and gave an odd half-bow with his head and shoulders. "My name is Hesha, truly; it is a milk name that my mother gave me. I have many others. Ruhadze I took from a friend of mine after his death; he had no sons and I wanted to honor his memory. I have been Hesha Abn Yusuf, Hesha Washington, Hesha Abraham....

"I was born between the First and Second Cataracts, in Nubia, that is now Sudan, in a village that no longer exists because of the Aswan Dam, to a people who are disappearing, to a religion that was not supposed to have survived. I have traveled in North Africa, in India, in Europe, and in America. I made my money in antiques, but my current holdings are diverse. I spend most of my time studying old languages and cultures; I try to keep buried dangers from being uncovered by the wrong hands. I am a bachelor by nature," he stressed. "I am considerably older than I look; and until this summer I enjoyed my life a great deal."

"Until this summer," Elizabeth said evenly.

"At solstice, one of the most terrible dangers I sought to confine was exposed. I have no idea who wields it now. At solstice, Erich Vegel, who was my partner and my only…friend," Hesha said, "accepted an invitation to a gala and kept a business appointment there on my behalf. He was killed that night or very soon after, I believe. It is possible that he fell into the hands of our enemies. It is possible that our business associates set him up; that people I trusted are now a threat. At solstice, a night-war started for control of the East Coast. At solstice, I met you. Since then," he said, holding up a finger for each transgression, "you have brought Kettridge back into my circle, disordered my house, invaded my sanctuary, and nearly caused the death of my servant Thompson." With four fingers up, he began another list, in identical tones, and folded down one finger for each item. "You have also discovered how to remove the white eye from the statue, located one of the two missing stones, extracted the ring from Vegel's boulder, and revealed weaknesses in our security system without actually killing anyone under my protection." He finished with his hand closed again.

Elizabeth ventured, "I'm sorry about your friend. And I don't know anything about your danger or your war," she said seriously. Her stomach tightened in painful knots. "As for the last…are you trying to say we're even? Because I don't understand you." She reached for the fist he still held in the air between them. "There's more to this situation than four for four." Her hand closed over his, and Hesha allowed it to remain.

"No. You are correct. I have taken things away. Your liberty and your safety, for example—and I will remain in your debt until such time as I return them to you." His voice, distant and formal, fell on her like ice water, but his eyes found hers and were smoldering hot.

They sat in silence for a long time.

Without words, Hesha opened the hand Elizabeth held. He reached for her other hand, and they went on sitting, saying nothing. The knots in Elizabeth's stomach vanished and were replaced by butterflies—not the ordinary breed born of fear or hope or past loves, but rabid butterflies that hurt and tore her at the same time she felt wonderful. Warm waves of contentment washed down her neck and shoulders to battle with a dreadful chill in her spine. She hoped he would speak. She was terrified of what he might say.

Hesha's hands held the mortal's lightly. His index fingers supported her wrists; he was enraptured by the rhythm of her heartbeat. *Pleasant music*, he thought. He waited patiently while the tempo changed. The matter could not be rushed…when the time was right, he brought out the words he had ready.

"Elizabeth," said the Setite softly, gazing into her eyes. "Don't ask me questions," he hesitated for a finely calculated second, "unless you're absolutely certain," again, a pause, "that you want the answers." He brought her hands together and brushed the knuckles lightly with his lips; he dropped them gently into her lap.

"I have a great deal of work to do tonight," said Hesha, rising. "But I would like to see you tomorrow. If you would care to work on the papyrus tomorrow at ten o'clock.?" She nodded gravely, and with as solemn a countenance he slipped through the barricade and away.

Hesha stared at the bag of blood waiting in his apartment.

"Thompson," he said loudly, into the empty air.

A circuit opened. "Sir."

"Have my car ready."

"Your car, sir?"

"Unless you particularly desire to watch me hunt, you will prepare my personal car instead of the chauffeur model."

"Your car, sir," said Thompson, quickly.

The intercom died with a click.

Footsteps on the stairs stopped Ron where he stood in the kitchen.

Elizabeth reached the top and found him staring at her.

"Hi," she said.

"Hey, Liz." Thompson answered. "Are you all right?"

"No. But what am I going to do about it?" Thompson kept quiet. "Any chance you could help me put my room back together?" Elizabeth looked up at him, wistfully. "I'm having trouble with the larger doors; I can't hold them up and stick the pins in the hinges at the same time."

"Sure."

"You talked to him?"

She nodded.

"Ron...I suppose I should have said this sooner...but thanks." She paused, and Thompson was struck by a fleeting resemblance to his master in the girl's face. "For the advice. And for getting the Asp off my back the other day. And...for pulling me out of there. The snake pit. Someday, Ron, explain to me why there's a room full of snakes in this house. Just not today. Thank you," she finished lamely, "for saving my life." She looked up at him. "God, that sounds so inadequate when you actually come out and say it, doesn't it?"

Thompson smiled and shook his head, but said nothing. He reached for the empty bottle. *Tuesday*, he thought. *By Tuesday, she will have thanked you for saving her life.' Damn him.*

Raphael rounded the corner from the elevator and slouched against the bunker wall. "What're you doing, Ron?"

"Agency reports. According to these jokers, Kettridge was in St. Louis, Philly, *and* Memphis yesterday. Damn kids. Wouldn't recognize their own mothers in a line-up."

The Asp poured sympathy into his voice. "You need a drink, Ron."

"I have a drink. And I'm not downing any of that paint-stripper you call booze," Ron said, until he saw the bottle Rafael was offering. "Holy shit. Where'd you get that?"

"Present from the boss. For bringing our girl back without breaking her." He shrugged. "I figure I owe you some; I'd probably have at least torn something if you hadn't stepped in." Raphael set a tumbler on the console and filled it with a generous double.

Thompson took a sip, nodded thanks, then picked up his reports again. The Asp plopped himself down in the spare chair and watched the screens. On the center monitor, Elizabeth and Hesha worked at the papyrus table. The sound was turned off, but the sitting figures seemed to be talking companionably enough.

"So." Raphael refilled his own glass contentedly. "Everything back to normal, hey, Ron?"

Elizabeth sighed and put Vegel's notes neatly aside. The manuscript was defeating her. She scooted her chair a foot or two farther down the scroll to a more heavily illustrated portion.

"Tired?" Hesha asked.

"Frustrated." Liz plucked a scrap of vaguely red-tinged papyrus from the side of the table. There was a small black line running across the edge...which failed to match the section she thought it would. "I had such a lucky run on this last Friday."

Her host continued working without comment.

"How old are you, Hesha?" Elizabeth asked suddenly.

"Thirty-three, I think. Perhaps thirty-four," said the Setite, meeting her gaze with an amused, puzzled expression. Elizabeth raised an eyebrow skeptically. "Not counting the years since I failed to die, of course."

"How long ago was that?"

His face hardened. "You want the truth?" Elizabeth nodded. "It may have been 1700 CE; I often suspect that it was earlier. The old calendars don't match each other very well." He watched her. "You're not surprised?"

"No. I was ready for that one; you've dropped enough hints." Liz took up her tongs again, and found a match for the red shard. "Your grandfather's North African household goods from the fifteenth century." She smiled at his reflection in the table. "What does this papyrus say?"

"You think I can read this?"

She laughed. "Yes." She matched two more red pieces together.

His black eyes flickered up at her. "Truth? This is a temple copy of a folk tale about Nepthys. The picture you're working on shows her leaving her brother Set's court, the court of Upper Egypt, to visit their married siblings Osiris and Isis in Lower Egypt. This piece—" he drew her attention to an assembled section—"is a prayer, and this—" another sound fragment—"is a recipe for incense to propitiate the goddess."

"Oh." Elizabeth reached for Vegel's notes and a new piece of paper. She copied down the symbols for the four deities and the two courts and started a search through the scraps for the names.

"How did you meet Professor Kettridge?"

"At a dig in Lebanon. Baalbek. It's a long story."

"Are you going anywhere?" She grinned at him.

"No." Hesha waited, giving her the opportunity, but when Elizabeth neither asked for the truth nor looked for it with her eyes, he went on freely. Jordan Kettridge might not have recognized the events described in the Setite's version, but Hesha made a thrilling story of them. Professor Kettridge shone as an honest archaeologist swept up in international events. Thompson made brave stands against unnamed terrorists; Erich Vegel protected the dig alone, by night, against overwhelming odds; and Hesha (with a fair amount of modesty) took the stage as the linguist, local guide, and quiet man behind the scenes. By the end of the account, Kettridge had discovered Hesha's secret, overreacted, and fled quite plausibly.

"And you haven't spoken to him since?"

The Setite paused. "I suspect I give him the same kind of nightmares I gave you," he looked up at her, "though for different reasons—" and the soft, embarrassed glance in his eyes was a masterwork of misdirection. With a slight, visible effort, he shook off the sentiment. "Kettridge is a scientist. I am...difficult to explain. I don't force the issue on him." Hesha set his tools down on the tabletop. "I think I'm done for the night," he said, stretching. Elizabeth watched his body move under his shirt, found herself staring, and looked quickly away. "You should get some rest, too."

They stood up together. Walking slowly, side by side, they traversed the length of the museum. At the point where Elizabeth would turn toward Vegel's room and Hesha would turn toward his own, she hesitated, and was relieved to find him still standing next to her. His hand reached up to her shoulder.

"Go," said Hesha, hoarsely.

Elizabeth bit her lip. She pulled her key from her pocket and took the steps down to her door. She listened to his soft footfalls take him farther, to his own threshold, and she turned the key in the lock. For another second she hesitated. *Go to bed, Lizzie. Don't think about it.* She snapped the key out of the wards and opened the door. Against her better judgment, she looked back—

—and saw him lying crumpled on the floor.

"Hesha!"

She screamed and ran at the same time, arrived breathless, and skidded to a stop on her hands and knees.

"Hesha!" Elizabeth's hands shook helplessly. No pulse to take, no breath sounds to listen for. His eyes—his eyes were shut; the lids and irises motionless. She struck the floor with her fist and jumped up again. *The bookshelf*—she flew to it and tried to slide it open. "Thompson! Thompson!" She kicked furiously at the heavy wooden case. "Damn it, Ron!" She whirled around, trying to remember...there were microphones everywhere, but where was the nearest intercom? Her apartment? Hesha's study? "Thompson!" she yelled again.

Elizabeth turned to run to her room. Behind her, the

bookshelf slid aside, and Thompson and the Asp dodged around her to reach their master. She was nearly knocked down; she hardly thought about it.

Ron Thompson knelt by Hesha—carefully, without touching him or his clothing—and held the other two off with a gesture. "Sir?"

No one breathed.

"Sir?"

The Setite's left hand crept to his collar. From the cords hung round his neck, at a glacial pace, he selected the newest. "Eye," he said.

Thompson waved Raphael in. "Take his legs." The Asp obeyed, and together they lifted Hesha's unresisting carcass off the ground. "Liz, get the door to his room."

Wednesday, 14 July 1999, 3:56 AM
Laurel Ridge Farm
Columbia, Maryland

"Light," said Thompson. "Sir? We're on the last step. We can't go any farther without…"

The creature in his arms hissed. Sibilant echoes filled the chamber.

"Thank you, sir." Thompson started moving again. "Careful where you step, Raf. They won't bite after he's said the word, but shuffle your feet just to be on the safe side. Turning right, now. Easy."

Elizabeth closed her eyes, took a deep breath, and waded—gently—into the ankle-deep confusion of snakes. The procession passed by the Eighth Hour and the Seventh. Elizabeth had to stop often to find a clear place to rest her feet. She felt as though the stars above moved with them and that the tangle of reptiles had eyes on her.

"Straight shot over to the sandbox, Raf. Liz? Crossing here." They stepped out into the empty center of the tomb. Elizabeth trailed after them, certain now that something was following her.

"Good. Set him down." Thompson laid his master on a long, thin, squat bench—nearly a cot—at the edge of a large, circular patch of white sand. From a tiny chest of drawers beside the circle, he took a bronze amulet on a black cord and a small bag shut tight by a drawstring. He handed them to Hesha without a word, and the Setite's fingers sprang into life.

"What's wrong with him?" Elizabeth whispered.

"Quiet," Thompson ordered. Looking at her face, he relented. "He's all right, he's just...concentrating. He doesn't have any energy to spare. Don't distract him." He pulled her up against the wall and cleared space for the two to sit. On the other side of the sand, the Asp did the same.

Hesha's hands stopped. For a moment, nothing happened. Then he sat bolt upright on the bench, stretched his hands out clenched tightly together, and moved his mouth as if he were speaking. The three mortals heard only a faint whistle, like a breeze. Hesha's right arm stuck straight out, steady as stone. Hesha's left arm descended, slowly, holding the bronze figure. The white eye of the statue had been tied into the knot above it. The tip of the amulet touched the sand; the Setite's left arm fell back to his lap, and though his body moved not at all, the pendulum began to sway wildly.

Elizabeth watched, fascinated. The little bob disobeyed half the laws of physics—after a quick whip to one side that stretched the cord to its full length, it zipped back just as fast to the center, changed direction, and swung sluggishly through a short arc. Slow, fast, short, long, making sharp turns, wide angles—*like a magnetic top*, she thought. *Like a toy.* She drew her knees in and braced both hands against the floor, sitting up straighter to see better. Fine black lines appeared on the sand wherever the amulet went—

When it stopped, it stopped suddenly. The eye and the weight made one last desperate pull toward the long line, and stayed there, quivering, dripping dark powder onto the sand. Hesha reached out and grasped the amulet, and the line between his hands went slack.

"Kettridge is in Philadelphia," he said, in a perfectly ordinary voice. "Have the agency provide protection for him. He is not to know the team is there; he is not to be interfered with—but he will need more eyes and firepower than I suspect he can muster on his own. Who saw him there?"

"Pauline Richards, sir. With your permission, I'd like her to head the team. She's one of the candidates I've been considering as a replacement."

"As you will." Hesha opened his eyes. *Kettridge took my*

advice. Interesting. The other red eye remained in New York City. He suspected that a warlock owned it; if true, it was completely inaccessible—but if true, why was it...unattended? There was no presence connected with it. The Eye itself lay in Atlanta. Very well. It could stay where it was, now that he understood the source. Hesha rubbed the white bead between his fingers. He took it off the cord and tied it again around his neck. The long line; the line too faint and too shaky to trace the first night in New York—now he knew where it ended.

He turned to the Asp. "Thank you for your assistance. Can you take the desk while Thompson and I conclude arrangements? Time is short." As an afterthought, he added, "Show her the safe way out, if you would."

"Yes, sir." Raphael danced nimbly away between the copperheads' bodies. Liz hesitated, hovering toward Hesha. "Good night, Elizabeth," said the creature, sternly. Her jaw clenched tight, but she rushed to catch up to her guide and they vanished up the stairs.

"Thompson. The Eye is in Atlanta, but the Eye's source of power lies in Calcutta. We leave for India immediately." The Setite found his feet and made a beeline for the sarcophagus. The snakes opened a path for him. Ron walked in the wake. "Call Janet as soon as you leave me; prepare equipment for yourself and the Asp. Expect the worst. Conference at sundown as usual, but have Miss Dimitros attend."

"Sir? Are we...we can't take her with us.?!"

"No?" Hesha perched on the edge of his stony couch. "We cannot leave her here alone, Thompson; we cannot send her back to New York until we are sure of her. The doctor is in Alaska. I doubt if her second-in-command would be quite so amenable to our usual storage solution...even if I cared to risk Elizabeth's health by placing her in a coma for the weeks or months of our absence. We could kill her, of course...but I think we will find her useful in Calcutta.

"Unless you would like me to reconsider, Thompson."

"No." Ron's ruddy face was pale. "No, sir, thank you."

"Leave me," said the monster, lying down. "The sun rises."

Elizabeth appeared—uncertain but poised—in the door between her room and Vegel's carved crypt. Thompson stood, indicated the empty chair beside his own, and smiled reassuringly. He handed a thick stack of documents to Liz, including her own genuine passport, shot records, and university records, which she had left in her apartment in New York. He opened his notebook—a new one, dedicated to Calcutta and nothing else—and sat back with an air of expectation. Raphael took a seat, and after a theatrically appropriate interval, Hesha himself joined the group.

"Good evening," said the Setite, taking his place on the stone bench. "Janet?" He said to the ceiling.

"Here, sir."

Hesha faced Liz and gestured to the disembodied speaker. "Elizabeth Dimitros, Janet Lindbergh. Circumstances forbid a more personal introduction, I'm afraid. Miss Dimitros, we leave for Calcutta this afternoon."

Elizabeth's brows climbed in surprise. Her chin came up sharply, defiantly. The golden glints in her eyes flashed at, through, and beyond the Setite's face, and she withdrew slightly. Still, she said nothing, and Hesha, who had had a quick and quiet speech ready to convince her if it became necessary, set those words aside and went on:

"Thompson and the Asp go with us; Mrs. Lindbergh and the Asp stay here as rear guard. Reports, please. Janet?"

Janet efficiently ticked off the arrangements and assumed identities they'd each be traveling under, including a diplomatic passport for the Asp.

"Diplomatic seal on all his baggage—including you, sir."

"Excellent," said Hesha. "Hotel?"

"The Oberoi Grand. Central, expensive, traditional but refurbished—and with an available suite exceeding Thompson's basic requirements, sir."

Ron spoke up. "We've hedged our bets with rooms under cover at various more appropriate places throughout town. I've got agents en route to take occupancy on schedule and form parts of the guard team. And there will be a H. M. Ruhadze making the appropriate border crossings to account for your public appearance and disappearance as needed."

"Munitions?"

Thompson glanced toward Elizabeth. He and the Asp had their choices ready, but...they were somewhat revealing. Instead of reading the list out loud, he passed his notebook to his employer. Hesha scanned it without expression. He reached toward Thompson without looking, and Ron handed the pencil to him.

"Bring extra supplies of the circled items; we may need them for trade on the black market. If not, we can distribute them for goodwill before we return.

"As for personal belongings: Be ready for anything. Asp, you can pass for local if you don't speak. I want your maximum range of costume ready as soon as we land. The same goes for my kit. We can pick up additional indigenous clothing once we reach the city, but we cannot do it without suspicion unless we blend in before we enter the shops.

"Thompson. Western dress. Tourist gear, business wear, bodyguard for any level from gutter to glitter. If you can pick up the accent we may add an Anglo-Indian range.

"Elizabeth. Pack your bags back up, but don't take all your books. Look over your supposed itinerary and select such volumes as would aid research on your dissertation at those places. Take from Vegel's library as you need, and bring anything we have on Bengali myth. You will study that and the hieroglyphs for most of our stay. As for clothes, I want your own things in your own cases. Thompson, see that she has a tourist, business, and jet-set wardrobe available at the Oberoi Grand when we arrive."

"I don't have jet-set clothes? Hesha," Elizabeth put in. "I suppose your men could steal my suits and things from my apartment—like they have my passport—but my silver dress is the only—"

He cut her off. "We will attend to that."

Elizabeth subsided. Thompson flipped to a new page in his notebook. The master of the house drilled them over baggage claim, shipping crates under separate labels, and the meeting dragged on.

A feeling like nostalgia settled into the old cop's bones. There was Hesha, captain of the expedition, his mind wrapped around every detail. The Asp, murderous but familiar, sleek and silent. Janet, sharp, thorough, thinking of everything almost as quickly as the boss himself. And if Vegel wasn't there to give efficiency a little twisted warmth, at least Elizabeth was finally on the team instead of pulling against it. He could see her, a year from now, working in the museum, chatting with poor lonely Janet, kidding around with the twins, learning from himself how to scan and shoot and run the system at the farm. He glanced down at the sleek, brown head beside him and smiled. *Little sister*, he thought. *Close* enough.

part three

calcutta

Friday, 16 July 1999, 8:06 PM (local time)
The Oberoi Grand Hotel
Calcutta, West Bengal

Hesha woke rapidly. The sun now setting over the Ganges delta had abandoned Baltimore some ten hours earlier; the long journey had taken them into and out of the night an unsettling number of times. Freed from sleep in the cargo compartments of the jets, he had had time to himself. Since the ruin of Atlanta, his prayers to Set had been too rare, his meditations interrupted too often by the Eye and all that came with it. He let his mind dwell a moment on the dreams his god had sent him—painful but promising visions—and the plans now concrete in his thoughts.

Rolling over, the Setite stretched himself. The casket, lined in suede and filled with fire-retardant gel, only gently confined his contortions. In a short time, he had hands, feet, and proper ears again. With a slickly scaled claw, he felt through the darkness. There was a small plug of gel and leather near his head; he pulled it aside and listened.

"Raf? What in hell did you bring *these* for?"

"Black market. They're very hot over here."

"Fine. You stow them. C'mere, Liz."

Hesha opened a tiny hatch that the plug had hidden. The light outside was dim and slightly blue. Satisfied, he prepared to make his appearance.

Thompson's assured baritone continued outside. "Calcutta has no phones worth speaking of, right? We wouldn't use them anyway. Take this. There's a list of numbers you'll need to memorize, I'll give them to you in a second. But the first and last security protocol for our phones is: no names. Ever. Someone dials up and calls you Dimitros, Elizabeth, Liz, Lizzie, anything—or asks you for any of us by name—you hang up. It's a trap call. After we've got the codes beaten into your head, I'll go over whether you leave the phone where it is, call us, call scram, or what. Now. First rule?"

"No names."

"Last rule."

"No names."

Hesha slipped from the aluminum travel-case into blue-curtained dimness. His personal items were strewn convincingly around the room. His truly private bags sat next to the gel-filled casket and had, by order, not been touched. The bedclothes, rumpled, testified to a jetlagged traveler. The bathroom showed enough signs of use; he seemed not to have had a shower before napping. He proceeded to take one now, and in half an hour a clean, rested Hesha, dressed well but lightly, opened the connecting door to the rest of his suite.

"Good evening."

His retainers stopped in their tasks. The Asp set an elaborate machine-gun back into its case. He dropped down beside it on a couch now cluttered with armament. Thompson put down a computer hook-up and found a chair near an empty sideboard. Elizabeth looked up from the central table. Her new phone, a notepad, guide-books and a stack of local newspapers lay piled in heaps around her place.

"Report, please. Thompson?"

"Janet's news is waiting on your laptop. Everything here—so far—has gone without a hitch, sir." He made a short, dismissive gesture with his hands. "We're only half-settled in, of course."

Hesha picked a pistol out of one of the Asp's cases and weighed it in his hands. "Reports at dawn, then." Discarding the weapon, he turned and left them.

Friday, 16 July 1999, 11:27 PM
The Albert Hall Coffee Shop
Calcutta, West Bengal

Hesha walked into the old, smoke-filled cafe with a book in his hand. It was a worn-out, rebound, foxed and tattered copy of Calcuttan folk tales. The Setite obtained a cup of coffee, a small table, and a straight, slat-back chair. He settled in as though he had all night to read. Through the haze and the variety of lights—none of the bulbs in the lamps seemed to have come from the same country, let alone the same box— Hesha made, without haste, eye contact with a man at the corner table farthest from the door. The Indian was white-haired and bearded, dark-skinned and hollow-eyed. He spoke, smiling pleasantly, to two earnest-looking young students both bearing, in case an onlooker might doubt, university crests and young-people's causes blazoned across their T-shirts, books, and bags. Hesha did not doubt; he was certain these two (whatever their former intentions) would never attend lectures in the sun-lit rooms of Calcutta's classrooms again. He raised his coffee cup to his lips and opened his book to a random page, but he kept one eye on the trio in the corner.

Slowly, courteously, the elder man shooed away his guests. They left, dissatisfied but saving face, without taking notice of the clean-shaven black newcomer who had cut short their audience.

Hesha waited respectfully for a nod from the bearded man, then crossed the tangled, noisy room to join him. Hesha Ruhadze bowed, cleared away some of the detritus left by the students, and companionably took up a seat backing the deep blue-and-green wall of the shop. The old man's view of the cafe was clear now…and so was Hesha's.

"*Nomoshkar,* Subhas Babu."

"*Nomoshkar,* Hesha Bhai. How have you been, little brother?"

"I do well, Subhas. I do very well. And you?"

"I confess that I bore easily; otherwise my life is sweet." He picked up a coffee, not his own, and Hesha followed suit. They pretended to drink, then set their cups down close to emptier vessels.

"I apologize if my unexpected appearance has caused you to lose friends or business, Subhas. I would have been happy to return later, if you wished it."

"On the contrary, little brother. Those children would chatter all night. I am grateful for the release." The old man brought a colder cup to his lips, set it down, and smiled. "It is funny. The more I insist to them that I have no Family, the more they convince themselves that I am of their own, but ashamed of them."

"Young warriors looking for philosophy in your venerable mind?"

"Rabble looking for a leader, Hesha. Don't flatter them as they flatter themselves. Flatter me all you like, of course." He laughed softly. "Now, what brings you forth, little brother? Surely not the Festival of Snakes; it is too early.

Conversation with you, Subhas."

"All the way from America? Next time, fly me to your doorstep; I should like to see the land of riches for myself."

Hesha tilted his head toward his companion. "It brings me forth tonight. Calcutta has changed since last I walked its streets…."

"It *has* streets," interrupted the elder.

"And I trust you to know all there is to know about it."

"You honor me." Subhas licked his lips, pushed his chair farther from the table, and crossed his legs. "Make yourself comfortable, little brother. Can you smoke?" Hesha nodded.

"It is the thing done here, you understand. Accha!" With a wrinkled, spotted hand, he called up an attendant.

"My dear girl," he said into her glazed eyes, "clear this mess away and bring us two lit pipes and two used cups."

When she's left them, Subhas began a catalog of Calcutta night life. "You might say the Camarilla is in possession, little brother. They certainly say it. They have a Prince; they keep court, and the same cast of characters plays out the same little comedy as in...oh, Lisbon, let us say. Ventrue says he wields the power. Tremere witches behind his back. Toreador pretends to rise above it all. Gangrel disdains to need the others. Malkav mystifies everyone, including herself. Brujah shakes a fist at Ventrue. And the Nosferatu watch and say nothing. But in Lisbon, of course, Ravnos is a rare and unwelcome visitor. Here I daresay he outnumbers the Europeans." The girl arrived and handed the empty cups and full, smoldering pipes to her patrons. "Forgive me, little brother. I let my poetry run away from me. This is not what you need.

"The eldest Anglo Kindred keep their lairs in the old White Town. Young leeches sleep anywhere they think is safe. They are often wrong. We have many, many dangerous places here. I will tell you these first. I know," he said, shaking his head at Hesha, "that you will *go* there first, so it may as well be. The Gypsies camp by the river, north of the racecourse, under the workings for the new bridge. Do not go near their homes if you wish to keep your senses and your skin. The Gangrel and the Ravnos keep up a fine little war defending the area from each other. Stay out of Chinatown. This is difficult; there are...maybe seven, maybe eight little neighborhoods that could vie for the title. Since you last left us, strange creatures have moved in from Bangladesh and Tibet. Beware of *them.* There are wizards in the south. I have not heard of attacks by them on our kin for some time—but only for as long as our kin have avoided the temples of Kali. The temple district is...uncertain.

"Sunderban jungle is filled with tigers. I need not explain myself, I trust?" Both took long, meaningless drags on their pipes and leaned back in their chairs.

"Hunting grounds?" Hesha asked, after a long silence.

"Everywhere. For a newcomer, if you seek crowds after dark, Park Street is good. The hotels are good. The grounds of the Maidan never quite empty, but I should not risk it. Too many trees, not enough masonry."

"Elysium?"

"Ah. You *want* to mingle with the Camarilla? Such poor taste, little brother. Very well. You are in luck, as usual. Tomorrow night the so-called Prince and his court gather to peck at each other. You will find them," he ended, well-bred contempt showing in every line of his face, "at the Bhooter Bari."

Hesha raised an eyebrow. "The Haunted House?" he translated.

"I am afraid so...I believe Malkav's courtier arranges the festivities during Monsoon."

They smoked again, presenting thoughtful faces to the passing mortals. At length, Hesha spoke. "I am greatly obliged to you for your time and wisdom, Subhas Babu."

"May I offer you the opportunity to redeem your debt at once?"

Hesha cast a noncommittal eye over the Calcuttan elder. "Please do, sir. Please do."

"I hear a great many rumors about the situation in the United States. Would you favor me with your considered opinion of events there?"

Hesha nodded, and wreathed himself in pipe smoke. "I speak from the outside, of course," he said, thus reserving the Eye and his own losses from the story, "but the facts as I know them are yours...."

Much later, on the dirty steps of a closed bookshop, in a crooked lane off Albert Street, a dark and ragged figure sat as if asleep. From his urchin's perch, the waiting spy watched a tall, dark, bald stranger stride past him and well away into the rainy night. When the black man was out of sight and hearing, the figure unfolded itself. Short, but taller than he had seemed sitting; poorly dressed, but less tattered than first glance would have shown; dirty and saturnine, but more handsome than the layers of grime would suggest—he flicked his wet hair out of his eyes, turned to an empty space in the air beside the steps, and asked it, "Him?"

Saturday, 17 July 1999, 11:33 PM
Bhagyakul Roy Palace, called Bhooter Bari
Calcutta, West Bengal

Hesha approached the palace from the south. The weeds that choked the pavement had been crushed down by many feet before him; he trod a well-worn path among the enthusiastic vines and grasses. Through the thick, gray veil of rain, he looked up at the old manse. The architect had graced it with cheap copies of classical Greek statues; squatters had added still uglier wire television antennas. The original owners had displayed their wealth in marble and rare stones; time, floods, gentle decay, and encroaching trees had destroyed the mortar and cracked the elegant facade. The windowless walls still stood, the columns and arches were intact, but in the portico where the original family's livery-clad footmen had waited on guests, two dozen shabby, unkempt men crowded close to take shelter from the storm. Smoke rose from pipes and damp cigarettes in their hands. Cheap speakers spewed out a woman's voice: bubble-gum pop with Bengali lyrics.

Hesha glanced back to the treeline and climbed the palace's broken steps. A large man, seated in a position of importance on a column base, rose to greet him.

"*Salaam*, sahib. Members only," he said dully, and prepared to sit down again.

"*Salaam*, bhai," Hesha uttered, in tones of command. The guard stopped moving. "I have a message for one of the members."

"Very good, sahib. You give it to me, I give it to him." Hesha climbed the final step and faced the poor man down. "I will give it to you," he said, "if you will take it immediately to your lord."

Seriously now, in tones of great respect, the guard placed his hands together over the note. "Very good, sahib." Grateful to go, he scrambled over his fellows and into the shadows beyond.

Half an hour later, the guard returned. He shot commands to the others. They scuttled back into the mansion like rats into holes. The leader himself disappeared, and, onto a clear stage, the Camarilla Court of Calcutta filed into sight.

Hesha waited for them, three steps down, wet but untroubled by it. If his robes were rain-heavy, they were that much harder to see through. If his cane and monocle and bare head glistened unnaturally in the house lights, so much more effective his lone figure would be. As a final touch, he made visible the coiling snake tattooed onto his bare scalp.

A long-faced, blond gentleman in a pale gray suit came to the front of the portico. He and his visitor exchanged long, unhurried silence, and then (clearly to the shock of the Kindred closest to him) he descended gracefully down the broad steps to where Hesha stood.

"Let us walk," said Lord James Abernethie, Prince of Calcutta. "And you will tell me why an openly professed Follower of Set seeks audience with me."

"I am," replied Hesha, "merely presenting myself to you upon arrival in your domain. That is one of your laws, is it not?"

The Prince smiled slightly. "Hardly one I would expect *you* to obey."

"In this case, it is purely a matter of practicality. I am here on legitimate business; I do not wish to alarm you, nor would I care to be attacked in the course of conducting my affairs."

Lord Abernethie drew to a halt. Neither he nor Hesha were inexperienced enough ever to look another Kindred in the eyes unless they were *certain* what they would find there, but the Prince came, in his ire, as close as safety allowed.

"And why in hell should I let one of your kind follow the rules?"

"It is," Hesha began, "your Elysium that would be broken. The sympathies of the Court would undoubtedly be behind you; but is it quite safe to have anyone standing," he paused, *"behind* you? As an added consideration, I bring three things. A gift..."

He clapped his hands, and a small, ill-tempered man stepped out of the trees. On a rolling cart, with immense difficulty, the servant pulled a large, olive-and-khaki-colored steel case through the weeds. Hesha pointed, and the Asp brought the cart to a skidding stop half-way to the house.

"Shoulder-to-air missiles. British make, not Russian. And a launcher, of course."

"And why would I need those from you?"

Hesha leaned thoughtfully on his stick. "Eastern problems, perhaps?"

The rain chattered around them, but James Abernethie said nothing for some time. "I accept," the Prince allowed, finally, "pending confirmation that they are as you say, and fully operational. What is the second item?"

"My promise that I do not intend to settle in Calcutta."

Lord Abernethie laughed out loud. "And the third?"

Hesha took from his vest pocket a thin plastic packet. He handed it to the Prince. Lord Abernethie opened the packet, using the envelope to shield the contents from the rain, and read—and recognized—the handwriting on the letters within. His death-pale skin blanched further, and he forgot himself so far as to look the other in the eyebrows.

"Welcome," he said shortly, "to my domain. Won't you come inside?"

"Thank you, your Lordship," said Hesha.

Lord Abernethie, after performing introductions between the visitor and the most distinguished of the guests—their hostess was missing and could not be found—handed his social duties over to one of his childer: the Rani Surama, a dark and dutiful daughter, native to the country (as Lord James was not), wrapped in a flame-orange sari and perfect manners. She took him round to meet each cluster of attendees, then established herself and Hesha in an out-of-the-way corner. Many of his new acquaintances made courtesy calls upon him, but his beautiful escort's discouragement kept the intrusions short, and one o'clock found them deep in conversation.

Surama's long and exquisite hands played lightly along the strings of a zither. It was an antique brought to the palace by her father, and the young Ventrue made use of it for music, for show, and to open a close and probing dialogue on Bengali antiquities. Hesha laughed, smiled, complimented the young lady on her talents and her homeland's treasures. Behind the civil mask, he kept track of the gorgeous creature's attacks and feints as clearly as though she dueled with swords instead of questions. She was checking his story, probably on orders from Lord Abernethie; she was curious on her own account—the waiting court had been given no hint of the Setite's three gifts; she was trying, poor infant, to seduce him.

Eventually, Hesha caught sight of a teenage boy in the crowd. Deferentially, the slim, bony figure made his way to where Hesha and Surama sat. He stared at the floor before him as he spoke. "Rani, your father is looking for you, you know."

"Is he really? Thank you, Michel." The Prince's childe took her leave of Hesha, and wandered away into the party. Michel's eyes followed her longingly; his heart lay in his face. Softly, in archaic Kurdish, he said: "What the hell are you doing, coming in the front like that?" His inflection suggested heartbroken poetry.

"Time is important," Hesha answered in the same language.

"Typhon's pet prophet in a hurry." The old Tremere wizard, a long-time debtor of Hesha's, shook his head. "I don't believe it."

"The Eye of Hazimel is loose in America."

"I'm glad I'm here, then." He paused, and then added: "Just so you know—I am the greenest neonate, no more than twenty years dead, sent here by the Chantry in New Delhi. Since my arrival I have become the little Rani's devoted slave."

"I shall do my best to reinforce the idea," said the Setite. "However. The directive force behind the Eye is in Calcutta."

Michel's face took on an even more mournful expression. "You are sure?"

Hesha did not bother to answer, and Michel took up Surama's discarded zither. "What do you want me to do?"

"Pinpoint the source. Then tell me where to find it."

"Mmm." Michel began to play a love song. "Hurry, if you are hurrying, and give me the details before she comes back."

"She won't be coming back."

"Why?" The warlock glanced at his companion, but the Setite didn't respond. "Sorry. How could I forget? 'Nothing-for-nothing' Hesha, as always. Let me see…. Lord Abernethie's blood weakness is girls—very young girls."

"Lord Abernethie's daughter, the Rani Surama, is an ambitious young leech with poor taste in friends. I brought proof of her treason with me tonight." Michel stared at him. "I would not make contact with you without providing the good Court something more interesting to watch while we spoke," said the Setite simply.

As the rumors began to fly through the assembled Kindred, Hesha gave the Tremere details enough, and no more. The commotion in the outer rooms grew louder, and the Setite finished:

"You will find me at the Oberoi Grand. I will dine in one of the restaurants each night with a brown-haired white woman as camouflage. Come to our table and talk to me about antiques. It should not compromise your position; I have encouraged half the leeches in town to do the same."

"Then you'll see me tomorrow. If the trace is as strong as you say, this won't take long," said the warlock confidently.

By the time one of Michel's "friends" came to tell him his lady-love was in danger, the two devils in the corner were ready to act their part. The boy ran, awestruck and anguished, to the Prince's audience chamber. He still clutched Surama's zither in hand. Hesha stood, found a gossiping circle of Cainites to mingle with, and settled in for a long, dramatic, and tedious evening.

Sunday, 18 July 1999, 9:16 PM
Hesha's suite, the Oberoi Grand Hotel
Calcutta, West Bengal

The last closed door to the big room opened, and Hesha came out in a loose, simple black suit that stopped a cut short of a tuxedo. He glanced at the woman waiting, then began filling his pockets with equipment. Phone, cigarette case, lighter...

"Turn, please," he directed.

Elizabeth obeyed. Layers of pale-blue and amber gauze followed leisurely. Thompson scratched his stubbled chin. The Asp leered freely. Hesha inspected her indifferently, and spoke in dull tones: "Janet. Her arms, shoulders, and chest are too bare for Bengal. Are all of your selections along these lines?"

Janet Lindbergh's voice sprang from the phone. "Yes, sir. Jet-set, you said. This is what 'Society' is wearing. Liz—" Elizabeth, no longer smiling, looked toward the phone to wrest her gaze away from Hesha. "Liz, there's a cloth-of-gold wrap in one of the cases. Wear that; I ordered it in case of cooler weather."

"I'll get it," Thompson offered.

"Elizabeth," said Hesha. "We are going to go downstairs and eat. Have you ever had Mughlai food before? Good. Then we will order two sample platters. Offer me things from your plate; I will do the same. In the end you will have eaten most of what is set before us. You are going to pretend to be yourself, one month ago. You know nothing of my house or the security team. You came to Calcutta from Rutherford House at my request, and you are here to assist me in purchasing antiques and transporting them to America.

"I expect that perhaps half-a-dozen people will come to see us tonight. Some of them will be perfectly innocent acquaintances of mine. When I introduce you to them, I will mention Amy Rutherford. Some of them will be less than innocent; I will refer to Agnes Rutherford and you will leave the table, visit the ladies' lounge, and then return to the conversation. If I mention Hermione Rutherford, you will leave the table, visit the lounge, and stay there, pretending to be ill, until you receive further instructions by phone."

Thompson appeared, offering her shawl. "You look lovely," he mouthed. She smiled weakly but stood tall.

"Come along," said Hesha, and she went.

Monday, 19 July 1999, 11:54 PM
La Rotisserie, the Oberoi Grand Hotel
Calcutta, West Bengal

Elizabeth toyed with the last mouthfuls of her coffee. It had been a long evening, full of visits from Hesha's endless stream of acquaintances. Seven times Agnes's name had come up—seven times Elizabeth had had to visit the ladies' room and flutter convincingly to stall, sink, or mirror. The smartly dressed, middle-aged attendant had politely, pointedly, refrained from comment. It would take little acting now to convince the woman that the vain, crazy American tourist was ill, as well.

Liz watched her companion with concern. These two nights—in public—Hesha had been as attentive and charming as when she first met him. He smiled, he laughed with her, his hand reached occasionally for hers...but his eyes were cold. She thought, finally, that she was learning to read him behind the mask. Under the surface, there was not, so far, a tender word for her, nor a sign of the soft and honest glance she hoped for. He was...worried?

Hesha considered, carefully, the personality of his contact. Michel was confident, skillful, and reliable. The Tremere had said that his magecraft would yield results by Sunday night. He had meant this, and Hesha, remembering their efforts together in the Ottoman Empire, had believed it. It might be that the ritual had taken longer than the cocky old boy had anticipated. But Sunday had gone, Monday would come to its end in mere minutes, and there was not only no sign of the warlock, there was no word. It might be that Michel was so new to town that any messenger was risky. But Hesha found it hard to believe that the wily ancient had so few resources.

The restaurant staff were closing the restaurant down around them, and his reverie ended.

"Elizabeth," he said quietly, touching her hand. She looked up at him, waiting for instructions. She was tired; they had been on display here for nearly four hours. She played the part very well, but the strain showed. For an instant, the memory of real smiles on her face came to him, and he noticed what she was wearing—truly noticed—for the first time. Tonight Janet had dressed the girl in strapless, wine-red silk and the Asp had bought a shawl from the bazaars to cover Elizabeth's shoulders. It was a figured brocade of blood-red and jet-black. Hesha began to suspect his servants of exercising their sense of humor at the girl's expense.

"We are leaving," he said. He held her chair and helped her to her feet. With downcast eyes she collected her bag and shawl, and Hesha offered his arm to escort her. "Fortunately, the rain has stopped for now. We can have dessert on the terrace, and gain a little more time."

She kept her chin up, but her shoulders sagged slightly. She leaned a fraction of her weight on his strong arm, and together they set out for the damp, steamy darkness of the cafe by the pool.

Hesha, dressed in sopping-wet, cheap clothes, leaning heavily on his cane, staggered uneasily down the narrow paths of the bazaar. His retainers would not have recognized him; a dissipated, surly mask hid his face from mortal eyes, his hands were gnarled with disease, he went barefoot through the dirty, stagnating water beginning to gather in the low places of Calcutta. At a rundown, half-height, hole-in-the-wall of a shop, he drew to a halt and wavered back and forth. Hesha looked up at the proprietor. He was a man of fifty, skinny, wizened, and bright-eyed; then he...it...was a near-skeletal creature covered in drooping gray flesh that looked more like wasps' nests than skin.

"All right. I see you, you see me," said a voice like a chainsaw in offal. "What do you want?"

"Information."

"Hah. Well. I have a good deal of that in stock," said the thing sitting in the doorway. "What did you have in mind, old Nag?"

"First, tell me: Are we enemies?"

"I know you, old Nag, and I heard your name in the gutter, but I don't know you that well." The Nosferatu shifted slightly in his seat. "Is there a reason we should be?"

Hesha shook his head. "None...that I know of. I have always regarded your people as the only allies worth having, but I fear your kinsmen have changed their minds toward me." He paused. "I do not look for vendetta, I look for help from you. Do you hear any news from Bombay?"

"I may."

"Bombay can speak for me, if they will. I did them a service some years back."

The gray creature gazed down on him, and slowly spoke. "I'll trade you all I know about your status with my clansmen for all the reasons you think we're on the outs with you."

"Done."

"I'd never heard of you before your visit to the Haunted House." Hesha's face darkened; the Nosferatu held up a crumbling hand. "I know, I know, sounds like a cheap trade. But on my oath, I'll make inquiries and find out whether there's trouble, and why, and give you the information under truce. If we're foes, I warn you first, all right?"

"Now the deal is in my favor, I think."

"No, no, no. I am dying of curiosity; there's a story behind this, I'm sure."

"Your people pressed an invitation on me. To a party in Atlanta, under so-called Elysium. They *insisted.* I had other business; I sent my lieutenant. The party was a death-trap, my cousin was killed in it, and I," admitted Hesha reluctantly, "do not yet know whether your kin meant to catch me in it. There has been no word, one way or the other."

Silence passed heavily between them. The noise of the bazaar at night, the rain on tin roofs, and the shouts and music from the red-light district in the next street surrounded them. The gray creature rustled, then cranked out the question:

"So what's the thing you really want? That we had to settle up truce even to start to talk about?"

"Do you know of a young man named Michel?

"Wet-behind-the-ears warlock? What about him?"

"We had an appointment. He failed to arrive. I don't care to wait pointlessly; I also feel that it is...unlike him to be less than punctual. I am worried that someone may be interfering with him, and thereby interfering with *me.* I want to find him—or find out what happened to him," Hesha finished blackly. "Now tell me," he said in more pleasant tones. "What can I do for you in return?"

"I hear that you're good at bringing things through customs.

I need merchandise." Hesha raised an eyebrow. "Banned books, underground newspapers, dirty magazines, that sort of thing," the monster rattled. "I peddle my papers to the kine as well, brother Nag."

The Setite smiled. "I'm conducting business out of the Oberoi Grand. Bring a list with you and I'll have my people ship you as many as you can stock; enough leeches are seeking those kinds of services that you will blend in beautifully."

Wednesday, 21 July 1999, 11:24 PM
The Ming Court Restaurant, the Oberoi Grand Hotel
Calcutta, West Bengal

Michel came in through the front door, exchanged words with the maître d', and started toward Hesha's table. He was dressed well, though his trouser cuffs were darkened with water and mud. Almost naturally, he threaded his way through the crowd of tables and diners—but Hesha, sensitive to the subtlest detail, caught the unnatural: Michel was nervous, almost frightened. The panicky gait put the Setite's teeth on edge.

"Mr. Ruhadze?" said the young man, hopefully.

Hesha stood. "Michel. Have a seat. Can I get you anything?" The Tremere shook his head, and the millionaire waved the waiters away imperiously. "Allow me to introduce you— Elizabeth, may I present Michel Singh. His family runs an excellent investment firm in Bombay; they have turned the younger generation loose to shine in Calcutta. Michel, this is Elizabeth Dimitros, an expert on antiques and antiquities. I was fortunate enough to convince Rutherford House to lend her to me for this trip—you know Hermione Rutherford, perhaps?"

"I'm afraid I haven't had the pleasure," mumbled the bashful boy in the third chair.

"So pleased to make your acquaintance, Michel," Elizabeth rang in, sparklingly.

Michel looked up and made an effort. "Oh, certainly, certainly. I'm charmed, Ms. Dimitros—Elizabeth," he amended, as she opened her mouth to suggest it. For a moment, the whole table smiled.

"Now," said Liz, as if searching her memory, "we were... oh, of course. Michel, I feel terrible running out just as we've met, but I was about to...ah..." she gestured gracefully toward the ladies' room, "powder my nose. Will you excuse me for a moment, gentlemen?"

As soon as the woman was out of earshot, Michel leaned in and began speaking. "I've been followed. I need your help."

Hesha stood immediately. "Come with me." His hands strayed to pockets—he hit the emergency code on the phone, readied weapons—and he maneuvered to put himself between the mass of the room and his companion. Weak. Michel looked tired and hunted, but his boy's face was haggard, and, above all, *weak.*

All this time, Michel talked. "I found what you're looking for, of course. That's why they're here. You were wrong, Hesha—I didn't think I'd live to see it, but you were dead wrong. When the Eye is active, it doesn't draw on Calcutta for power. Calcutta sends power out to it."

Hesha steered the boy toward the kitchen door for safety. The service elevator...fewer crowds...fewer witnesses...they reached the wall, and with half the angles of attack covered, Hesha permitted himself to scan the room, then looked down at Michel in surprise. Michel had lost control—and consciousness— and the print of a small and bloody palm had appeared on his cheek.

Hesha snatched at the air where the invisible hand had rested. Nothing. He forced his eyes to find the stalker...and failed. He grabbed Michel by the waist and shoulders but found the warlock weighed down by another, unseen body. Hesha kept one hand on his contact's shoulders—pulled him up, down, sideways—discovered the opposing force moved too fast for him. Wounds appeared on the boy's skin—double punctures— and the Setite, frustrated, lifted Michel's helpless body over his head. He spun and began running for the doors.

In the corner of his eye, he caught sight of the thing.

She was tiny—no more than eight years old, had she been human—naked as a frog, and twice as fast as dragonflies. Her hair had been hacked off near the roots, her skin was dark, shading to ebon black at the fingertips and toes—and her tiny, delicate jaws were clamped on Michel's dangling arm.

In the moment before she knew she had been seen, Hesha seized her by the neck and broke her. The miniature assassin dropped off and ran. Her steps faltered, her head rocked from side to side, but she twisted through the rising crowds faster than the Setite could follow.

Hesha reached the front door, pushed his way past the confused hotel staff, and found Thompson waiting for him on the other side. Without a word, he thrust Michel's unresisting carcass into the bodyguard's arms and dashed after the child.

Elizabeth emerged from the lounge just in time to see him run past her. She followed without thinking, the emergency tone shrilling from her phone. He was in trouble. She ran, and fought to keep him in sight.

Outside, the monsoon rains poured down. The streets were ankle-deep in water; running feet threw knee-high spray that glittered in the city lights. Over the flood, there was a small shadow—Hesha trailed that. The Assamite could move faster than he, but she couldn't keep it up forever, and his legs were long. If he could keep her in sight.... So long as she stayed on the streets, there would be the splashing footsteps. Hesha swore. The imp's trail turned west, down a narrow alley. He could follow her through that, but her destination must be the park— the Maidan—poorly lit, grassy, spotted with trees, and huge. He called on Set to lend him speed, and kept running.

Elizabeth dove down the dark alley. Hesha was only a silhouette in the downpour before her; there were lights on the next street, at least. She gathered up her skirts, cursed the heavy, water-logged satin, and leapt over the trash and rats. Out, and up the street, and down another crazy lane, across a boulevard, through traffic—and into a morass of vegetation and mud. Hesha was still just visible, heading for a tangled mess of trees, across a triangle of water. Elizabeth kicked her shoes off and sped after him. Her stockings struck gravel and tore, her bare feet hit the mud, and she fell sideways into the pool. When she looked up, Hesha was gone. Thunder rolled across the commons, and she limped painfully out of the dirty water.

The Setite, blinded by the rain and whipping branches, followed the scent of Michel's blood through the trees. On the other side of the thin stand, he caught sight of the girl again. He sprinted, closed the yards she'd won in the wood, and began to close the gap.

Lightning struck.

Hesha shrieked at the flash. His eyes shut down and burned in their sockets, his world blanked away, and the Beast took him running. The curse drove him blindly, colliding into trees, into stones, into bodies, and the life they found the Beast took with them. In control of himself at last, utterly sightless, he fell to four limbs for safety, slipped, and ended in a puddle. Burrowing into the mud, pressing his raw-red lids into the cool water, he waited, face down, for the pain to fade, praying to Set to intercede against the light.

From far away, he heard a high, chiming laugh and, through the ground, footsteps only slightly heavier than the rain pelted away.

Thursday, 22 July 1999, 2:48 AM
The Oberoi Grand Hotel
Calcutta, West Bengal

"Don't bother, Ron. They're nothing." Elizabeth pulled her scratched feet out of the old cop's hands. She tucked her bare legs back under the wreckage of her dress—brass-green watered satin, it had been; crusty, mud-yellow, spoiled and stiff now—and slumped wearily over the sofa's arm.

"Nothing, hell. There's plague rats on the Maidan. Right foot, Liz. And eat your breakfast."

Time crawled by. Elizabeth ate little. Thompson tended the girl's left foot. Both of them watched their phones—as if watching would help—and waited. The Asp, on his, conducted short, whispered, coded conversations with hushed voices in other parts of the city. Twice, Thompson took calls: Janet Lindbergh, worried; Pauline Miles, offering the information that Kettridge had left Philadelphia for Albany.

"Thompson…" Elizabeth began cautiously, "does he *have* to be in by dawn?"

Ron lowered his eyes. "Of course not. He's supposed to check in. But he makes the rules; he can break them. Go take a shower, Liz. Hot water'll make your feet heal faster." He helped her up, and propelled her toward her room.

Thompson and the Asp stayed awake until they were sure, despite the clouds, that the sun had conquered the horizon. Without a word to each other, they sought out their beds. Sleep took hours to come.

"Elizabeth Ariadne..." said the man with the moon on his head. "What do you do here?"

Liz looked up from her seat in the lobby of the hotel and let her notebook fall to the ground. It, and the chair, and the ground beneath them faded away. She stood up—one stands, when a god speaks—one stands, also, when one has no chair— and tried to see the figure's face more clearly, but the moon's rays filled her eyes, and the voice was all she knew.

"I...I came to watch the dancers perform. Tonight they were acting out the Curse of the Deer from the Mahabharata."

"Doomed love. I see." The man with the moon on his head turned and walked. Elizabeth, without moving her feet, came with him. They trod on a soft surface, like skin, but it was likewise the cold, hard, night-blue sky. The stars scattered, just as Hesha's snakes scattered when he passed among them.

The moon-god came to a halt and spoke again. "The dancers are too early in the cycle. Tonight begins a different chapter, Elizabeth Ariadne. Look down at my feet." She obeyed—she could do nothing else—and saw, in a blank space where the other stars would not go—from which the other stars had fled to do the moon his due reverence—a small, dim, red, insolent star that burned her eyes.

"The dance tonight, Elizabeth Ariadne, is taken from the War of the *Rakshasa*. The King Ravana has returned...the Demon Ravana is awake...the *Rakshas* Ravana wages war again." The shining hand of the stranger covered her gaze, and the red star let her go. "Can you remember this?"

Elizabeth shook her head in doubt. "I am dreaming."

"You are dreaming," said the god. "But there will be a way. In your hands, there will be a way—" He stopped suddenly. "They are coming for you, Elizabeth Ariadne. Remember, Elizabeth..."

"Elizabeth...Liz...wake up."

In her seat in the lobby of the Oberoi Grand, Elizabeth opened her eyes and saw Thompson's ruddy face and grizzled brows staring down anxiously.

"He's back," said Thompson. "Meeting in half an hour."

Elizabeth knocked quietly on the door of the suite. The Asp opened it, checked the hallway, pulled her through, shut and bolted the door fast behind her. He brushed past her, left the woman standing in the foyer, and signaled into the common room. Conversation sprang up immediately—hushed, urgent tones, starting in mid-sentence, starting at the exact word they had left off before the knock and the tiny crisis of opening the door.

"...Spent the day in a drainpipe?"

"Better than in the river. Remember it when your time comes."

Unacknowledged and alone, Liz stepped timidly into the conference and sat down.

"Where is Michel?" Hesha asked of Thompson.

"He's dead, sir. He was weak when you handed him over. We took him upstairs, washed the hand print off and tried to... revive him, but before we could do much with him, his body disintegrated." Thompson shook his head. "He wasn't dry, either. He bled, but one of the stains wasn't his blood. I think it was some sort of acid. There were glass fragments on the shirt before the stuff ate it away."

A long, uneasy silence took the room. Hesha, standing straight and solemn by the window, looked out on Calcutta. Huge drops of rain slammed into the glass. Beyond the falling streaks and the gale-tossed deluge, the city lights were dim. Colored neon, traffic signals, garish signs, and bright street lights, all wavered like fountain lamps. Calcutta seemed a city underwater, and the Setite could not see even so far as the horizon.

"Report."

Thompson and the Asp weighed in with the news of the last twenty-four hours. Names of strangers buzzed across Elizabeth's ears: Pauline Miles had lost a man; Das Gupta and Forrest checked in; the team covering the White Town sighted Smith, Jones, and Robinson but had lost track of Tom, Dick, and Harry... Johnson, Jackson, Jameson...Alex, Abigail, and Albert Street. Ramona, Ramana, Ravena, Ravana.... Elizabeth's attention strayed to her notebook, her hieroglyphs, her pen. The stream of information poured down around her like rain.

"What are you doing, Elizabeth?" Hesha's voice, curt and angry, broke into her reverie.

"I came to watch the dancers perform," she replied without thinking. "Tonight they are acting out the Rising of Ravana."

"Elizabeth!" This time, the Setite's tone cut through her, and she jumped. Her eyes met his like a cornered animal's, and she stared. Hesha picked up her papers. The top three sheets were loose, covered in gibberish, shot through with fragments of thoughts in English, and overlaid with line drawings of the three-eyed demon statue. Impulsively, he tore them in half in front of her, then stalked back to the window. "Report, Elizabeth."

Deliberately, Elizabeth Dimitros closed her notebook. She stood, angry-pale and tightly held together, leaning slightly on the glossy edge of the table.

"I will not." Her jaw clamped shut. "I will not call you 'sir,' either. I am not a secret agent. I am not a decoy. So far, the closest I have come to my own profession is browsing the antique shop downstairs. I don't know why you brought me here," she drew a heavy breath, "and by now I cherish no illusions that you will ever tell me the real reason. I was doing what I could on the papyrus from here; I was memorizing Vegel's transliteration notes. I was doing my best to ignore your illegal, impossible, inexplicable—since you never do explain when I ask—activities. You want to stop that, go ahead. I have work of my own I can do." She limped around the chairs to her room. "But I'll be damned if I'll sit here anymore."

The door shut behind her, and the lock turned audibly.

Thompson and the Asp kept quiet. They looked briefly at each other, then kept watch—a fleeting, corner-of-the-eye, nervous watch—on Hesha. With control and precision, he folded the torn papers between his hands. He halved, quartered, and tucked them into the breast pocket of his jacket. Finished, he addressed the open phone as if nothing had happened.

"Janet. Report."

Thursday, 22 July 1999, 4:02 AM
A subterranean grotto
New York City, New York

The dilapidated desk, large as it was, barely accommodated the stacks of books and papers piled all around the old, manual typewriter. The battered lamp nearby performed its duty even less adequately. Darkness threatened to swallow the desk, as well as the misshapen figure behind it.

The occupant, however, seemed to take no notice of its environs other than to prop its sizeable feet on the desk, very nearly shattering the fragile equilibrium of the various stacks. One piece of paper alone—the sheet held by gnarled, grime-encrusted fingers—held the creature's attention.

INSERT IMAGE 1

22 July 1999

Re: Hesha Ruhadze

Report from Calcutta via Cairo——Hesha
arrived and presented himself to Prince
Abernethie; one of Prince's childer
subsequently terminated; coincidence?
Also: H. contacted local Tremere who was
then assassinated; Assamite suspected.

Rolph reports from Atlanta——probable
Assamite involvement in destruction of
Hannah, Tremere regent. Hesha's man
Vegel was there at the time.

Hesha allied w/ Assamites?
danger to us?
TRACK MOVEMENTS
as possible

Friday, 23 July 1999, 3:43 AM
The Oberoi Grand Hotel
Calcutta, West Bengal

L ate and unannounced, Hesha strode into his suite. Thompson
and the Asp, waiting, stood to receive him. With a nod, he
dismissed the pair. Gratefully, they secured the area and went
off to sleep.

"Good night, sir," said Thompson, leaving.

No, thought Hesha, *it was not.* He stripped his raincoat of
equipment, stowed the tools, and hung the dripping trench to
dry. Emptying his suit pockets, he glanced at Elizabeth's place
at the table. Slowly, he set down two handfuls of tiny supplies.
Abandoning shoes and jacket, he selected a thin, crooked piece
of steel and stepped over to the woman's door. With an ear and
a hand, he listened through the wood, and found no sound but
slow, deep breathing and faint, steady heartbeat. The steel drew
back the dead bolt, and the Setite opened the door a crack.

Scents spilled out of the room: young woman, old books, ink
and new paper, faint fear and anger and tears. Hesha followed
the trail; here she had stood in fury, here she had begun to cry,
here was terror.... He pulled the darkness safely around him,
and crouched by the edge of her bed.

Hesha watched her thoughtfully.

It would be too much to say that he regretted losing his
temper with her. His analysis, conducted behind the walls of
his self-control, found his own conduct...unsatisfactory. It was
unnecessary to bring the woman to the sundown conferences;
it might, in fact, be dangerous. She had no need to know the

greater picture, even in such limited views as his retainers were given. Elizabeth's duties could be explained just as easily in private, face-to-face. She now lay farther from his influence than ever, across a rift, put there by his own lack of restraint. He had let the masks slip away over a trifle, over nothing. And he could not even put the blame on the curse. It was his own temper; the Beast had simply laid back and laughed at the show. Michel's death was no excuse, no surprise. As he had lain last night in the flooded drainpipe, Hesha had known the Assamite child would finish her mission, one way or another, and had come to terms with all the implications, all the difficulties entailed.

Temper. Plain anger had gotten to him, and after the meeting, as he searched Calcutta, he had both carried it with him and found it everywhere. His Nosferatu contact had not appeared. That he—she?—was unavailable was reasonable, yet Hesha's reaction was unreasoning annoyance. He drifted down to Albert Street and found Subhas holding sway in the coffee-house. The courtesy and deference of the white-haired gentleman slowly disintegrated; Hesha's own civilized face fell, and the two old allies found themselves on the verge of all-out battle. Only the split-second's hesitation, the fighting instinct that sized up the enemy before striking, kept them back. In the dead pause, the experienced, careful pair recognized the false feel of the argument. Hostility quickly turned to mystified calculation—something outside their close-guarded psyches pricked them toward war. Subhas laid his hands on the table, Hesha eased his chair away, and they parted without bloodshed.

As the Setite left the coffee-house, he'd noticed the two students coming in, and the sounds of the young Brujah losing their control—the fleeing patrons of the shop, the howls of the rabble-childer caught by Subhas in a fighting mood, the shattered windows and broken bones—followed Hesha's keen ears down the street.

Seeking more clues, Hesha had waded through the rising water to the bridgeworks. Chaos reigned. The typhoon rained. The gypsy camps were flooding with the rest of the city, but what should have been an accustomed, annual retreat to drier perches was a screaming, surging confusion. A lone Gangrel, furiously calm, turned Hesha back the way he came. The cat-like creature had given out that the tribes were going mad, Bhanjaras and Khana Buddos all together. She blamed the Ravnos, and spat curses on them over her shoulder. Hesha left her before the rage could outweigh her determination to defend her charges.

No longer doubting the *influence* that pervaded Calcutta, the Setite turned to give the curse its due. He hit Park Street and the old cabarets, hunting as clumsily as a night-old Cainite. In his gut grew a fire such as he could not remember; beyond ordinary hunger, beyond the Beast's gluttony—an awkward, unfrenzied, foundering desire. It drove him into a bar. He'd come out with a light-skinned, long-haired girl of Elizabeth's age and build. Hesha pushed her into an alley and drained her dry without remorse. The Beast didn't take him over, didn't even try. Why fight for control when they were of one mind already? Complacent and contented, it curled around Hesha's new anger like a cobra around her eggs. And that made the Setite angrier still. *Unnatural*, he thought. Something deep and sinister was wrong in Calcutta. Hesha, on his guard now, believed he could fight its effects, but he prayed to Set that whatever it was would end soon. He prayed, too, that the elder denizens of the city knew themselves well enough to resist.

Elizabeth kicked slightly, and rolled onto her shoulder. Hesha stared down at her. Sleep had banished her worries… given her peace. Without consulting him, his hand reached out and stroked the hair away from the placid face. Her eyes twitched behind the lids, and her face began to twist into less happy lines. *More nightmares. How does she know?* The creature pulled his hand away, reset the locks, and sought oblivion in his own rest.

"Hesha…" said the god in the mask. "Blood of my blood."

"Lord?" Hesha opened his eyes and sat upright. "What do you want of me?" His traveling casket and hotel room were gone; the blackness of dead dreams surrounded him.

"Look upon me."

Hesha turned toward the voice, and made out shapes in the

darkness. A vast, serpentine creature with a body like tar filled his vision. The night and the monster's flesh met only at the horizon. Directly beneath him, the figure of a giant with the red mane of a lion, the beak of a bird, and the horns of a ram lay fettered in its coils. As he watched, the god in the mask writhed in his trap, his muscles straining until the veins stood sharply up. The god freed one arm, and the ropy limbs of his opponent flailed about him until they found better purchase on his neck. Freeing his neck, the god sacrificed the arm again, and the fight returned to its starting point.

"My lord," said Hesha, kneeling. His own legs, he saw, were wrapped with the coal-black tendrils of the beast.

"Stand! You cannot afford to bow to me until I am free! Look, instead, upon my companions."

On every side of the god in the mask, there were other figures. Some, lying quietly but with their eyes open, were nearly free of the creature. Others, equally still, were so covered by the tarry scales that nothing showed of their own bodies; the monster had conquered all, and only the shape of the victim remained. A few—very few—wrestled as the giant did.

"And look, now, at what stands behind you." Hesha turned, and found only the empty darkness he had seen on waking. "Look *up*, blood of my blood, and understand."

And Hesha followed the god's commands, and realized that the night in front of him had a shape. It was a twisted pillar formed from the body of the thing below him, and it rose higher than a mountain into the dull sky of the dead. At its peak, wrapped almost entirely in the coils, was a figure the Setite knew well; he possessed a statue carved as its portrait. The demon, four-armed and hung with horrendous weapons, glinted black and blue and dripped red rivers of blood down the column that supported it. *Rivers,* thought Hesha. *The blood of a hundred thousand men…a million…*

"Grandfather sets now," said the god in the mask. Hesha turned back to see his master, and as the dream faded, heard the muffled voice of Set shout from beneath the twining body of Apep: "Remember!"

"Is there something wrong, Thompson?"

Ron's eyebrows shot skyward, and he swallowed hard. "You don't remember, sir?" He perched on the edge of the table, and shook his head. "Hell." He composed himself. "You woke up at sunset, and you shouted something—not in English—so loud the windows rattled. I came in to check on you." His gaze flickered worriedly over his master's face. "You don't remember that? Well...you seemed to be meditating, and you didn't seem to be under attack of any kind, so I left. That was about half an hour ago."

The Setite combed through his memory. There was a dream...something important...gone. He picked last night's suit jacket up off a chair, and sat down. Perhaps if he *did* meditate, the image would return. He doubted, though, whether the angry influence laid over Calcutta would permit calm, studied reflection, and the hotel, noisy with air conditioning and other people's conversation, was a poor seat for contemplation at any time. Some woman was carrying on now, close enough to be heard. Hesha folded the coat between his hands and tried to clear his thoughts. Paper crackled under the cloth. He pulled the folded sheets out of the pocket and turned them over.

Elizabeth had drawn the statue—*The statue was in my dream.* In English, she had written her own name, Hesha's names, 'Dances of India, 6:30 Daily,' rough alphabets, and then 'the red king' seven times and 'the red star' eleven. The printing, carefully formed, looked like scribe's practice. Each iteration of the "r" in "red" grew more refined, and the English words trailed off into repetitions of the single letter, which became mixed with a pointed, horizontal oval—the mouth sign that stood for "r" in hieroglyphs.

Hesha looked back to the gibberish Egyptian. Of course... the woman, memorizing the characters, had practiced writing a language she was comfortable with: English. The writing was not nonsense; it was accidental code. He frowned, and started transliteration. "'Ris'bth" was her own name. "Hsh'" was his, though the symbology chosen was atrocious. "Rwn'" should be "Reauna," but...there was the same pattern, one letter different, "rfn'" which suggested, in India, "Ravana." Her consonant shifts tended toward German...with difficulty, he extracted "red star," "*rakshasha*," "king," 'Mahabharata,' and 'awake.'

The Setite sat for a moment longer, listening to the echoes of the words in his head. Whatever had been sent to him during the day was lost for good, but he knew, without understanding why, that Elizabeth's notes paralleled the dream.

"Ask Miss Dimitros to step in, if she would."

Thompson grimaced, and began, painfully, "I...I don't think she can, sir." Hesha's eyes pinned him, and he went on, "She's delirious. She slept all day, and when you yelled, she woke up and started ranting about demons and ghosts and kings. I think she caught fever when she ran after you the other night."

The Setite rushed past him and into Elizabeth's room. She was sitting on the bed, trying to talk around the Asp, who was struggling, rather helplessly, to get her to lie down.

"...And the four travelers came to the City of Dreadful Night, to find the Prince of Ra—stop it. Stop it! Hey! But the King of the—let me go, you snake—but the King of the *Rakshash* slept under the heart of the mountain, and he heard the—" She broke off her story long enough to bite Raphael's arm, and the Asp retreated, cursing in Italian. "But the Herald of Ravana sent the Monkey-devil to destroy the accursed wizard...."

"Leave us," commanded Hesha, turning a cold, hard gaze on his minions. "I'll see to her."

Hesha picked his way over to the bed; the woman or the Asp had flung the blankets and sheets to the floor. Elizabeth, left to herself, sat tailor-fashion on the mattress, smoothed down her crooked nightshirt, and began reciting again.

"Once, in the City That Never Slept, there lived a young girl of humble family...."

"Elizabeth." Hesha sat opposite her, and searched her eyes. There seemed to be nothing behind them. "Who sleeps under the heart of the mountain?"

"Ravana, King of *Rakshasa*, slept under the heart of the mountain for ten thousand years, but now he slept no longer. The mountain tore open from root to tip, and the King strode forth to meet the Three from the East."

"Who is the Prince?"

"The Prince of the *Rakshasa*, Hazimel, who turned against his father and sleeps beneath the City of Dreadful Night."

"What is the Red Star?"

Her face contorted nearly into tears. "The red star disobeys the Moon, Hesha. I walked on the floor of your ceiling, and the red star bored into the sky." The empty eyes filled with pain. "Hesha?"

"I'm here with you, Elizabeth, but I can't see very well." He took her hands. "You'll have to tell me where we are."

"We're in the fields outside the Prince's tomb. There's a storm coming, and it's getting darker. The clouds are blotting out the sky."

"Good. The red star will not see us. There should be a building very close by; a temple," suggested the Setite. "It has lotus columns and statues leading to it. You can see the temple, Elizabeth."

"Yes…" she hesitated. "But it wasn't there…."

"It was *always* there, but you had not noticed it. We are going to shelter from the storm inside that temple, Elizabeth. I am walking toward it. Follow me out of the fields."

Her expression changed. "This is a nightmare," she said slowly.

"Come out of it, then. Can you see me? Follow me out of the dream."

Elizabeth came to herself, suddenly, as though she were a rope let loose in a tug-of-war. Hesha kept watching her, wary that the trance would pull her back again. Her eyes cleared completely, and he forgot to look away, wondering what it was that made them light and dark at the same time. Surely, in three hundred years, he had seen eyes like hers before….

"Where have I been?"

He shook his head. "I'm not sure. Thompson thinks you were fevered; I think you were caught in visions. I had something of the same experience myself today." Elizabeth looked down at their hands, still joined together. "Let me apologize for my temper last night. No one is quite themselves in Calcutta anymore." Her gaze rose to his again, and he said, slowly, "I understand you followed me last night, after Michel was attacked. That was very brave of you." He squeezed her hands. "Don't ever do it again," then added, "I want to know that you are safe."

Hesha rose and opened the connecting door. "Thompson, Elizabeth and I are going out to dinner. You and Mercurio are welcome to do whatever you want," he said, without turning to face his bodyguard. "Close your mouth. Calcutta is sufficiently dangerous tonight that you would not be able to protect us even if you had an army—and I think that Calcutta is *in* enough danger that it will leave us alone."

Ron Thompson paced along the Maidan with the slow, rolling gait of a cop on the beat—on his beat, in the rain, on a bad day, after an argument with the sergeant, during a gang war. With one eye, he kept tabs on the Asp in point position. With the other eye, he watched Hesha and Elizabeth strolling ahead of him. They seemed, despite all sense, to be enjoying themselves. Over the open circuit of his phone, he caught a steady stream of muttering curses. Mercurio, not content to express his disgust with mere body language, vented his spleen into the ether.

Hesha Ruhadze walked between his men. He chose to ignore them; he carried a huge golf umbrella with a ridiculous pink-and-white canopy. His attention centered entirely on the girl by his side. She wore a thin black dress and a thin black raincoat. Elizabeth's sandals flowed with the Hooghly's water, but the tears that had threatened since they came to Calcutta were dry at last. They wandered into the Maidan grounds, and the Friday-night carnival air swept around them despite the rain. The snake charmers, beggars, flower sellers, and street performers gave him a thousand scenes to show her, and enough things to talk about that avoided...unpleasantness.

A bead-seller, draped with hundreds of strings of his own wares, approached them, hawking his cheap glass fervently at the lady. The Asp closed in, and Hesha felt Thompson's lingering resentment step nearer. Elizabeth listened to the man's pitch and smiled, but shook her head. "Na, *dhonyabad.*"

Hesha chuckled, and moved her along. "Your Bengali pronunciation is very interesting."

"Why doesn't that sound like a compliment?"

"I am sure the man was flattered that you made the attempt. Most Americans don't." They turned, passed out of the little pavilion village, and struck out toward the city lights again. "Didn't you want any souvenirs?"

Cheap beads? I can buy the same kind in New York...if I ever get back to New York." She frowned up at him.

"You'll go back to New York." Hesha assured her. He switched his grip on the umbrella and clasped her hand. "I promise." Elizabeth, neither satisfied nor seeking to argue about it, let him keep hold of her hand as they walked. "Let's go up to the bazaars and take a look. The shops may be closing, but I'll find you a souvenir worth having. Something nice for your apartment? A rug? A handmade leather desk set for Sleipnir? Do you," he asked seriously, "care at all for brass?"

"Brass?"

"India is very good for brass...." He led her north through a maze of little streets, and they came out on a wider avenue lined with shops. As they went, the Asp scouted ahead of them. Thompson checked their trail to be sure they were not followed. Hesha kept his own eyes open. And Elizabeth, without thinking about them much, noticed two things: First, that the signs over the stores and on the billboards used a little less Sanskrit and English type and more Arabic letters; second, that Hesha, whom she had never seen wearing jewelry anywhere but around his neck, had on a string bracelet. As they walked hand in hand, their wrists rubbed against each other, and the beads knotted into the bracelet chafed her skin.

They made their way up the little bazaar, taking a last look around establishments closing for the night, window-shopping at the Muslim stores that had shut at sundown for the holy day. Then Elizabeth, at first content to follow where her companion led, started choosing their path. To begin with, her side-trips made sense—an antique store, a sari weaver's, a stall parting with the last of its sweet pa'an desserts—but gradually, any little thing could catch her eye and send them down an alley and up the next street without explanation.

Hesha gave her sightseeing full rein, even when the excursions lost reason and Elizabeth seemed to wonder, herself, why this building or that intersection was so interesting. She came to a halt near an old, ill-kept mosque, made a comment on the architecture, and suddenly decided to duck into a tiny passage nearby. The Setite joined her in splashing down the sidewalk—acting, to Elizabeth, as if a wild dash through the dark gap between two old houses was normal. The tiny lane bent halfway through, where the tenements facing one street met, crookedly, the backs of those facing the other way.

And in an instant, Elizabeth felt Hesha's hand leave hers. By the time her eyes could find him again, his arms held writhing darkness. Thompson and the Asp's strangely subdued flashlights drove the shadows back, and Liz saw in horror that Hesha's changing hands clutched a child.

Hesha pinned the tiny girl to a cracked stucco wall, and the skinny, charcoal-colored waif let out a thin cry. Doubling up her little body, the child got her knees beneath her and leaped out. The plaster shattered, but the force of her stick-thin legs was enough to propel herself and the Setite across the alley. They slammed against brick stairs on the other side. The child, her head down and fastened like a tick to Hesha's forearm, pushed away again. The wrestlers swung round against a softer surface—Elizabeth—and hurled the mortal woman into the wreckage of the first wall.

The lights moved in, wavering, and then stopped abruptly. Liz felt the Asp beside her and found a hand reaching down to lift her to her feet. Standing again, she looked toward the battle. The smaller figure, despite the warm lights, was only gray-brown, barely visible. The taller figure stood over his enemy on weirdly jointed legs and struck at her with scaled talons. He tore wounds across the child's naked skin with a whip-like, forked tongue two feet long.

Elizabeth drew breath to scream, but the Asp was faster—his arm curled about her neck and his callused palm covered her mouth before the sound escaped her. She choked, tried to bite him, but stopped. Pressure on her nostrils warned that he could suffocate her as easily as silence. In his other fist, she saw the silhouette of a gun, changing aim with almost mechanical precision as the fighters moved back and forth. When it stopped, when the furious spray from the whirling monsters died down, Mercurio shoved her forward, and Liz saw that the fight was over.

"Gloves," ordered Hesha.

He dropped the body of his enemy into the water beneath him. It twitched, and the Setite walked onto it with his thick-soled sandals. One heel ground the child's chin into the pavement. Elizabeth flinched. The victor rinsed his claws off in the stream, and Thompson stepped forward, snapping latex gloves onto his master's re-forming hands. Hesha immediately threw down his blood-stained raincoat, peeled out of his shirt and trousers and let them fall into the rushing flood. He checked himself over and carefully washed away the red-black ichor from his wounds.

"Clean, sir." Thompson confirmed.

Elizabeth shuddered. Hesha's scaly hide had begun to seal itself; the gashes and bites inflicted by the creature under his foot closed up. None of them had bled. The scales melted away, and with the change in his skin, the odd joints and height disappeared. Ron signaled to the Asp. Raphael took aim on a spot under the water. Thompson slipped out of his own coat, draped it over his boss, and returned to the staircase and a steady, two-fisted grip on his pistol.

Protected by the gloves, Hesha reached down, seized the girl by the forehead and jaw, and pinned her against the brick steps. Her infant muscles worked terribly against the pressure, and half-formed sounds fought their way through clenched teeth. Without warning, the Setite released his grip on her chin and the child's mouth flew open. Faster than the watching mortals could see, his fingers darted in and came out holding a gray, flapping piece of dead tissue: her tongue. He threw it into the gutter, clamped down on her skull again, and looked into her eyes. She shut them quickly.

"Thompson. Give me a gun and silencer. And pry her eyes open." Ron said something beneath his breath, but Hesha caught it. "Cut the lids off, then."

The old cop moved in. He fit the weapon together and laid it on the step below Hesha's hand; he took a small knife from his sleeve and bent over the child's head. The Setite leaned closer to the gray face and spoke short words, commanding words, at the girl. Her lips still formed the beginnings of syllables. He shouted Arabic at her, whispered it, searched the ruined eyes for signs of obedience or uncertainty. "Quiet," he tried in English.

"Hold her head," he said shortly. Again, he let her jaw free. With a crack, the little girl's jaw disintegrated as the bullet passed through, and when the blur of movement stopped, a quarter of her face lay splattered on the plaster wall across the alley. Hesha tried his commands again. Finally, as her captor concentrated on overpowering her will, the small, determined creature on the steps managed to make a sound.

Hesha jabbed at her with a careless, impatient claw. He regretted it instantly—there had not been enough left of the girl to take the ragged cut. She shrieked, shriveled up, and dried to powder on the spot.

In the empty moment afterward, there was hardly any noise in the alley.

The rain rattled and plonked over the wreckage. It had before; it would again. In Calcutta, in July, the sky falls on the city. Rain fell on the dust that had been an Assamite and turned it to mud.

Elizabeth, still the Asp's prisoner, sobbed in terrible, heart-broken gasps. Her breath hurt her; the water on her face was not the rain. Her full and stinging eyes flickered slowly around the circle of light. She feared what lay outside it, and she feared the three men standing in it with her. Hesha moved toward the Asp, and behind him Thompson gathered up the tools of the gruesome surgery. Liz's gaze retreated; she would not look at either of them.

"Let her go," said Hesha. "Let her go."

Released, she staggered, and the monster caught her by the arms. Gently, he turned her down the alley, away from the fast-eroding corpse on the steps, and started the long walk back to the hotel.

Saturday, 24 July 1999, 2:24 AM
The Oberoi Grand Hotel
Calcutta, West Bengal

Elizabeth, bending over the sink, looked up from the drain to the faucet. A dark-brown hand held a wet washcloth out to her—her eyes flickered up to the mirror and saw Hesha standing behind her. She was sick again, and he held her shoulders while her body fought to void an already empty stomach. The acid trickled into the running water. The damp cloth moved coolly across her forehead. Her convulsions stopped, and he waited while the woman rinsed the bile from her mouth.

"Don't touch me!" She wrenched violently away from the creature's unresisting hands.

Hesha stayed where he was and let her put the whole length of the room between them.

"She was just a baby. A *baby!*" Elizabeth shrieked the last word.

"No," said Hesha.

"You killed a little girl," she spat at him, "a child. You tortured a baby girl to death."

"No," repeated the monster, calmly. "This is part of the nightmare you had earlier."

"Goddamn you! Goddamn you, this was real. I saw you do it." She burst into tears. "Why did you *kill* her?!" Hesha stepped forward, carefully. He stopped at a finely chosen point—exactly the distance she would allow. "This is part of the nightmare. Your Red King under the mountain. The Monkey-woman, sent to kill the wizard. Nothing in the nightmare is what it looks like."

"I *saw* you kill her," Elizabeth whispered dangerously. "And I saw *you*." She swallowed against the churning of her guts, and trembled. "What are you?"

The Setite shook his head. "Another part of the nightmare."

"No!" Her hands, clenched into white fists, beat against her legs in frustration. "Truth! What are you? What are you? *What are you?*"

He closed the space between them and gathered her into his embrace. They stood there for perhaps five minutes—the mortal woman shaking, shrinking from him, arms wrapped tightly around her body to protect herself from him, but crying on his shoulder just the same. Hesha said nothing, yet he held her together against the wracking sobs. They slowed, the anguished cries subsided into weeping, and when he knew she was mistress of herself again, he released her.

Elizabeth tried to retreat without having any place to go. She collapsed onto the carpet in the corner, and said dully, "Leave me alone."

Hesha knelt on the floor, just out of arm's reach. He was aware, suddenly, of the warmth left on his skin by her body and of the hot, damp tears soaked into his shirt. Under the sound of the woman's ragged breath, he began to notice her heartbeat. He shook off the rhythm of her blood and broke the silence.

"I killed that creature," said the Setite evenly, "because she had tasted my blood, and she had endangered my mission and my people, and because she killed Michel." He spaced the words out, let them fall on her slowly. "Who was Michel to you?"

"The wizard. And she was the Monkey-woman sent to destroy him. She—it—was not a child; not a baby girl for you to cry over. She might have been a child, a century ago. But my enemies took that child, trained her, killed her, and turned her into an assassin under their control." He paused. "A tool for killing."

From where his heart used to be, there came a whisper: *What kind of tool will you turn Elizabeth into?*

"I told you I keep buried dangers from coming into the wrong hands. I came to Calcutta because one of the worst of them is loose in the world. The Red Star that terrifies you in your dreams." He looked at her. She was listening, at least. The mention of the star struck her, and she might be prepared, finally, to believe in what he had come for. "Michel would have found its source for me. Together we could have learned enough, I think, to stop the Eye—the star—if it were being used for harm." His voice hardened. "The assassin put an end to that hope. More people will suffer because of that girl and whoever paid her to kill my friend. They destroyed him to keep him from talking to me." He wondered as he said it if that might even be fact.

Hesha leaned back against the heavy curtains, and stretched his legs. Heavily, sadly, he told her, "But you...you shouldn't have had to see that. It was terrible, and I *am* sorry that you have come so close to the center of this." He studied the bedspread, her night stand, the room beyond. After a precise interval, he looked back to the woman in the corner, and held a hand out to her. "Forgive me, Elizabeth," he pleaded. He shook his head, and said again, "You shouldn't have had to see that." *Lord*, he prayed, *you sent me a seer when you knew I had lost Vegel, and I am grateful. But why this woman? And why did she have to see so much so soon?*

Hesha felt warm fingers clasp his, and he sighed with what breath he had. He looked to her; he followed her glance to their joined hands; he smiled ruefully.

Elizabeth took his hand in both of hers. The cuff of his shirt lay over the wrist, but she thought, underneath...there it was. A bracelet of knotted hemp and polished white beads. The largest hung low, and she pulled the string around to see it better. Without surprise, she recognized the white eye of the statue.

Neither spoke. The room had been peacefully calm a moment earlier. It was dead calm now, charged for a storm.

"You always," said Elizabeth, "wear that on a thong around your neck. Why is it on your wrist tonight?" Before he could answer, she pursued the logic. "You put that on your wrist. You took me walking, and you put it up against my wrist." More slowly, "And after that, I started...going sideways. Going places for no reason." She closed her eyes and pulled her arms back around her knees. "That was why you were nice to me tonight.

So you could hold my hand and put that in it. I was just...the string on the pendulum....

"You used me."

Hesha grew a claw and cut the bracelet off. He closed his scaled hands around it.

"Yes," he said.

"To find the girl."

"No. I didn't know what you would take me to." The Setite paused, rubbing the stones in the bracelet against each other. They clicked like the blue prayer beads of his long-lost home. "Given time I could find anything in the world myself. I don't have time, Elizabeth. I am looking for short cuts. I need fast answers. I put you...in circuit...with the eye stone to trace the source. I did not expect to find the assassin; that is the truth."

Very quietly, Elizabeth murmured: "But I am still just the string of the pendulum to you."

"No. The string in the pendulum is any cord, any thread. You are irreplaceable, Elizabeth." And as he designed the lie, he realized that it was true.

"Irreplaceable," she repeated, laughing low in her throat. Hesha started—her tone had changed completely. From high hysterics, she had descended to a cynical, unpredictable level he wasn't sure he could reach.

"Why is that funny?" he asked sharply.

"Please," said Elizabeth, shaking her head. "Go away now. I'm tired."

The phone rang in the next room. Hesha looked toward the door, reluctantly. She laughed again, and climbed onto the bed.

"Go, Hesha. The *rakshasa* are calling you, and someone wants me to sleep."

"Hesha Ruhadze?" It was a man's voice, heavily accented but speaking English well enough.

"Here."

"I need to talk to you in person. Right away. I don't think my name would mean anything to you. But I talked to Michel a few nights ago, and I think you need to talk me at least as much," said the stranger cockily, "as I need to talk to you." He let that rest for a moment. "I'm in the Pink Elephant, downstairs. Come in the next ten minutes, or don't come at all."

Hesha sidled diffidently into the darkened, music-drowned club. The persistent drumbeat crept up from the wooden floor into the soles of his feet. The smoke and colored, moving lights played tricks on his eyes. He scouted out the bar, called for a whisky and soda, and scanned the room for familiar faces. Relieved to find none, he pretended to sip his drink. With the attitude and expression of a determined late-night drinker, he stalked around the dance floor to a small, empty patch of booths and tables. The Setite sat in the crook of a curved bench, leaned against the wall, and proceeded to make the booze disappear.

After a casual delay, a figure detached itself from a group of girls gyrating in the flashing lights. With swaggering steps, the man approached Hesha's table and swiveled his hips under the table.

"Ruhadze. Nice of you to drop by."

The newcomer was dark-haired and handsome, but slovenly. He wore a wicked-looking, greasy imperial and his jet-black, arched eyebrows seemed as pointed as the mustache and beard. Locks of curling, untamed hair fell over the unnaturally pale brow, and he brushed them back as he smiled. Hesha examined him without comment. Tested by silence, the stranger lost. He hurried on anxiously:

"All right. I'm here to make a deal with you." He scratched at his chin. "You're looking for something. I know where it is. I can take you to it."

"Your name," prompted Hesha.

"Aren't you interested? I thought you were hot to find the…"

"Your name," the Setite ordered.

"Ravana. Khalil Ravana."

"Go on, Khalil. And call me Hesha, if you would." His momentum broken, the stranger with the *rakshash* name hesitated. Hesha filled in the gap. "Why do you believe that I am looking for something?"

"Michel," Khalil replied. "He came to me asking a pack of questions about…about a place I know. He'd had plenty of time to ask before, but he wasn't interested until you showed up. Then he gets killed here, on your doorstep. Word has it he didn't even get to sit down before they got him. So, I figure. You're looking for what he was looking for. And he didn't get the info to you before they got him. Now, I don't know who 'they' are, but I can guess. And I have a feeling that I'm not a *healthy* dead man anymore. I'm here to spill my guts so they can go after you, instead."

"How kind." Hesha steepled his fingers. "And what is it that you want from me?"

"Well, I'm not sure yet. Maybe you can owe me one." Hesha shook his head. "Name your price."

Khalil shrugged. "Look. I'll show you the merchandise. I'll take you there. If it's what you want, we can work out the deal then. Call this," he seemed to be listening to someone on his left, "a service done in return for…future considerations." He wrinkled his mustache. "For one thing, you can get me the hell out of Calcutta."

"I am capable of doing that," confirmed the Setite.

"Right. So." Khalil nodded. "I'll meet you in here tomorrow, right after sunset, and take you to the spot." Hesha lifted an eyebrow. "No. Tomorrow, at nine o'clock, we will meet you outside the hotel."

"Who is 'we'?"

"Who *are* we." The Setite folded his hands and stared the unlucky Ravnos into momentary silence. "That," he said, "is my concern. Meet us outside, next to the bookseller, at nine o'clock."

"I never said anything about—"

"And I did not ask you about other people, either. Still, you will escort me and my followers from the bookseller, not this meat market, at nine o'clock. If you and your friend—" Hesha gestured to Khalil's left side— "wait for me here, you will find yourselves left behind when I leave Calcutta."

"Just one fucking minute, you dirty snake." The Ravnos's temper, magnified by the anger overlying the city, brought him to his feet, shouting. "I don't have to put up with this shit from you. There's no one else can take you to the—I could walk out of here right now, and where the hell would you be?"

"For some reason, Mr. Ravana, I don't think you *can* walk away from this. Inform your employer that I prefer to deal with principals; I will make an exception in this case for his or her sake. There can't be many truly...*expendable* peons at his disposal at a time like this." The Setite stood, bowed mockingly to the man he could see, sincerely to the invisible listener, and departed.

Behind him, mixed with the sounds of the music, he heard Khalil kick the table. It flew across the room, breaking glass and heads along the way, and a stream of curses followed it. When the Setite looked back, the younger monster was surrounded by half-formed shapes and blobs of color that had nothing to do with the club's lights.

Hesha fitted his monocle into place, turned to climb the great Dutch-tile staircase, and permitted himself half a smile.

Ron Thompson sat, cold and wet, on the backboard of a shuddering donkey cart. His mood was as black as the night around him, which was saying a great deal. The typhoon—a thousand-year storm, by CNN's reckoning—had rolled in at dawn. If the sun had risen, though, Thompson hadn't seen it. The clouds were too thick. Despite having hovered over land for eighteen hours, Typhoon Justin showed no signs of slackening. The Himalayas had trapped the rain and wind on their way north. The gales that drove them could not force the system over the mountains, but neither were they giving up the struggle. The water ran three feet deep over the city. The lights in the more civilized portions of the city flickered and threatened to give out. And in the slums the madman with the reins drove them through, the power was gone completely. Visibility: zero. In disgust, Thompson gave up his sentry-post and hunkered down beside the Asp. The water and floating vegetable mess swirled about his ankles, but the bright green boards of the cart's sides afforded some protection from the wind, at least. The little green wagon pulled up next to a massive, complicated ruin of an apartment building. Water poured over the cracked walls in sheets, gushed out and around the few rain spouts and tin gutters. Thompson and the Asp waited, looking up at the broken windows, torn awnings, and feeble shutters. When it became clear that the cart had really and truly stopped, they clambered down off the back of it. The Asp took up guard, so far as the rain would allow, and Thompson lent Liz a hand as she jumped into the knee-high brown flood. Hesha stepped out alone, on the opposite side.

Khalil Ravana leapt from the buckboard to the back of the unfortunate donkey. With quick, practiced fingers, he unhitched the animal from the traces. He kicked her flanks—she refused to move—and he whispered horrors into her ears. Wild and white-eyed, the jenny fled the tiger's roar, up a short flight of stairs and into the half-shelter of an open hallway. He vaulted off, tied the beast to a railing, and turned to hop back down the stairs.

"Aiii!" A high-pitched complaint and a stocky, gesticulating female blocked his path. In Hindustani, she demanded an explanation of the donkey. Khalil snapped his fingers, and a heavily muscled man with an ax crested the stairs behind him. The phantom licked his lips and raised the bloody weapon over his head. "Aiiiiiiii!" Twice as loud and three times as shrill, the screaming woman disappeared behind the corner and into a dark doorway.

Khalil turned a smug face to the four waiting in the street. He sauntered down the steps, opened a thick, surprisingly solid-looking door, and picked Hesha out of the little group by eye. "We're here. Come on." All four started toward the open portal. The Ravnos laughed. "No. Just you, Ruhadze."

The Setite stared wordlessly at his guide.

"What? What? You want to go back to the hotel empty-handed? You come alone or you don't come at all. I tried to tell you this last night, you cocky ass."

Hesha stepped closer to the doorway, examining the wood, the crumbling building, and the Ravnos's sneer. "*She* comes with me," said the Setite. His eyes scrutinized every muscle of the younger creature's face. Khalil's lids flickered, and a tic began over his right temple. For a moment, Hesha thought the man might lose control entirely—but as he teetered on the verge, the look the Setite expected came over him. Again, Khalil seemed to listen to someone close by, and his expression cleared.

"All right," he agreed, evidently to his own surprise. "But only her. The others stay here."

Hesha called out: "Give Miss Dimitros a flashlight and a camera."

Thompson and the Asp said nothing...so loudly that Elizabeth caught every word. The boss was nuts. The whole thing was a trap. The girl wasn't ready. The girl, at least, was dressed in jeans and sturdy shoes tonight. The girl wouldn't go. The girl would go. As their constrained, well-trained faces spoke all this, the two men strapped Liz into a web belt hung with tools, slung a rugged old camera—waterproof—around her neck, and clipped a fanny pack full of film under her raincoat. The last thing she read from them before the Asp pushed her forward was a kind of commiseration: not to each other, but identical glances, right at her, that said they had been where she was, and they hadn't liked it, and they wished she were anywhere but there. Oddly comforted, Elizabeth followed Hesha down the passage. She kept her hand on her phone, and repeated Thompson's list of alarm codes to herself keep her calm.

The dimly lit hallway ended in a staircase up. *I am being followed*, thought Liz. Seven-two-two. The staircase brought them to a half-balcony, broken at the outer edge. Someone *is in the room with me: eight-three-four*. Khalil led them into an abandoned apartment and over a roof. *The police have arrived: three-zero-six*. The roof came to a broken, twisted fire-escape. *I am wounded:* one-one-one. The guide wrenched a ladder free of the iron wreckage and propped it against a wall. *Hesha is wounded:* nine-nine- nine. They climbed up, walked along a bastion of old brick between two buildings, and paused at a dead end. *Fire: five-two-eight.*

Khalil disappeared into the bricks. His head and hands still stuck out above the baked clay. Hesha took hold of the callused fingers, and stepped into the illusion. He reached back for Elizabeth, and she took hold. Inside the bricks, she could see nothing, and so reached for her flashlight. They were on a spiral staircase with a very low ceiling; it led down into the masonry. The bricks gave way to stone, the stone to brick again, and the steps curled away beyond the stifled lamp's glow. Their feet made little noise on the dusty cleats. Soaked clothing failed to rustle; after a time it stopped dripping, and Elizabeth could hear, very clearly, that hers was the only breath taken in the musty chimney.

I confirm your call, she thought in defense. *Four-nine- four*.

At long last, the descent stopped, and the three crawled along a tunnel. It kept to the horizontal, for the most part, and wound through ruins that had nothing to do with cement, bricks, or the tenements above them. Between stretches of rubble and blank stone, Elizabeth noticed figure carvings and words written in something like Sanskrit. She would have stopped to study them, but the other two set a pace on all fours she found hard to keep up with.

I have lost eye contact: Eight-one-eight.

Suddenly, the elbow-bruising, knee-scraping passage opened out. Liz unbent, stretched, and played her flash over the path ahead. This place, tall enough to stand in, was a quarter-sphere: one flat wall, vertical; a tile floor, almost at right angles to the wall; and breathing-space carved out of the rubble. Behind them, the hole they had entered by. Ahead, the outline of a door. Its history leapt to the eye: sealed with stone, broken into, filled in again with brick and clay, broken a second time, a third— possibly more often. It was open now between shoulder height and the lintel, and Hesha had just climbed up the rubble and through.

Elizabeth set her foot on a stable-looking chunk of debris, held onto the jamb for safety, and gained the top of the broken seal wall. She crouched there for a moment, rearranging her gear. The flashlight, swinging from its clip, played across the curved, vaulted ceiling. The beam bobbed across Khalil's cheerful face and laid-back posture; he reclined easily along the top of a carved balustrade at the other end of the room. Liz aimed the light lower, looking for a spot to jump down to, and screamed—

Corpses covered the floor—some fresh, some skeletal, some in putrescent states of decay—and were covered in turn by rats, unhealthy, hairless, lesion-covered creatures that scurried into empty jaws, hollow ribcages, and festering flesh-tunnels at the sound of her cry. After a second's pause, they showed themselves again. Eyes red in retina-flash turned toward her meaningfully. A handful advanced on her; the rest went back to their feast.

Hesha's voice carried across the claw-clicking scrabbles of the vermin: "Leave her alone," he commanded.

Instantly, the horrors disappeared. Elizabeth shuddered. The bare stone floor lay clear now. She fell gratefully to it. Suspiciously, nervously, she took in her real surroundings. The ceiling remained the same; the walls, revealed, were carved rock, not rat-ridden earth. Khalil still lounged on his railing, but his expression lacked cheer. Disappointment lingered on his face. And Hesha, unseen before, occupied the far right corner of the chamber. His forefinger ran along the painted reliefs, not quite touching them, and his brow furrowed in concentration. Liz crouched by the door, watching him.

Khalil, for a good five minutes, had the patience to do the same. Then the Ravnos cleared his throat. "Good?" he asked brightly.

Hesha stopped and faced the Ravnos. "Good. But this is still not the source."

Khalil clicked his tongue. "Nope." But he showed no signs of moving.

"What do you want?"

"Well," Khalil sat up. "You're hunting for the Eye. It sticks out all over you." He shrugged his shoulders. "I could be a valuable guy to have along for *that* ride. It's our Eye, after all, not yours. So I might know things you'll need later." He scratched his chin. "So. If I show you the last room, you take me out of Calcutta with you. And you protect me. And you make *nice* to me," he snapped out, losing his genial mask to spite for a moment. "And I'll help you find that Evil old Eye."

Hesha considered for a moment, and then spoke—slowly, in carefully chosen words. "I will take you with me," he intoned, "and protect you," he paused, "as long as you continue to aid me in my quest for the Eye of Hazimel."

"Deal," shouted Khalil. He burst out laughing, and looked up at his new partner in a fit of camaraderie. "Imagine the look on old Abernethie's face—a gypsy and a snake taking each other's word for bond. Well, come on. It's down here." He tapped the floor with his toe, and a pit opened beneath his feet: rock-cut steps, leading down...filled, at the moment, with floodwater. Khalil dropped into it lightly, waist-deep, and grinned at Elizabeth. "Bring your aqualung with you, sweetheart?"

Hesha caught her eye. "Photograph this room. I want details of the murals." She nodded, and he followed Khalil down the hole.

Left by herself, Elizabeth propped her flashlight against one wall and began recording the other on film. When all four were done, she cross-lit and started again. With waterproof pencil and notebook, she made notes on the estimated measurements of the room. She waited nervously with the camera and lamp in her lap. The pool of water lay undisturbed. Eventually, she rose, changed the angle of the light again, and took a third set of portraits, this time with her notebook in each shot for scale. The time crawled by.

Am waiting at rendezvous: Two-seven-one.

Sunday, 25 July, 1999 12:34 AM
The burial chamber of an unmarked tomb
Calcutta, West Bengal

Khalil, bored beyond belief, lay full length on the stone lid of a muddy sarcophagus. His companion's light roved around the chamber like a darting yellow firefly; he himself would rather be back at the disco—better still, loose in New York. *There* was a city of sin for you. The Ravnos folded his hands over his belt and dreamt of America.

Hesha floated from wall to wall, scrutinizing the symbols, the designs, the scenes, and, finally, rows of script carved into the rock. Satisfied at last, he sighed. The burial chamber, even though he suspected it might be a false one, came from the same culture as the *rakshasa* statue—some of the work seemed to be by the identical artist, in fact. The few breaths of air he had held in his lungs for talking bubbled away, and his dead body settled more surely on the slippery floor. He kicked his sandals off to gain better purchase, drew his own camera out, and proceeded to go around the tomb in detail.

On the third wall, near the corner, he found the crucial passage. Instructions. Hesha paused, reading them, and stood stock-still for a moment…. He had sought the Eye for more than a century; the shock of success (though the Setite had always been confident of succeeding *eventually*) gave him pause.

Instructions for the containment, sealing up, and safe transportation of the Eye of Hazimel.

Hesha very nearly laughed. The task was tremendously simple…once you knew the secret. It had taken him more skill to translate the old script than he would need to catch the Eye. It was peasant magic, hedge sorcery, literally child's play—mud pies. Holy river water mixed with earth (*silt from the Ganges*, he thought, *from the Nile*) touched to the orb would close the lid. A thick coating plastered around the Eye would put it to "sleep." The dry and hardened clay would protect the artifact from harm...and the magician from the artifact. The scribe went on to detail a story about the rescue of the Eye from thieves, a tale of a mighty *rakshasa* who commanded it wisely, an invocation to Hazimel. The inscription continued below another relief, but the additional text was lost. Directly over a legend about the origin of the Eye, some illiterate hand had taken a chisel to the mural. The shallow scratches described a variation of a Bengali folk tale—the destruction of a demon-queen's heart with a palm-leaf sword. Hesha photographed that section carefully, cursing the graffiti writer. Perhaps he could decipher the broken carvings later. He moved on to the next panel, then the ceiling, and the sides of the sarcophagus itself. He took his time.

Elizabeth loaded another roll of film into the camera. She'd used half the supply already; better, she thought, to save rest of the exposures in case there were more rooms Khalil hadn't bothered to mention yet. If there were an angle of this chamber she hadn't caught, it wasn't for lack of trying. Or time.

She clipped the camera back onto her chest and picked up the light. Curiosity brought her to the first (or last) panel of the series. It was hard to know where the narrative—she was certain the carvings depicted a definite myth, not disjointed scenes—began, but you could start with this corner. Reading left to right, she traced a story in her own mind, at least.

In the first relief, a city fell to invaders. On the left side, it showed tall, beautiful buildings, on the right, the warriors outside the gates. In the second panel, the towers fell, the warriors controlled the streets, and the refugees poured out. Larger than the rest, and so, probably, more important, ran a strange man. Elizabeth studied him carefully. He bore a few of the symbols assigned to demons—*rakshasa* or *asura* or the evil dead—but his eyes were clearly the most important feature

in the artist's mind. They didn't match. One was at least three
sizes larger than the other, and the remains of the paint showed
irises of different colors. In the third scene, the *asura* stood in
jungle, surrounded by mountains, and in several poses across
the landscape seemed to be commanding the construction of a
temple or palace in the distance. In the fourth panel, the demon,
large and central, took the left side to fight a band of invaders
from the captured city, shown in miniature high in a corner of
the design. On the right, he dispensed justice to prisoners tied
to columns of his nearly finished building.

In the fifth section, by far the busiest and most difficult to
interpret, an army from the distant city came to conquer him.
Even understanding that the scene progressed side-to-side,
Elizabeth found herself defeated. There was an army; there
was the palace of the *asura;* the *asura* fought; but on whose side
did the animals battle? If the demon commanded the beasts of
the field, why were some of them in aggressive postures *inside*
the palace's courtyard? If the creatures fought for the army,
why were so many facing away from the *asura* and attacking,
apparently, their own?

Unfortunately (Elizabeth listened to the sound of that
word, and admitted she was biased against the demon with
the mismatched eyes), the last panel showed a clear triumph
for the *asura*. In his finished temple, he held court. Behind him,
a large (or immensely important—size could mean anything at
this level of pictography) demon-god with a hundred heads and
arms stood in state. He, or she, or it, Liz concluded, must have
sent the animals to help the demon win the battle. At least half
its heads weren't human, and she picked out a number of rats,
dogs, cats, monkeys, and asses among the crush.

Without warning, Elizabeth found herself flying back from
the wall. Sprawled on her back by the steps, she looked around
frantically, wondering who'd hit her. She realized, in terror, that
the earth itself was moving. The tremors raised dust from the
cracks in the floor and pelted the flagstones with grit from the
ceiling. Elizabeth crab-walked to the balustrade and grabbed
it for support. She braced for the worst. The Lord's Prayer shot
to her lips, and "Hail Mary" followed it. The last shock rolled

through the ground as she got to "now and at the hour of our death." The vault blocks stayed where they belonged, the floodwater stopped jumping out of the staircase, and the gravel near the broken door lay still.

Her phone beeped, and she jumped. After the angry earth-rumbles, the modem, *friendly*, staccato tone seemed absurd. Elizabeth almost giggled in relief.

"Hello?" Thompson's voice, she thought. The static was so bad it was hard to tell. "Still with us?"

"I'm here," she answered.

"Hello? Hello? Anyone there?" The signal broke up entirely for a second, then: "Circuit's open, just...no one...can't get an answer."

"I'm here!" Liz shouted into the phone. "I'm here. What happened? Can you hear me?"

Thinly, through the noise, the Asp's voice: "Try again... street...."

The line went dead, and Liz stared at the little handset in disappointment. She racked her brain for *Have survived earthquake and can hear you. Connection too bad to speak*, but the situation seemed too specific. She sent four-nine-four, then holstered the phone and looked at the pool. The sloshing water revealed nothing of the situation below. She checked her camera for damage, retrieved her light from the corner it had bounced to, then pulled her legs up and sat tailor-fashion on the railing. Adrenaline—the second jolt of it that night—spread out from her stomach.

Elizabeth waited patiently for half an hour or more, just watching the water calm down. At length, she noticed a new ripple on the surface. She felt the railing cautiously for new tremors, found none her fingers could detect, and smiled as the pool moved more dramatically. The other two were returning; in a little while they could be out from under the ruins. She slid off the balustrade onto the flagstones, and walked around the railing to meet Hesha and the gypsy as they came out.

The water surged, and Khalil leapt up from it like a rocket. He shook himself like an animal in the air, flinging spray across the room. Liz shielded her eyes with her hand and kept her attention on the pool. A heavy thud reached her ears—she looked up and saw the guide bashing his body against the door seal. He hauled back and threw his shoulder against it again— he was trying to batter his way out, though the opening was in his arm's reach.

Elizabeth gasped, "What are you do—" and broke off when she caught sight of his face. Khalil's eyes stared out at nothing, so far open that the whites showed all around the iris. Stark, unreasoning terror filled them, and his wild-animal glance returned to the pit over and over again. His mouth hung open like a panting dog's, and his bared teeth were clear enough in the light: The canines, elongated into fangs, glittered cruelly.

"Oh, my god," whispered the mortal woman. She backed away from the monster *and* from the unseen danger down the stairs.

The Ravnos ran against the wall another time, so forcefully that he bounced back and fell howling onto the floor. His eyes began to change—the lids narrowed— now predatory slits, they searched the room for prey, not escape. The creature rushed Elizabeth, picked her up in clawed hands, and threw her into a corner. He pounced on the huddled body, stuck his nose into the crook of her neck, smelt her, pawed her collar half off her shoulders, and licked her bare skin. She scrabbled away along the wall. His face grew puzzled for a moment. Then all expression dropped from it, and the animal came back. Khalil jumped to her side again, seized her shoulder, and—a noise came from the pit, and his eyes changed again. He began to turn around.

Instantly, Elizabeth was aware of Hesha as a blur between herself and the monster. The scene froze: Khalil Ravana, spread-eagled on the floor, Elizabeth pressed up against the wall, Hesha in front of her, his hand still holding the blunt end of something pale piercing the other man's breast.

"Don't scream," the Setite said calmly. "The earthquake may have weakened the tunnels. Have you been wounded?"

"Just bruised, I think."

"Good. Now help me with him." Hesha dragged the Ravnos's corpse as far as the door. "Climb over. Now, steady the body as I pass it to you. Don't try to take the weight yourself."

Together they manhandled the stiff through the opening, and
Hesha began tying nylon cord around the dead man's torso.
Elizabeth looked at the weapon in Khalil's chest and confirmed
her suspicions.

"He's a vampire," she said, and her tone was so strange that
for an instant Hesha stopped what he was doing.

Smoothly, he went on with his knots. Equally smoothly, he
told her, "No. He's a *shilmulo*."

"He grew fangs. You staked him and he's dead, Hesha. He's
a vampire," she insisted coldly.

"Elizabeth," said the Setite, with a trace of impatience, "if
I staked you, would you still move around after the fact? If I
pierced your heart, would you survive? Khalil will, *shilmub* do,
humans do not." He tied the rope ends to his own feet, and bent
down to enter the tunnel. "Watch the stake. If it shows signs of
coming loose, tell me immediately. I would rather not have to
repeat the procedure in a more confined space." Liz hesitated,
and he caught her eye. "What is it now, Elizabeth?"

"Does he drink blood? And don't go on about mosquitoes or
leeches or Maasai. You know what I mean. Truth, Hesha."

Hesha looked down at the gypsy's face. Maverick eyes
stared back at him, and flickered hungrily.

"He does," said the Setite, and he crawled into the hole,
dragging the paralyzed Ravnos after him.

Sunday, 25 July, 1999 4:45 AM
The Oberoi Grand Hotel
Calcutta, West Bengal

"The room is secure, sir," Thompson's voice came from three earpieces in three different parts of the resort. "Hallway unobserved."

"Bring him around. Transport, watch for opening doors. Distraction, report and delay anyone coming up. I will come by the center route to provide a more attractive target."

Transport, in the form of the Asp, a bellboy's cart, and a suspiciously bulging garment bag, crossed the lobby and entered the service lift safely. Distraction, in the form of Elizabeth, stationed herself by the passenger elevators and played convincingly with camera, watch, notebook, sandal strap, and the morning newspaper. An early hotel maid found herself accosted for directions to a prominent shrine in an unmappable portion of the city. As Hesha passed by, Liz professed her thanks, double-checked a street name, and let the woman go.

"He's in," Ron announced. "Everyone come home."

"Distraction" strolled along the corridor to the suite. The Asp opened the door for her, smiled wearily, and they bolted behind them in unison. Elizabeth moved to the big table and began unstrapping gadget after gadget. She threw the film into the refrigerator, ducked into her room and changed her mud-stained clothes for fresh pajamas, and collapsed onto the couch to watch the others. Khalil, unwrapped but still frozen, lay on the floor in the middle of a bed quilt. Thompson and the Asp counted down, lifted, and carried the body into Hesha's quarters. They took the corner into the sitting room, and Liz picked up the sounds of final adjustments to couch, windows, and *shilmulo*. Thoughtfully, her fingers played over the keys of the little computer in front of her.

"Asp," said Hesha, "our guest will not be in the best of health or temper when sunset comes. Find a blood bank or hospital and steal ten or fifteen units from their stores. Cold supper will serve better than none...."

"Yes, sir." Raphael vanished into his bedroom.

"Thompson—I want you and Janet to find out everything you can about the tremors tonight. I want local coverage here, I want local from the source, if Calcutta was not the center. Full report on BBC, CNN, Voice of America, NPR, Chinese governmental, Russian public and private and pirate stations. Pick up the wire services, as well."

The old cop nodded, picked up his phone, received the laptop from Liz, and walked out, dialing.

Hesha turned, seemed to notice the last member of the team for the first time, and looked at her curiously. "Elizabeth? What do you want?" the Setite asked cautiously.

"You saved my life tonight, didn't you?" Elizabeth said, her voice full of wondering gratitude.

Hesha nodded. He felt better; he was on solid ground again. A thankful attitude opened up vast avenues of control over the girl. He raised one hand in a subtle, nobly deprecating gesture, and stepped closer to the couch. He decided to sit on the cushion beside her. He moved to do so, and she smiled at him. "You nearly got me killed tonight, didn't you?" she said, in an utterly different tone.

Hesha sat down on the coffee table. Warily, he waited for the rest of it.

"I looked *shilmulo* up on the Internet just now. Five links to various Rom dictionaries...several dozen links to pages devoted to vampires, Hesha."

"There is no such thing as a vampire, Elizabeth. It is a buzz word that incompetent translators to English tack on to any mythological creature that survives by feeding on something in a fashion repugnant. The monster need not even drink blood to qualify for the honor, nor human blood, nor be undead—"

"Stop," Liz said abruptly. "Listen," she asked earnestly, looking into his ebon eyes with her amber-brown ones, "I...I think I may be in love with you." Just as solemnly, with the same serious yet uncertain cadence, she went on: "I think, also, that I would be better dead than feeling this way toward you... that I would rather see you dead, than to feel like this. And I don't understand why, after everything I have seen, I can still feel anything toward you." She took a moment's breath, and the creature in front of her thought of a little blue glass left in a refrigerator in Brooklyn, and thought he knew the answer. "Please, Hesha...tell me the truth. What are you?" The Setite paused, weighed the moment carefully, and slowly let his everyday mask slip away. Revealed, his skin was slightly lighter-colored. His bare scalp sported a detailed, coiling snake tattoo in deep black ink that had never faded. Open and unguarded, honest eyes looked out at the woman on the couch, and as he spoke his voice trembled a little.

"I am the dead priest of a dead god. That is the truth."

Elizabeth smiled bitterly. "You give me a different answer every time." A tear rolled down her cheek, and she rose to go.

"They might all be true," he said softly.

She kept walking and did not answer. Hesha stood, caught her door before she shut it, and gazed at her in appeal. "Close your eyes," whispered the Setite, slipping into the girl's room.

In surrender or weariness or hatred or lust or love, her lids dropped, and Hesha leaned down to kiss her lips. After a moment's hesitation, she kissed him back. The Setite felt her mouth move, but felt nothing beneath the surface of his skin. The Beast drove forward, listening hungrily to her heartbeat, thrusting the sound to the forefront of his consciousness. Elizabeth's arms stole up his back, drawing their bodies closer, and the Beast picked out the vibration of her life and savored it—cut off Hesha's connection to the floor, to the feel of her nightshirt under his fingers, even took the simple pressures of holding her, and of the fingers digging into his back. With an immense effort, he drew away—shook the veils from his senses—and took the clear moment to carry her to the bed. The

Beast threw itself at his mind, but to the Setite's surprise and relief, the anger over Calcutta was gone. Without that aid, the curse was weaker than himself, and he locked it away.

His hand crept under her shirt. Her heartbeat pulsed through her ribs and flesh and into his palm. Hesha sought the woman's mouth again, and found it soft, warm, and more eager than before. His fangs slid down, and he tore the slightest wounds in her lower lip. She flinched, but he brought blood through the pin-prick holes. He drank slowly, hardly drawing more from the cuts than they bled of their own, and the mortal's gasping, shuddering breath told him the struggle was over. Elizabeth relaxed into his arms, unresisting, still holding him.

Hesha sipped delicately from the veins of his lover; the monster went on devouring his victim. Hesha savored the taste of Elizabeth's strangely sweet, adrenaline-sour blood; the Setite fed off a captive. Hesha felt the pounding of the girl's heart and was glad to know she shared the ecstasy; the calculating coldness of his mind counted the beats and measured their strength. When the steady rhythm broke and fluttered, he licked her lips clean, sealing the cuts.

He looked into her puzzled face, smiled, and whispered sleep to her. Elizabeth curled up under the blanket, and he put an arm over her. She slipped off into dreams, and Hesha looked sluggishly to the window. Dawn…he might make it to his room…but the drapes were closed tight here, the blanket thick…mortal women placed a particular importance on staying after…it might be useful…for controlling her…with his free hand, he pulled the discarded counterpane around himself in double and triple folds and piled the pillows over his head. Ra gained the horizon, and his descendant fell safely into slumber.

Thompson, checking around the suite for the last time before retiring himself, found Hesha's casket open. In dreadful anticipation, he opened the door to Liz's room. He watched her breathing for a moment, then went back and dug a mylar sheet out of the emergency case. With an air of duty done despite better judgment, he made Hesha's burrow sun-proof, and left them together.

Alone, sitting on his own bed, he stared at his hands. If he bent the wrists back and held them up at an angle, Ron could just see the pulse under the skin. He stood up suddenly, opened the curtains, and let the morning light strike him. He lay down and the sun came up, and he fell asleep basking in it.

Sunday, 25 July 1999, 8:32 PM
The Oberoi Grand Hotel
Calcutta, West Bengal

"Khalil? Can you hear me?" Hesha bent delicately over his guest's paralyzed body. "Have you recovered? Look to your left, twice, if you understand me."

The jetty eyes signaled intelligently enough.

"Good. Brace yourself." The Setite put one hand on the gypsy's chest, the other on the stake. He pulled.

Whatever mysterious...compulsion, *aggressive* compulsion, had taken hold of the undead in Calcutta seemed mostly to have abated. Hesha thought Khalil should be harmless enough now.

The Ravnos sprang free, flailing wildly to get away from the older monster. Khalil scurried, rat-like, to the opposite corner of the room, and crouched defensively.

Hesha let him go, backed up a trifle, and sat down on the arm of the couch with his hands in view. "I apologize," he began, "for the manner in which I put an end to your...seizure...last night. You passed very quickly beyond reason, and, having promised to protect you, I could hardly let you run out into Calcutta in such a state." At his feet lay a small blue cooler; he opened it, drew out a blood bag, and tossed it underhand to his guest. "I assure you, none of that is mine."

"Yeah. Right."

Hesha snapped the stake in two and shrugged. "I assume, Khalil, that your employer has you fully bound to his service. You hear his voice from a distance; you obey him when you clearly would prefer not to. I have a great deal to accomplish and no blood to waste where another has gone before me. Drink that and fix your chest. There are more in here." The Setite leaned down and picked up a bag for himself, then pushed the cooler halfway across the room. He sank his teeth into the plastic and winced at the taste. Khalil, after a moment, joined him. The Ravnos was a messy eater. He tossed the empty bag aside, seized the cooler and went through six or seven more before stopping.

"There are fresh clothes hanging in the closet for you, if you would like to dress. And a shower, of course. Hesha eyed the mud-caked hair and dirty feet of the *shilmub* pointedly. "It is my custom to hold a meeting among my staff at sunset. If you have anything you care to contribute, you are welcome to attend, provided you mind your manners—I do not allow my retainers to be interfered with, even by allies.

"If you wish to leave, you are free to do so." The Setite caught clearly the flash of panic on the other's face, and let the sentence end itself. Khalil was deathly afraid of something outside. Hesha rose to join the mortals in conference. The Ravnos remained in the corner, looking more like a trapped animal than ever.

The Asp, Thompson, and Janet Lindbergh were waiting for him—the first two in chairs at the main table, the last by phone, an open net connection, and a miniature laser printer.

"Good evening," said Hesha. "Report."

"Yes sir," Janet responded promptly. "Ron, the first file for him, please.

"The following facts are undisputed by any sources. First, Typhoon Justin, centered over West Bengal and Bangladesh, lost momentum at last and returned to tropical storm status. Second, Bangladesh suffered massive, deadly mudslides in nearly every corner of the country. Third, Bangladesh was at the epicenter of a considerable earthquake whose effects were felt as far as Rangoon and Delhi."

Hesha contemplated the report before him. Without looking up, he asked, "How are our people?"

"Everyone checked in on time, sir," Thompson answered.

"Elizabeth?" inquired the Setite, in the same detached tone.

"Sleeping. When we try to wake her, she starts talking about Ravana again. I thought it best to let her be, sir." To Thompson's relief, his master remained at the table, and the conference went on without further reference to the girl.

Hesha shook the dreaming woman by the shoulder. "Elizabeth? Can you hear me?"

Liz mumbled incomprehensibly.

"Elizabeth!" Hesha said sharply. She stirred. "Good. Talk to me. Tell me about Ravana."

"Ravana…the three overcame Ravana. They tore him down from the mountain, cut him open, and gave his heart to the sun to eat. The Prince of Storms let go his hold on the kingdom… Ravana died in the center of his power, in the midst of his children. They had not come to aid him. He put his curse on them, from the center of his power: They should go mad; they should be no more; and so it was. Their nights will dwindle unto nothing…even *rakshasa* cannot fight the power of three curses at once…murder, calumny, and the madness…" She flickered briefly into a normal voice: "It's a common enough metaphor, Professor. The rebellious children cursed by a grandparent— usually part of a colonization cycle. Campbell makes too much of it, but Graves is sound…." Clarity faded to fairy tale—chapters Hesha had heard before—and decayed further into meaningless murmurs.

Monday, 26 July 1999, 10:02 PM
Unfinished works of the second Hooghly Bridge
Calcutta, West Bengal

Hesha approached the gypsy camps by the same route he had tried on the Friday. He walked to and through the site of his previous encounter, down through the northern half of the camp, and under the bridgework itself without being accosted by the feral guardians. He passed through the center— well south—out through the other side, and no Ravnos called him out or tried to do *anything* to him. It was against all possibility that every *shilmulo* in the settlement could restrain itself when presented such a pretty mark as a serious, public, devout Follower of Set.

Hesha stopped on the southern limits, and looked back thoughtfully. There were, he realized, a great many fires lit among the shacks and tents and wagons—not cookfires, which need not be so large—not drying fires, since the flood-dampened stores weren't hung near them. Hesha had avoided them on the way through as a matter of course. Now he turned his steps back to the nearest, drawing as close to it as his courage would allow, and squinted into the heart of the light.

It was a scrap-wood bonfire, knee-high and not quite four feet across. Piles of fabric lay atop the board-ends and broken crates, charring and melting in the heat—a cardboard suitcase, a broken violin, a pile of books, photographs, a set of hairbrushes, half a dozen decks of cards—as each sheet of paper smoldered through, the ashes peeled away into the wind, and wisps of old cloth drifted with the smoke.

Hesha retreated into more comfortable shadows and watched the people in the vicinity. He was almost certain that the fire was the end of a gypsy wake...the dead man or woman's possessions destroyed by smashing and burning them...but no one grieved at the blaze or in the tents around it. No mourners stood here or at any other open fire he could see—and the passersby averted their eyes from the sight.

Half an hour later, the Setite walked into the Albert Hall Coffee Shop.

Subhas's table was empty.

After a moment's contemplation, Hesha sat down in the old man's usual seat. He placed his hands on the table, and the waitress he remembered Subhas dealing with came over to serve him.

"*Nomoshkar,* sahib. What would you like me to bring to you this evening?"

"Turkish coffee, please." As she started to go, Hesha cleared his throat. "Pardon me, but could you tell me where my friend, the gentleman who usually sits here, might be?"

The polite, dark-skinned girl shook her head. "Oh, no, sir." She seemed upset, and turned back with plenty of conversation on her face. "It's funny that you should ask that. We have all been worried—he was a very kind and generous gentleman, and no one has seen him since the night of the earthquake." Hesha encouraged her with a nod. "Every night he comes in just as the lights go on, and leaves just as we close the doors. He never misses a night...not until the quake came. And tonight is the second evening he has been gone. I am afraid something might be wrong with him. The owner thinks that the old Babu—pardon me, sir—the old gentleman may have lost family in East Bengal." Her eyes showed more than that; the Setite saw that she feared Subhas had died. "If you see him, sir, do tell him that all of us here are very, very concerned for him. Please ask him to send us word if he is all right."

"I will," said Hesha. "If I see him."

Tuesday, 27 July 1999, 1:02 AM
Five Star Market, Kidderpore
Calcutta, West Bengal

"Old Nag!" The peddler stared in amazement for a moment longer, and then shook his head. "Damned if I'm not glad to see you," the Nosferatu declared wonderingly.

"And I am extraordinarily relieved to see you," Hesha replied.

They regarded each other in silence for what seemed like a long time, even for creatures of their patience. Then the gray-skinned monster rasped out: "About our arrangements..."

"Yes?" Hesha's tone implied a limited bargaining distance, and the face in the little bookshop bobbed nervously.

"You found Michel before I did, I hear. Which renders that deal null and void, I'm afraid. But the other...I won't be able to fulfill your wishes for some months, at least. All my contacts are temporarily unavailable."

"I accept that as an excuse for nonpayment of the debt," Hesha said, and the monster amid the magazines appeared relieved. "Tell me, though, where were you Sunday morning... when the quake hit?"

Warily, the Nosferatu answered: "In a drainage tunnel."

"Underground and underwater?"

With even more caution: "Yes."

"There are no creatures of the night in Calcutta but ourselves, are there?"

After a terrible, rattling sigh: "No. No one. I was on my way to meet some friends that night. I came up to street level, and they were gone. Every one. The Ravnos are gone, the Court is gone, the Prince is dead...." With a hint of hysteria in its voice, the bookseller shouted, "I am the Prince of the City, old Nag!" In a lower tone, he added, "My first act is to abdicate my throne. How about it? Want a city, Prince Hesha? Lord Ruhadze?"

"I'm leaving town, I think. I'll see that you receive at least partial payment for your attempts on my behalf." Hesha leaned on his stick and resumed walking toward the hotel. "If you ever find yourself in a position to tell me what I asked about, the Grand will have a method available; ask after me at the front desk."

The short, gray, spindly creature looked down at him, and the Setite's long strides halted. Trembling, licking its lips, nervous, the Nosferatu leaned in. It asked, "What did you *do* to Calcutta, old Nag?"

Hesha stared at the hideous face for a moment, shook his head, and moved on.

Tuesday, 27 July 1999, 2:51 AM
The Oberoi Grand Hotel
Calcutta, West Bengal

Elizabeth lay swathed in blankets. Her eyes moved like a dreamer's, but her face never relaxed into peaceful sleep. The covers were undisturbed; she could not have moved much since Thompson and his master had checked on her at sundown. She had not eaten since Sunday. She took water only when bullied into it, and even then in small sips. Hesha looked at his pet antiquarian with concern; if the trance were unbroken another day, they would be forced to put her in a hospital to keep her from dying of dehydration.

He pulled her by the shoulders into a sitting position, then propped her up with mounds of pillows. Liz showed no reaction. He called her by name—softly, sharply, commandingly, even (though it took an effort) with tenderness in his voice to bait her. The Setite took her hands—she neither resisted nor clasped back. The expressions on her face reflected things she saw outside the room, not horror or happiness that Hesha was near.

Without guilt—simply as a point of information—he recalled drinking a fair amount from her. Nothing more dangerous than a pint or two, but a weakened body might not protect against the...trance...so well as a healthy one. Hesha went to the washroom and filled a glass with water. Slowly, with a few spills, he persuaded her unconscious mouth to swallow properly. He brought more, managed to give it to the woman without choking her, and sat beside her for a while, holding the empty cup in his hands. A faint clicking sound caught his attention, and he glanced down...his claws, extended, tapped a rhythm on the thin glass. Hesha lanced one wrist with the other thumb and let the blood flow into the cup. He held the reddish-black fluid under Elizabeth's nose, and called her again. Faint signs of recognition rewarded him—he put the glass in her hands and held the rim to her lips.

"Elizabeth? Can you hear me? Try to drink this."

Ron Thompson came into the sickroom quietly, looking for his employer. He found a scene that disturbed him more than anything else he had known in Calcutta: Elizabeth, apparently awake, sitting up, seeing nothing, talking nonsense about kings and monsters and page-boys and demons—amulets draped around her neck—a tape recorder on the bedside table—traces of red on the girl's lips—Hesha sitting at the foot of the bed, listening intently and holding an empty, bloodstained cup.

Hesha caught his driver's eye and signaled silence. He mouthed, "What is it?"

Thompson glared at him like a thundercloud. He beckoned brusquely. Hesha eased off the bed carefully, so as not to disturb the recitation, and joined him on the other side of the door.

"Sir," began Thompson in darkest tones.

Hesha scanned the conference room over Ron's shoulder. Janet's line was open; the Asp and Khalil sat at the main table, playing cards.

"Thompson," Hesha whispered warningly, "you know how deeply I value your opinion. However. This is not the time, the place, or the *company*," his eyes flicked meaningfully toward the Ravnos, "in which I would desire to hear your views. Understood? We will take this up in private, later.

"Now," he said, resuming conversational volume, "what was it you came to see me about?"

Ron hesitated, stumbling over the sudden change in gears. He pulled his notepad from his breast pocket to reassure himself. "Our agents have their exit assignments, sir. We're prepared to close up shop on your word." He turned to the marked pages, but hardly glanced at them. "The 'good-will' items we brought with us have been delivered to the bookseller in the Five Star.

The gentleman was rather overwhelmed by the consignment, but we persuaded him to accept."

"So...you progress," said Hesha.

"Yes, sir. But so far...the agents know where they're going, but you haven't given me any information yet to start arrangements for us. What's the next step, sir?"

The Setite stepped away from the wall, seeming to grow taller and more commanding. He approached the table and looked down at the card game in mild disapproval. Thompson, guessing ahead, unobtrusively took his place at the foot of the table. The Asp laid his cards face down and waited respectfully for his employer to speak. Khalil Ravana, sensing the shift in atmosphere, fanned his cards perfectly, and elegantly, and set the hand to one side. He made himself comfortable, relaxing into the soft chair, resting his arms on the padded rests, and letting his quick fingers play amongst the poker stake in front of him.

"Bullets?" Hesha remarked.

Khalil picked up a 45mm round and spun on its point like a top. "He wouldn't play for money."

"I warned him not to."

"And Khalil here didn't want to play with matches," the Asp sneered.

"I see." Hesha seated himself, dialed Janet into the conference, and began: "As you are all aware, my primary project at this time involves tracking down the Eye of Hazimel. Khalil Ravana," he nodded at the Ravnos, "has provided substantial aid in this direction. In return for his services, we will provide transportation and sufficient false papers to allow him to emigrate to the United States.

"What none of you have been told yet is that Calcutta, as a nucleus of Family activity, no longer exists." The Setite regarded his guest reservedly. "Perhaps you need confirmation of this?" The Ravnos shook his head, and Hesha smiled inwardly. There were, as he had thought, at least *four* survivors—the bookseller, himself, this errand-boy, and Khalil's master. Of course, Khalil's master need not have been in the city at the time...Hesha shelved the speculation for later and continued his speech.

"When we concluded the second half of our agreement, Khalil, you implied that your knowledge of the Eye and its properties would make you useful to me as I searched for it. I have called this meeting to discuss our next move toward the artifact, and I would be grateful if you would contribute to that discussion."

Raphael's face twitched slightly at his master's implied invitation to "discuss" anything.

Thompson, more accustomed to Hesha's tactics with third parties—and more often asked in fact for an opinion, despite the scene over Elizabeth moments before—cleared his throat and started talking. "Well, sir, maybe the time has come to go to Atlanta ourselves. If you knew for certain what had happened to…" he paused, looking for terms to hide behind, "…your associate, you might learn something. Isn't that where the first trace led?"

"That is true," said Hesha.

Thompson snatched at straws to keep going. "California? The professor's notes will be there; you know from Liz that he had relevant info. He probably didn't tell her all of it." The Asp translated "discuss" in his head: Play up and play dumb.

"I like the idea of Atlanta," he said slowly. "But I can't help but wonder about the little nest of lines running around New York City. There were traces headed that way we never followed up."

Hesha nodded, and Raphael let his pent-up breath go. He'd taken it—whatever it was—in the right direction. Let Ron pick it up again….

With a sleek and superior air, Khalil held both hands up to stop the conversation. He shook his head condescendingly. "Gentlemen, gentlemen…you're on the wrong track entirely. Professor's notes? Cold killings? You're lucky I'm here. Atlanta is old, old news. And New York is no good; the Eye has never been in the city, whatever you may think." He let his voice lilt up, and his final word rolled off his tongue momentously: "Chicago."

"Chicago?" Hesha inquired evenly.

"Chicago." Khalil smiled.

"You are certain of this?"

"The Eye is in Chicago," said the cocky young gypsy. "I swear. See? I told you I'd be useful. Atlanta, hell..."

Hesha studied his partner. "Very well," he said. "Thompson. Janet. Reservations and security through Chicago." Hesha had no more use for Calcutta. His discovery in the underwater chamber of the tomb had prepared him for this next, and perhaps final, leg of his quest. "I want to be out of India by sundown. Khalil, you have two hours until dawn. Be ready by the time the sun catches us. If you have more things to do than can be accomplished in the time, make a list of them and the team will attend to it."

The Setite rose. "Questions?" No one spoke. "Then I look forward to seeing you all...Wednesday night, I believe."

As the dead filed into the next suite to rest, Hesha clapped a hand on his bodyguard's shoulder, and Ron felt a paper pressed into his palm. After the door closed on them and the sun rose, he sat down at the table to read it.

Thompson,

Ignore Khalil. Find out from Miles where Kettridge is and arrange for our transportation there. If the good professor has gone to ground in Chicago, very well—the Ravnos is telling the truth. Simply be sure that we arrive before him.

Send Khalil to Chicago no matter where we go.

The cabin was small, rough, new, and intended to look both older and more rustic than was plausible. It smelt of disinfectant, detergent, dog, tourist, grass, fish, and dirt. Over "country" print curtains black duct tape stuck black plastic sheeting to walls and windows. Patches of sunshield on the door and near the ceiling testified to the scrupulous care with which the creature's servants looked after his interests. When Ra released the Setite from sleep, Ron Thompson was there, waiting patiently.

"Good evening, sir. I've brought you breakfast."

"Local bank?"

"Your own vintage, sir. I had it driven up with the car. We're in upstate New York, by the way."

"You've been busy. Report."

"Yes sir. Pauline Miles and her team tracked Kettridge here. Presumably, Chicago was a blind by Khalil, and I hope the left-luggage office opens that skunk's crate in the daytime." Thompson ran a hand through his grizzled hair.

"Pauline's team has been weakened by the losses you already know about. I sent all but the die-hards home for a break. They need it…they saw more than they should have. Kettridge has been amazingly popular these three weeks.

"I kept Pauline here; she's in the know now, for certain, and she's weathered the storm well enough. She's still my top pick to manage the detective work if I buy it, but there's a lot to be said for brute force and the ability to manage that.

So I've brought in Matthew Voss for a tryout. He comes from the executive-protection side of the business. His team is fresh and ready to come in, but so far I've kept his people away from what's left of Pauline's squad to minimize the risk of Family rumors spreading. We have a small army of security, a fair-sized arsenal, both the cars, Miles and Voss, the Asp—who has already sighted in half the guns for his own aim—Janet taking care of the baggage difficulties, myself, and you, sir."

"Where is Elizabeth?"

"Awake and in her right mind," said Ron with satisfaction, "having dinner with the others."

Hesha rose, stretched, and selected a map from a pile on the unfinished table. "As your replacement, are you suggesting Miles, Voss, or both?"

"Both, I think."

"I am inclined to agree with you." Hesha pored over the country as represented by contour lines, tree cover, water table, fault zones, stratification, highways, local roads, footpaths, fire breaks, school districts, police jurisdiction, zip code. At last, he picked out an ordinary trail map showing points of natural interest, and sat staring at it. "When the others have finished eating, we will go. Voss's team for back-up. You, the Asp, Pauline, and Elizabeth will travel with me." His shoulders twitched. "I can feel your disapproval, Thompson, but she has proved to be an invaluable sensitive. If there is trouble, she will know; probably before we do.

"Also," said Hesha, "if these two are satisfactory, you might look forward to joining the ranks of Set once the Eye is secured."

Thompson sat very still. "Thank you, sir. I will certainly keep thinking about it."

Elizabeth hiked last along the steep, winding trail. No clouds marred the night. The full moon shone so brightly overhead that none of the hikers had turned on their flashlights. Hesha appeared for a moment, above her, on a switchback of the path. She looked up at him, admiring the figure he cut as he moved— proud, silent, sure-footed—his skin gleaming blue-black and the whites of his eyes glowing like stars. He vanished beyond the curve. Thompson filed into view close behind, and Liz could see every gray hair silvered by the moonlight; she saw, and pitied, the bent back, the tired set of his shoulders. The Asp, lighter-stepping, stealthier, more sly in every movement, passed his partner at the turn. He pulled Ron's pack open, dug something out of it, and stuffed the item into his own gear. The older man marched more easily, and his thick hand reached up to Raphael's shoulder. The Asp pretended not to notice, and moved out of sight.

In front of Elizabeth, Pauline Miles kept steady pace. While it was hard to hear the Asp make his way along the path, it was difficult to see Pauline. She was short, thin, naturally dark, and her dull, dark-blue clothes blended easily with the shadows.

The track widened just after the bend, and the two women matched step for the last few yards. Their three companions had stopped ahead of them in a break between the trees. Pauline and Elizabeth caught up, found places opposite Ron and Raphael, and held their position quietly. Hesha waited, stock-still, for a full minute, and then moved across the meadow in a straight, unfaltering line.

Elizabeth brushed through clusters of some plant that smelled terribly sweet, and picked a branch from one to carry with her. She looked at their destination—another climb, she supposed—a majestic, tumbled mass of stone and forest rising above the shallow valley. Hesha was two-thirds of the way to the foot of it already.

"Liz—watch your laces," Pauline whispered.

Elizabeth stooped to one knee to tie her shoe. For a brief second, she felt a wave of heat. The earth beneath her hands felt more like asphalt than anything else. Liz blinked and saw stars—shook her head, and felt the ground again. Grassy, rooty soil. Her fingers dug in and found a worm, a few pillbugs—she knelt until her cheek nearly touched the dirt, and no scorching sensation came to her face. Liz rose in doubt and walked the rest of the way trying to see out of the corners of her eyes.

Hesha approached an opening under a tilted rock, peered inside, and then confidently beckoned to the others. He led them around and to right, pulled himself up and over a sizable boulder, and looked down into a passage the width of a city sidewalk and the height of two men. A wall of rock had, long ago, split in two. The forces that had riven it had forced the pieces closer together at the top, wider apart at the bottom, forming an irregular tunnel sloping down into the earth. The "floor" was dirt and rubble washed in by water. The walls sported moss and small plants only so far as light might enter the crack.

The Setite observed all this without pausing. He turned on his light and led the others into the hill. One by one, four lamps clicked on behind him.

At the end of the descent, the tunnel opened out into a large, ungainly chamber. The five lights—very small and dim in comparison to the dark expanse they had to contend with—played over the billowing curves of the cave. Elizabeth recognized the smooth, weird shapes of water-cut and water-built limestone. She fanned her flash's beam out as far as it would go, and turned it on the ceiling, which soared to the right past the limit of the light. To her left, it swooped down to within four feet of the floor. A bizarre combination of claustrophobia, agoraphobia, and vertigo washed over her. She looked to her footing, sharpened the focus again, and tried to keep the light on the same level as her eyes. The others stepped out, each taking a slightly different route to avoid the stalagmites and columns jutting up from the floor. Hesha picked his way to a narrow, nearly invisible opening and the team followed—though it was a tight and difficult squeeze for Thompson.

On the other side was a disturbingly familiar chamber. Elizabeth felt as though she had walked into a natural chapel, the cave's roof vaulted like a cathedral's. More stalactites, stalagmites, and columns had formed here than in the first room, and the largest of them formed two uneven lines...like rows of pillars in a ruin. The few formations down the center of the room lay low; pillows, rope coils, and buttons dotted the gently rolling floor, and the icicles and curtains suspended from the ceiling hung no lower than the tops of the "pillars" on either side.

"Wait here," said Hesha. His voice echoed. He lowered it,

and went on: "The professor will be easier for me to handle by myself. I don't care to have him harmed by one of you," he said, glancing toward the Asp, "even by accident, and I do not want any of you shot or burned by him in an attempt on me."

Elizabeth clambered up and found a damp seat on a stone stump. She watched as Hesha picked through one of the packs, strapped a large and heavy rubberized-canvas sack to his back, and set out across the "chapel." He traversed the slippery, rounded terrain without a misstep, selected a deep shadow in the right rear corner of the cave, and headed unswervingly toward it. By the moving shadows, she realized that what she had taken for the "back wall" of the cathedral must be a free-standing column of enormous size. She squinted to see better.

Hesha reached the side passage he had chosen and turned back to look at the giant pillar himself. His lamp caught the thing in sharp profile, and Elizabeth gasped. For an instant, the sidelit formation had seemed to move; an optical illusion gave it a hundred monstrous faces and distorted limbs. The Setite moved on and darkness settled on the far end of the cavern once more, but Liz dropped off her perch. She knew that ghastly image; she had seen it last in a mural under a tenement in Calcutta. She popped the filter off the powerful lens in her hand, and started running along the "aisle" of the chapel.

The hot halogen bulb flooded the huge hall with light. It stripped the shadows away from the pillar and threw them into the corners of the room. It picked out dirt and rust imprisoned under the translucent calcite film. But the faces were gone. Elizabeth studied the surface of the hundred-headed demon— of the natural, two-story, stone pillar that must have grown for eons and stood for millennia—and tried desperately to find an angle from which she might see the faces again. The harshest light refused to bring out the contours that could have fooled her eye. The softest light, filtered again, as Hesha's lamp had been, failed to duplicate the conditions. Thompson, confused but willing to help, took the flash and stood where Liz thought their employer had been, and though she returned to the stump and called out directions to him, the faces never reappeared in the stone.

Ron came back, curious and slightly worried. He asked, "What was it?"

"I thought I saw something."

"Moving?" The Asp jumped in.

"No. Just...there."

Elizabeth said nothing more, and Thompson stayed by her while Raphael and Pauline went off to search the room for more practical things, like exits. Their voices ricocheted up and around and back to Ron and Liz's ears, and the girl flinched.

"You've got a feeling about something?" The old cop asked softly.

She grimaced. "No. It's just...the echoes...sounded as though there were more than four people in here. Can we go back to the first cave?"

"Sure," said Thompson, and they jumped down off their stumps together.

Hesha followed the trail of the red eyestone easily— almost smugly, with a full-belly kind of contentment. The bead around his neck seemed to tug him along the track, and the sensation of cool, carved, blood-colored chalcedony hovered like a beacon when his steps aligned with the correct direction.

The Setite savored the potential for triumph. He had nothing, yet, and he knew the danger of assuming victory before the battle had been fought—but by night's end, he might have accomplished his goal. It was *possible* that the Eye would be Set's by daybreak. It was *possible* that his quest would end, and that was an astonishing possibility.

He cherished, too, the confrontation ahead. Hesha could admit to himself that he looked forward to seeing Jordan Kettridge again. The young man—no, not so young, realized the creature—was an unusual specimen. Rarely did Hesha encounter a human so hard-headed, so unshakable. Kettridge could be won over, but not bought. He could be convinced by evidence, but not turned by anything Hesha could find to tempt him. Any mortal could be broken, of course, but they were of so little use afterwards. So for the past sixteen years, Hesha had made Kettridge's career into something of a hobby. The Setite amused himself by funding Jordan's work, supplying him with grants and minor clues to support the archaeologist's theories. He smoothed over governmental difficulties, kept the academic wolves at bay, and used his influence to help the professor obtain any visa to any nation he wished.

Someday, he might tell Jordan all that he had done for the man—but he liked the picture of a dead Kettridge standing before Osiris (if Osiris ever regained proper control of the underworld again), faced with the feather of Ma'at, reciting the list of his deeds, being questioned by the gods about his relationship to a Child of Set called Hesha Ruhadze…and giving, innocently, all the wrong answers.

The red line fell to a level below. Hesha wedged himself into the corners of a ladder-like, easily climbed chimney, and descended carefully to the slick stone beneath.

He found a dead end.

In a den-shaped space the size of a double bed, a man's body lay prostrate on the rock. The Setite braced himself for what might come, and touched the outflung arm of the ragged figure. His fingers gripped flesh as cold as stone, but not rigid. An old corpse? It smelt very dead…but the texture of the skin suggested withering flesh beneath, not the corruption of the grave. A Cainite…dormant…or meeting Final Death in a way Hesha had never seen before.

The Setite swung his light around to examine the carcass. The stick-thin, haggard shape was bare-chested but wore loose trousers, sneakers, and a belt. Filth, caked mud, and dried gore hid the original colors of his clothes and encrusted most of the body. More significantly, to Hesha's mind, an old swath of something paler overlaid the other stains like a sash. The fat-yellow stream began at the man's swollen, ravaged left eyesocket and dripped down his face, neck and shoulder as if a tallow candle had melted out of the blinding wound. Some of it still glistened as if fresh, and new drops of the stuff had fallen onto the cave floor as though the candle had been wrested from the corpse very recently.

Hesha leaned over the body and picked up the red eyestone. He held the bead between his palms and attuned himself to it for a moment, then attached it to the cord that held the white eye and the amulet. He retraced his steps as far as the top of the chimney, turned completely around twice, and realized that he had a new problem. The white stone was as good as a bloodhound for tracking the red ones. The red one around his neck felt the call of the Eye itself, gave a location, and general bearings—but only as the crow flew. In the labyrinths of a limestone cave, Hesha could not walk a straight line toward the source.

The Setite pulled out a compass and his phone.

"Either the professor is being very, very clever," he said to his team, "or we're dealing with someone else altogether. Someone more dangerous. There is a dormant Cainite here. The prize is gone, but there's no sign of a struggle. How our friend might have managed that, I don't know, but he has the object we are looking for. I want you to have the backup team come up and cover the cave entrance. They are to prevent any other persons from entering the caverns. If our subject tries to leave, allow him to do so, but alert me immediately, have him trailed, and keep him closely guarded. Do not, on any account, fire on him.

"In the meantime," Hesha continued, "you and the others are to split into even groups and begin a search for our friend. His position at the moment is to my southwest, up roughly eighty feet, and half a mile away. From the point at which I left you, I approximate him to be due west, forty feet above you, and just under a mile away. Concentrate in that area and mark everyone's feet before you go. I will contact you again if I scent any of your paths or if our target alters his position."

Thursday, 29 July 1999, 12:41 AM
Upstate New York

Ron Thompson slid warily down a steep incline. It was scattered with loose stones and extremely treacherous. He knew this because he had spent the last half hour climbing carefully up it to see whether the shadow at the top led anywhere.

"Blind alley," he said to his partner. "Let's go back to the junction and try the center."

Liz tried to move like the Asp. She discarded the example and tried moving like Pauline Miles, and felt better. Bare rock to bare rock—loose stone was bad; it slipped under your shoes—avoiding damp places and pools—she could still hear herself, but not so loudly as Thompson's heavy footsteps.

The middle way went nowhere, but quickly. The crevasse at the end of it was too wide and deep for them to cross; logic argued that Kettridge could not have crossed it either, and they returned to the junction. The first of the left-hand holes descended. They believed they were still underneath Kettridge's level, so they took the second. An hour later, mentally exhausted by the vast variety of hiding places in the honeycomb they had just explored, they turned to the down-slope. That, at least, was wide, smooth, and easy to walk along.

It looked as though it would dead end in a pit, but Thompson flashed his light around the bottom of the tunnel, found another shadow he couldn't explain, and the two of them scuttled down into it. The light revealed the shadow as more stream-bed; they crawled beneath the low but narrow, knife-like knee of the ceiling, and stood up in a chimney with a near-perfect ladder wall rising higher than the lights would reach.

Thompson clipped his flash to his chest and started the ascent. He pointed, ordering Elizabeth to another route, not directly beneath his. She took hold of a ledge, got her feet beneath her, and mounted the steep stairs. Reach, step, reach, step...her light bothered her, her fingertips chafed on the rough stone, and her jeans weren't as loose, climbing, as they had seemed while hiking. Liz began to lag behind. She looked over at Ron, realized he had two full lengths on her. While she watched, he stopped moving straight up and started pulling himself forward—he'd reached the top. Elizabeth grinned and picked up the pace. Twelve feet to go, at the most...

Sounds from above:

"K—"

Spang. Thwack. Thud.

Elizabeth froze.

"Shit." A man's voice—familiar, but not Thompson.

"Liz—" Thompson, sounding strange.

She fairly ran the last eight feet to the top, slipping twice in her haste, pushing her head over the top without thought for the consequences. Thompson lay there, twisted to one side, lying in a curled, half-fetal position. His right hand, speckled with sticky crimson, touched the blunt end of a golden-brown stake in his chest. Liz shoved her light above the edge and saw another man—Jordan Kettridge—running to and kneeling at, the body of her friend.

"You're a rotten shot," said Thompson angrily. "Feels like all lung."

Jordan choked. "I thought he'd come alone. Oh, shit. Ron...I dropped the aim when I saw it was you, I swear to God...but the trigger—"

"Save it, Jordan." Ron coughed, and Elizabeth swarmed up beside him. She held his head off the ground and tried to keep his body still. Tears poured down her face. She fumbled frantically with the buttons of her phone. "Wait," Ron groaned. "Stop. Don't call him."

Elizabeth misdialed, cleared, and started over. "He might be able to *help* you—" she pleaded. "You told me, he healed you after the snake bites—"

"Maybe he'll heal me. Maybe he'll kill me." Thompson looked up at her, trying to explain. "He wants to replace Vegel." His glance caught Kettridge's, and the younger man looked away. "I thought I wanted that. Since then…" he gasped, and a little more blood spilled from the edge of the wound, "I know that I don't. But I don't think…that Hesha…will just let anyone go…."

His hand closed over Elizabeth's. She let the phone fall into her lap.

"Let me tell you something," he said gently. "You think he cares about you? You haven't seen him lie enough. I thought there was something to him. Then I saw how he manipulated you. I don't believe much of him anymore…I don't want anymore to be like him …." His voice trailed off like a sleepy child's, and his eyes shut for a moment.

Then, wide-eyed and suddenly stronger, he asked, "You love him?" Elizabeth's eyes shifted uneasily. "You don't really love him. His blood—their blood—does things to people. One sip, you care about them. Two, you love them. Three drinks makes a slave out of you. That's how *he* put it, little sister."

"I haven't—"

"You have. *Twice.*" Ron's voice dropped to a harsh whisper. "The hangover cure, that night in New York." She opened her mouth to protest, but the dying man overran her. "Then, in Calcutta, I caught him feeding it to you while you were in that trance, telling stories…two drinks, Liz.

I've lied to you, too, of course. You start to do that, around him…for the best of reasons. But I'm just a liar, Liz. The Asp is a cat burglar and an assassin. And Hesha's a vampire, no matter what fancy words he puts over it or whose definition you use. *He's* the thing from the late show. So don't call him. Give me a quiet grave, first." Thompson rolled a little, toward Jordan Kettridge, and his lined, fading face fairly begged. "Get her away from him," he whispered. "Get the hell out of here. Leave the Eye…just don't risk yourself or her…get Liz away…." His hand pulled Elizabeth down to him, and she wrapped her arms around him tightly. "Ron...please... we'll get an ambulance...."

"They're gonna airlift me out of a cave?" he tried to joke. He coughed again, and this time blood spilled freely from his mouth. "Don't worry, little sister. I'm getting away. Watch me run. Watch me—"

Ronald Thompson ran out of his life smiling, with his eyes fixed on Elizabeth's face.

Kettridge covered the old cop's face, and Elizabeth hung her head, crying bitterly.

Jordan walked away and left her alone for a long time.

"Miss Dimitros..." Kettridge approached the kneeling woman cautiously.

"Yes," she answered, dully.

"I am sorry. Ron and I...were friends, a long time ago. If he had wanted Hesha—"

Elizabeth turned her head to look at him. "That's easy to say now."

"I mean it." His gray-green eyes locked on hers, and she discovered sincerity there.

"What now?"

"If you will let me, I'll try again for Ruhadze."

"To kill him?"

"Yes." Jordan nodded, adding, "and to destroy the Eye for good. There's a way out uphill from here. If I can stake the vampire, I'll be leaving by it. If I can't, I'm going to die here," he said calmly. "You can go now, if I can trust you not to warn him."

Liz took a deep breath and let go of Thompson's cooling hand. "I want to help you."

"Are you sure?" Elizabeth nodded vigorously, and stood up. She took a gun off Thompson's hip, and Kettridge stepped back, despite himself. "Then call him. Tell him something... convincing."

Liz stared at her phone. Hesha's number—she dialed it in, and waited.

"Yes," answered the rich, deep voice she remembered.

Elizabeth looked down at Thompson. *No names*, she thought. *I could use his name and warn him—* "Hello." Somewhere in the labyrinth, Hesha paused. For the woman to call was...unusual. "Report," he said guardedly.

"We found a campsite. My partner is looking it over; we think you should take a look. Without the supply you're carrying," she said, thinking of the sack of wet Ganges mud, "he's afraid to go into the bags."

"Why are you making the contact?"

"The phone wouldn't work in the area. There may be too much rock between you and it—or the object may be there and interfering. He sent me back to the last junction to try." She gave detailed directions and then cut the call off. Kettridge laid a hand on her shoulder, led her around a corner, and set her down by a backpack and rolled-up sleeping bag. A *campsite*, she thought in surprise. *True enough.* Then the professor dragged Thompson's body out of sight of the chimney, cocked and loaded a crossbow, and settled in for a wait.

Sounds from the chimney:

Nothing, for almost an hour.

A faint, scraping footfall.

Kettridge turned, aimed, and fired. *Spang. Thwack. Thud.* He loaded another stake into the bow, then flashed Thompson's bright, unfiltered light at the prone figure by the stair edge. The body lay still. Elizabeth joined him at the corner, checking the color of Hesha's skin. It was fainter and grayer than the tone he affected while waking...it was, in fact, the shade she remembered from the dream of his death, and the night in Calcutta when he let his illusion go. The tattoo stood out in the flash.

Liz crept forward and tried to lift the body. It came up all in one piece, rigid and stiff as a board. Hesha's eyes complained to her, and she looked quickly away.

Jordan Kettridge lowered the crossbow. He brought Hesha into the center of the chamber he'd used as a camp, and from a pack at his waist, he pulled out a clear, zip-lock bag. It bulged with pale goo and an Eye the size of a baseball. He laid it down three feet from Hesha's corpse.

"We're leaving." He shoved Liz back down the passage, threw his backpack on, and started running up a side path. He took a gray metal box with three lights and four buttons from the same pack that had held the artifact, armed it with the first button, pressed a second, and glanced back to see fire and rockfall consume the room behind them. He turned up another corridor, and started running, nudging the girl along whenever she faltered. He pressed one and three, and the passage they had just left collapsed. At the end of the tunnel, a tiny hole led out into moonlight. Liz scrambled through it, Kettridge shoved his pack ahead of him, and fell out headfirst himself.

The slope under them was grassy and steep, and they ran down to the valley floor in minutes. Breathing heavily, falling down under the weight of his bag, Jordan triggered the last charge, and half the hill seemed to shake and fall in on itself.

Later, in a rented car on its way to Manhattan, Jordan kept a close watch on his passenger. She wept some of the time, and she talked about Thompson, trying to arrange for herself the things she thought she knew about the man. She ranted at other moments, and though a fair amount of the anger came at Kettridge himself, she was most bitter and furious at Hesha. *She hates him*, thought the hunter. *She's definitely not still under his control.* With a great deal of relief, Jordan relaxed behind the wheel. Hesha Ruhadze had died for the last time beside his victim, Ron Thompson. Hesha Ruhadze would never haunt antique-shop assistants or obscure Berkeley anthropology professors again.

Home again, thought Elizabeth. She stopped for a moment on the threshold—she had never thought to see her rooms again. They were, for that instant, the most beautiful place on Earth. Then she looked down at herself, shuddered, and ran for the bedroom.

Liz stripped off her blood-stiffened clothes, threw them into the trash, and plunged under the full force of the shower. First it was too cold, then scalding hot—she adjusted the knobs, but she didn't care—Thompson's blood had soaked through her jeans. It was in her hair. It was under her fingernails. She scrubbed away the gore, then washed again, trying to forget that Hesha had ever touched her, anywhere. After forty minutes, she got out, pruny from the water and rubbed raw by the washcloth. She went to her wardrobe, realized that most of it was in Hesha's house...with her dissertation notes...and her favorite dress... and her grandmother's silver jewelry.... Liz pulled on a white dress shirt that she'd bought to give to her sister-in-law and a pair of khakis that had somehow escaped being packed off to Baltimore.

She rambled to the kitchen and started her answering machine. It told her there were forty-seven messages, and she hit PLAY as she opened the refrigerator. An old boyfriend called to see if she still existed, and the fridge was empty. There was a note inside from Amy explaining that she'd had it cleaned out. A series of clicks represented wrong numbers and telemarketers. Liz pulled a cardboard dinner from the freezer and slammed it into the microwave. More clicks. Her brother had called. The museum wanted to know if she could fill in while a permanent staffer took a sabbatical. Liz made juice from a frozen tube of concentrate, poured herself a glass. She snagged her dinner and sat down at the coffee table to sort through her mail. Later, satisfied, somehow, by the ordinariness of the junk, the coupons, the credit-card offers, the sales notices—fur coats and dishwashers had so little to do with dead men in the mountains—she drifted over to her workshop.

Antonio, the delivery foreman at Rutherford House, had left a stack of small pieces and a few notes. Liz looked through them and put the pieces away for later. She saw the eye molds still sitting on her workbench; she threw them out hastily.

Sleipnir caught her eye, and she ran a hand happily over her desk. She sat down on the polished top and gazed out the huge, gorgeous windows. Her thoughts turned to Amy...better to call her tomorrow, when all the things that had happened had settled a little more. She knew, thinking about it, that it would be hard to talk to someone *outside*—and now Amy *was* outside—about everything. Kettridge had offered his phone number; had let her talk, she had needed badly to talk, and Jordan had even listened. After the shock, he understood. He was still intense and a little awkward, but very nice, very kind. Paranoid, too, she realized—trying to give her tips on sunlight and fire and how to get the right weapons if she ever needed them. He was running scared and didn't know how to stop. Elizabeth supposed that a thing like Hesha might do that to a person.

New York settled down under a golden afternoon. People left their buildings and walked to buses; unlocked and un-Clubbed their cars. The locals stepped down to the corner grocers and back, and drifters simply did. Elizabeth watched them all, and a sinister feeling crept up her back. On impulse, she reached for a spray can from the shelves, found a lighter by the candles in the library, and put them together experimentally. A very satisfactory jet of flame rewarded her. She sat for a long time on Sleipnir's broad back, cradling the can to her chest and holding the lighter white-knuckle-tight in her left hand.

The sun began to fade. The warehouse shadow grew longer and longer, and streetlights glimmered on one by one. Suddenly Elizabeth felt called to action. She gathered up all her spray cans, matches, lighters, lamp oil, and candles and set them out strategically. She doublechecked the bolts on the (thank god!) inch-thick steel door to her apartment, locked all the windows down tight, and piled a heap of light, noisy junk in front of the swinging pane that led onto the fire escape. She ran down the curtains and retreated to the sofa, keeping her improvised flame-throwers close at hand. At the slightest noise her hand reached for them; she started whenever unexplained silence fell on her. The vampire had taught her to sleep by day—free at last to fix that, exhausted, and bone-weary, Elizabeth realized that she would not shut her eyes until they closed of themselves.

Elizabeth felt her left shoulder tighten up. She flinched and looked back, sure that something had come up behind her. There was nothing—she looked to her right—and suddenly, Hesha's face appeared in front of her own. His eyes were yellow, with inhuman, slit pupils. Her heart jumped as she stared at the apparition. She thought of the fire, but her body had turned to lead and refused to obey her. She could not even look away.

Hesha said nothing.

Liz sat frozen like a statue, in a paralysis so complete her lungs gave her only short, quick breaths—as she panicked, the rhythm quickened, her head grew light. Terror dug deep claws into her, and the vampire's golden eyes bored through her brain. She was dizzy and felt like falling, but her body refused even to collapse.

The monster spoke at last. "Good evening, Elizabeth." He reached out and took the can and lighter from her. "Clever, as always. And you paid attention during our time together. That you failed is not your fault; you cannot fight what you cannot see." He placed his hands on her chest and pushed her unresisting body back on the couch. "Be comfortable."

He knocked the woman's petty arsenal off the coffee table with one sweeping arm. The cans clanged horribly on the floorboards, and the raucous noise echoed down from the rafters.

Hesha seated himself on the table, and kept his unblinking eyes on his prisoner.

"It has become necessary for me to kill you. I doubt that you would appreciate many of the reasons for this. It is not in my nature to explain, and it would not be within your ability to comprehend me should I speak the whole truth to you." He paused. "While you await your death, however, you may desire something to take your mind off your situation, and I invite you to consider this: If you had not allowed Thompson to die—yes, I know about that—I would not be here to kill you now.

"You betrayed me. I understand that, and I fault myself—my handling of you has been flawed from the beginning. I sinned. I almost fell into compassion. I allowed myself and my meditations to be distracted by the Eye. I underestimated a mortal—the same mortal—more than once. I saw clear signs and misunderstood them.

"You killed Thompson, Elizabeth," he murmured, puzzled, "and I had not seen even the shadow of that in you. I see most things...." The golden eyes came closer, until Elizabeth felt she were drowning in them. "Have you anything to say?" His irises deepened slowly to black. "If you sit still, you may whisper."

Elizabeth tried to leap up and scream at the top of her lungs. Hesha seemed disappointed. He raised an eyebrow.

"How did you know about Ron?" She could hardly hear her voice herself.

"I found Kettridge's cave at the same time you did. He believed there were only two entrances. He neglected to consider holes a human body could not squeeze through. I listened to it all."

"Why did you let him die?"

"Why did you?" he asked in a tone of genuine curiosity.

She swallowed hard. "How did you escape?"

"You staked me. I am not a vampire; I am a Child of Set. I have no heart for Kettridge to spear me by, and I am difficult to destroy. No more questions. No more explanations. Do you have anything to *say*?"

Elizabeth thought for a moment. "Kill me quickly."

"No." Hesha's gaze turned gold again.

"You die tonight for Thompson's sake," intoned the Setite. "You die tonight that I may redeem myself in my Lord's grace. You die tonight because alive you are a temptation to me." He began to chant in a language Elizabeth did not know. Then: "You are beyond my control. You are a burden on my will." The strange language flowed through her ears again. His voice rose, repeated one phrase half a dozen times, and fell to silence.

Hesha's fingers traced the line of her jaw. His hand tilted her head back, and his arms snaked around her. Elizabeth watched terrible, sharp fangs like a viper's drop down from behind his canines. She closed her eyes and braced herself for pain, for a torn throat and a severed windpipe; she prayed for unconsciousness to come soon, even if the monster were determined that death should await some plan of his own.

She felt an unexpected softness, a tender kiss, on her mouth, and the shock was worse than a wound. Hesha, pretending to want her, in a room in Calcutta...his lips slid along her cheek, kissed her again beneath the ear, and finally bit into the vein.

Elizabeth screamed for what seemed like an eternity, but was less than a second; the scream never passed her lips. Her breath caught. A gasp escaped her. The worst of the attack wasn't pain, but heart-wrenching, bittersweet ecstasy. She clutched at him desperately, drawing him closer, and forgot everything... she pressed herself against him...her heart ached—it couldn't beat fast enough.... Her cheek rubbed against his, and she felt his skin grow warm with what he stole from her. She flushed for a moment, and felt it fade as more blood left her. Elizabeth lost the strength to hold him, and sagged into the strong cocoon of his arms. Time slowed—or Hesha sipped more delicately—and she seemed to float in a luxurious sea. Bells rang in her ears, and lights danced before her eyes. In a moment, the chimes and colors fell behind her, and there was nothing left but the sea—she couldn't feel the pressure of his hands or the tingling of her own fingertips—there was the sea of ecstasy, darkness, and the faintest memory of a body...somewhere...with a tiny, stinging pain in the side of its throat. She held onto that a minute longer, dizzy and dwindling, thinking not of her life ending, but of the touch of him going away forever...she could remember his arms....

Then there was nothing—just enough of it, for just long enough, for her to know always what nothing was like—

—and a single drop of fire landed in her mouth.

She had a mouth, she had a body. It was a mass of sharp pain and chill, stiff, dull agony. She kicked and clawed at something she couldn't see—it tore back at her, trying to destroy what little there was of her—and the fire came back to her mouth. Wine, pure water, strawberries, acid, thickened passion, mother's milk, bitter gall, vinegar, burning hatred...singing guilt...a power... other men's memories...deliciously and unspeakably wrong to drink, but impossible not to swallow. The stuff filled her heart and coursed through her veins, and the sharp pains went away. It went on flowing, and the agony subsided.

Elizabeth opened her eyes.

She was sitting in her father's old office chair. Hesha's face, devoid of expression, looked into hers. His eyes were gold. His hands held chains and shackles, and while she tried to understand why he hadn't killed her yet, he clamped them on her wrists, through the back of the chair, and around the steel pillar in the center of her apartment.

Hesha left without another word.

Saturday, 31 July 1999, 3:56 AM
A studio apartment in Red Hook, Brooklyn
New York City, New York

Elizabeth Dimitros sat in the exact center of her apartment and waited. She was through remembering. She could not even guess how much light would be too much—twilight, or the glow before dawn, or the full rays of the sun—but she would know, soon, just how much was needed to kill a vampire—how deadly Ra was to the body of an infant Child of Set.

From time to time she listened for footsteps in the hall. If one of the other tenants passed by, she could yell and try to find shelter before sunup. Antonio sometimes started his rounds at five o'clock—would that be too late? If Hesha were going to come back (*Hesha isn't going to come back*, she thought bitterly) he might use the door, as he had in leaving.

The sky grew paler.

Perhaps it was best this way....

Footsteps—coming closer. Elizabeth's heart leapt. Should she call out? No, the walker was already coming to her place—there was nothing else at this end of the hall. She turned herself in the chair and looked desperately at the opening door.

She didn't recognize him at first—she only knew she wasn't seeing Hesha.

The man smiled, looked her up and down, slowly, glanced at the shackles, and licked his curling lips.

"Hello, sweetheart," said Khalil Ravana. He grinned evilly. "Did you miss me?"

About the Author

Kathleen Ryan has worked for, with, and around White Wolf Publishing since 1993. Her first fiction pieces, about a young mage named Amanda, appeared as book- openers in *Mage: The Ascension*, first edition. Through cajolery and threats she has managed to get an Amanda piece in every major Mage release since then, wrangled all the fun parts of Tradition Book: *Euthanatos* for her¬self, and snuck most of Changing Breed Book: *Kitsune* into the back of *Hengeyokai: Shapeshifters of the East*. *Clan Novel: Setite* is her first novel-length published work.

Curious about other Crossroad Press books?
Stop by our site:
http://store.crossroadpress.com
We offer quality writing
in digital, audio, and print formats.

Printed in Great Britain
by Amazon

72299162R00159